ADVENTURE TALES 7   **SUMMER 2014**

Contents

The Blotter

Welcome to the 7th issue of *Adventure Tales*! We are, as usual, managing to keep to our "irregular" schedule with an issue that's "only" 4 years in following the last one. Hopefully that won't happen again. (Blame the economy...we've had to focus on things that actually make money, rather than the publisher's time-consuming pulp-magazine hobby!)

This time, we have a very special lineup. Wildside Press recently purchased the literary estate of Mack Reynolds, one of the top science fiction writers of the 1960s and 1970s, and we have been going through his early pulp stories (and finding some great reads!)—so we are making him the Featured Author in this issue, with no less than 2 essays and 6 of his early stories...plus a bibliography of all of his novels.

But first off is "Air Trail," by Arthur O. Friel, one of my favorite pulp writers. It comes from the November 25, 1939 issue of *Short Stories*. As usual with Friel, it features a south-of-the-border adventure.

Spaceman Lancelot Biggs returns in Nelson Bond's "F.O.B. Venus," part of Bond's long-running space opera series. This entry comes from *Fantastic Adventures*, November 1939.

Horror-master Frank Belknap Long, who was part of H.P. Lovecraft's circle and penned the classic Cthulhu Mythos story "The Hounds of Tindalos," offers a change-of-pace story with the touching "Night-Fear," from *Dynamic Science Fiction*, October 1953.

"In Destiny's Clutch," by Rafael Sabatini, originally appeared in *Top-Notch*, May 15, 1921.

"The Haunted Landscape," by Greye La Spina, is from *The Thrill Book*, June 1, 1919.

"The Phantom Hearse," by Mary Fortune (writing as "W.W."), originally appeared in *The Australian Journal*, Sept. 1889.

"The Gothic Horror," by George Wetzel, originally appeared in *Fan-Fare*, Vol. 3, No. 3, May 1953.

"Heritage," by Arthur T. Hillman, originally appeared in *The Acolyte* #10 (Summer 1945). It was billed as a prose poem, but it's actually a Lord Dunsany-inspired little tale.

Verse

"In Recognition of Death," by Fritz Leiber, originally appeared in *The Acolyte* #10 (Spring 1945). "The Nether Garden," by Frank Robinson, originally appeared in *Chanticleer* #3, December 1945. "Quest," by Wanita Norris, originally appeared in *Fan To See*, Vol. 1, No. 2, February 1953. "The Sea at Evening," by Andrew Duane, originally appeared in *Fan-Fare*, Vol. 3, No. 3, May 1953. "Alexandrines," by Clark Ashton Smith, originally appeared in *Odes and Sonnets* (1918).

IN RECOGNITION OF DEATH

by Fritz Leiber, Jr.

I

It is a wonderful train ride
With the farms sliding by in the cold dusk
And animals grazing in the yellow sun
And little wooden-floored stations,
The boards brushed with frost or odorous
*   with rain,*
And strange turbulent cities by night
With steel bridges over rivers reflecting
*   lights*
And vast mysterious depots.

But the conductor is always coming up
*   behind me.*
I can hear the click of his punch.
And I wonder if he will pass me by,
Or if he will take up my ticket
And I will have to get off and enter the
*   landscape,*
Become stationary forever.

So I gaze more greedily
And talk to the person opposite
And rummage in my baggage,
And insincerely yawn,
And furiously think.

II

Death is my real friend,
Always doing things for my own good
Whether I like them or not.
He prods me toward the future,
He goads me to accomplishment,
He keeps reminding me of my unfulfilled
*   potentialities,*
Promises, hopes, intentions, and resolves.
He makes no promises.
He never threatens.
Yet he is eloquent.
If I lived ten thousand years,

His voice owuld only be more urgent.

III

Death, a stern counsellor, is alwayus at my
*   elbow, whispering,*
"The time is, was, and shall be," in his
*   clipped accent.*
"You died ten years ago, tomorrow, now."
Often I have refused to see him, calling
*   others to mask him from me.*
Sloth and placidity are fat councilmen.
Their gross bodies easily cover his lean
*   one.*
But where I to put granite walls between us,
His words would be as true.
Forget mortal counsellors.
Death is the only true ally.
He deals in verities.
He recognized accomplishment.
He knows there are things he cannot kill,
Or, killing, must remember and so make
*   immortal.*

IV

The killers creep toward me throught the
*   dark,*
Red-smeared, with hate in their hearts.
But death is dignified and does not hate me.
The killers are ignorant and cruel.
But death knows all and regards me fairly.
The killers are not his agents—
It may happen that they will die at the
*   hand of their intended victim.*
Death will not kill me, but something that
*   has life or movement—*
A stone, a force, a micro-organism, the
*   macro-organism.*
Life will mangle me, and death will
*   befriend me.*

                                                     ✗

AIR TRAIL
by Arthur O. Friel

CHAPTER I

Dugan sat on the riverbank, looking south. Over him a thick-leaved tropic hardwood tree fended off torrid sun. Below him the opaque Orinoco, master stream of Venezuela, flowed toward the distant ocean. Far across, another steep yellow shore topped by dull greenery stretched in utter monotony. Farther still, hulking hills rose in blue haze. On those half-seen bulks, receding into the dim mystery of untamed interior South America, the loafing man's eyes stayed dreamily set.

Behind him, northward, lay flat Spanish leagues of parched *llanos*. Many a weary day's travel across sunburned earth intervened before a horseman could reach the Caribbean Mountains. And then what? Caracas. Politicians and their servants—police, soldiers, other hired jailors or killers of rebels against their power. As in Europe. And as, perhaps, in North America, if would-be lifelong rulers could force their will on millions of smoldering dissenters.

Dugan chuckled and deliberately spat sidewise. Rebel Irish, rebel American, rebel against all oppressive authority, he now derisively consigned all cities, north or south, to the devil. Especially those of North America, where old police circulars still offered reward for the capture of one James Patrick Dugan, oil worker, whose fists had knocked an ugly political boss permanently out. Down here, too, more than one antagonist had met fatal shock from similar thunderbolt punches. But down here such accidents were pardonable. And along the Rio Orinoco sudden deaths were mere incidents.

Incidents remarkable, however, if caused by bare hands. Bullet or knife was the customary concluder of local disagreements. So now this wandering Norteamericano had become known here and there as El Macho—He-Mule, or Sledgehammer, or Hard Hitter.

And now, gazing away into the utterly lawless mountains beyond the man-eating yellow river, the lounger unconsciously stretched and clenched his powerful fingers. Restless reflex of fighting muscles, recently inactive, worked on his nerves as the hazy hinterland lured his adventurous mind. Out—away from all scheming governments—out into no man's land, fighting savage Indians or murderous half-breeds, but free!

"Huh-huh-huh-huh-huh-huh!"

The harsh chuckle sounded close behind him.

His outstretched arms froze; then casually sank to the ground. The next second he was up.

Springing, ducking, suddenly set, he faced toward the unseen laughter. Low beside his right hip a big-bored revolver leveled itself with trigger tight-drawn.

"Huh-huh-huh!" he mocked. "What's funny around here?"

No answer came. Nothing was there. Nothing but trees, shade, empty ground slant-lit by the sun broiling the outer plains. Warily scanning the tree butts, he saw no lurking gun-muzzles.

Then the voice again spoke. And again it was behind him.

"Huh-huh! Beg for your life, you—"

Nasty names followed. Suddenly shrilled a ghastly scream. Then fell new silence.

Dugan, wheeling at the first word, again faced nothing human. Brown eyes dilated, square jaw grim, heavy shoulders hunched, he stabbed the surrounding shadows with penetrating gaze. Once more he saw only the thick waterside timber.

Off at his left something thudded earth. A horse hoof, stamping once. Dugan's own horse, resting upstream, had risen at that shriek and now stood ready.

No other horses could be near. Otherwise that intelligent animal would have signaled sooner. These two far-farers were one in emergency. So now in the hot stillness the man felt a strange chill.

Voices. Nothing else. One malicious voice speaking Venezuelan; a language strange to book-Spanish students but well known to El Macho. Another voice of different timbre, inarticulate in agony. Both voices oddly hollow, as if transmitted through a faulty radio machine. Out of the air—

Dugan's low-hung head jerked up, searching the leafy boughs. At that instant something grasped his right shoulder. His left fist darted up—halted short. The ghostly talkers were only a bird.

A parrot. A royal parrot, green-bodied, red-shouldered, small but brainy. Now, wise little eyes glinting into the man's stare, it nodded and plaintively asked:

"Crrrawk?"

Dugan's hostile scowl smoothed out. His tall body quivered with suppressed mirth, and his gun dropped into its holster. Gently he closed both hands on the little body, drew it down, and asked:

"Hungry?"

A peck at his breast answered. Then the feathered poll sank and the light weight subsided in the comforting nest of broad hands.

"Poor little devil!" murmured Dugan.

The little devil was indeed poor. Its feathers were faded, dirty, and ragged. Its skin, tight-drawn over bones, was gashed by half-healed rips. "Hmmm! Been treated rough, haven't you, boy? Somebody's house pet. Took a ride for yourself and got ganged by wild parrots. Well, come on."

Cradling the bird, the man stepped softly through the grove to his hammock-roll of supplies. There lay a half-hand of fig-bananas; short, sweet, nutritious fruits seldom if ever seen in North America. Avidly the starved bird attacked a proffered pulp. Others followed. At length, full fed, the small stranger wiped its beak, walked to Dugan's saddle, squatted and slept.

Dugan, sitting down against a tree, rolled a *cigarrillo* and slowly smoked. His horse had resumed its rest, and nothing else moved. Even the overhead leaves hung almost motionless in the dazing heat of afternoon; and the great river alongside flowed noiseless. Drowsy, yet awake, the man burned up his brown cigarette and then patiently waited.

At length a sweep of late-day wind clattered leaves and roused the bird. Leaping aloft, it perched on a bough. Busily it cleaned itself, dressing wounds, smoothing ragged feathers. Satisfied, it launched out in brief flight; then, finding itself none too strong, veered back to drop at the man's feet.

The man extended his trigger-finger. The bird jumped, gripped, cocked its head and inquired:

"Crrrawk?"

"No, hombre. No more handouts. Unless you tell me a story. You know one. Let's hear it."

Softly stroking the scarred head, Dugan quietly continued:

"You're a decent lad, and clean, and you've got a brain. And I know how it is, when you're just trying to live your own way but get knocked around by dirty gangs. Now where's that nasty guy that makes men screech? I think I'd like a look at him. Just show me."

His slow words were *llanos* language. The bird stayed motionless. Rising, Dugan tossed it upward. It flew and vanished among the leaves.

Leisurely he prepared to ride. Saddling,

he teased:

"Want a ride, *lorito*? Huh-huh-huh!"

His concluding tone echoed the chuckle first heard behind him. From above dropped response:

"Huh huh! Feet getting warm? Another rub with the iron, Zorro. Between the toes—"

"*Waaaah! Ai Dios!*"

The last outcry was another voice, yelling in intolerable pain.

Dugan, tight-mouthed, walked his horse away. Bright on his supply-pack rested the tempting yellow fig-bananas. Out into the roasting open he rode, downriver.

Sombrero tilted backward against western sun, body loosely resistant to grilling heat-rays, he left the bird behind. Soon a light weight settled again on his shoulder.

Drawing rein, he stopped.

"I mean that, lad," he said. "No story, no ride. And no eats. Think it over."

The peering parrot-eyes looked into his own, then shrank behind closing lids. The small head drew down in struggling thought. All at once came new words in new tone:

"*Lorito, lorito, Estas muy bonito!*"

Sweetly feminine, with a lilting uplift, this voice was truly Spanish; clear, without throaty local slurs. The rhyme was childish, meaning: "Little parrot, you are very handsome." But, having said it, the bird cocked its head proudly at the listener.

"Well, I'll be damned," drawled the outlander. "All right, you get another handout for that one. But— No, not now. Show me what you mean. Then I'll pay off."

Again he threw his hands aloft. The flyer veered, beat its way higher; wavered uncertainly— then chose its goal and went.

Ragged wings laboring but sure, it flew toward a dull clump of trees on the hazy horizon. Marking its course, the man glanced at the sinking sun and the shadow-slant of his horse's legs on the burned earth. Soon the flying dot disappeared.

"North-northeast, I'd say," he judged.

"Anyway, from here to there, old horse. Watch your step."

His left hand stroked his horse's neck. The animal softly snorted and walked as directed. Dugan drew his sidearm, clicked its cylinder around, smelled its smooth-oiled readiness, dropped it back into its holster.

At those deliberate clicks the experienced *llanos* horse slightly lengthened steps and cocked ears forward.

Stride, stride, stride, the long-gaited gelding journeyed steadily. But at length, when the northeast wind veered more northerly, the regular steps shortened, slowed, stopped. Nostrils sniffing, the horse then backed.

Half a mile ahead, the close-bunched trees stood hostile against all intruders. West, the red-hot sun slid fast down. And fast from the west, high in the hard blue, suddenly sped a fleet of macaws; huge parrots, wide-winged, long-tailed, harsh-voiced, screeching with every wing-flap; savages, wild as the South American jaguar but more noisy.

Dugan, breathing the wind, caught a faint odor and scowled. Glancing up at the yelping macaws, he scowled more blackly and reached for his belt-gun. Jarring threats always aroused his antagonism. But the homing birds were high out of gun-range. So his hand dropped away.

"*Grrrah!*" he growled. "You're the gang that beat up my little *lorito*, hey? Try and do it again!" Kicking, he jolted his horse ahead. The macaws shrieked more harshly but swirled higher.

At the tree edge the two halted. Among close-grown trunks and sparse brush nothing moved. Pushing on in, they found damp ground and a small shallow pool. Scouting around the water, then moving westward, they stopped short.

Before them lay a dead man.

CHAPTER II

Sprawled in a short brown hammock,

the corpse stared sightless up into the leafy canopy which had concealed it from the *llanos* vultures. Now out of those leaves something dropped on Dugan's right shoulder. Startled, he jerked half around, then grumbled:

"Damn it, *Lorito*, don't jump me again like that!"

Beak open, head drooping, the tired bird snuggled against his neck. Then the gashed green poll lifted and screeched defiance at the unseen but furiously clamoring birds above. Now its language was that of the macaws, raucous yells which matched and out-dared the loudmouthed bullies.

Dugan grinned.

"Give 'em hell, lad!" he encouraged. "I'll back you up."

For a moment the royal flyer redoubled its challenge to the mob. Then, gasping, it subsided.

Vindictive replies in the leaf-blotted sky died out. The macaw gang had gone without a fight. Dugan, swinging down, left his horse to drink untended while he studied the dead man.

Tall, light-skinned, dark-haired, this was a young Spanish white man; stubborn-mouthed, big-nosed, straight-browed, and straight-eyed even in death. His fixed gaze still looked straight up, asking dumb sun or stars where to go. His body was somewhat swollen by postmortem gases, but his long legs were hardly more than sharp-shinned bones; and his bare feet had been worn raw before death.

A tramp—dead from starvation. Dead about two days, but well preserved by dry *llanos* winds. Stepping closer, the observer rapidly examined the cheaply clad form, then swung away with a glance all around.

Starvation, yes. No wounds. And no food, no camp-kettle, no trace of a fire, no horse-track.

Nothing but a young fellow gone into nowhere, a bird still trustfully grasping an older man who had come from nowhere, and echoes in the live man's mind.

Soberly Dugan remounted. Out into the plains he rode, northward. Then the sun set, and from the swiftly darkening east came night.

A mile or two upwind he stopped beside a single scrawny sapling and made dry camp. Unsaddling, he turned his horse loose; squatted, ate Orinoco travel-fare—cassava and cheese—drank from his gourd canteen; fed the parrot with another banana; then asked:

"How come, *Lorito*? How did that lad happen to starve—and you, too?"

No answer came. In the dimness the bird nodded, seemed sluggishly trying to think. Then, flying into the stunted treelet, it roosted and slept.

"All right. Take it easy."

Dugan lay down; head pillowed on hammock-roll, body supine on hot earth, gun negligently pendant between outstretched legs. In this sun-roasted ground were no fever germs, and on its foodless surface were few snakes. As for night-prowling, horse-killing *tigres*, he knew his canny animal would run to him for defense.

Nothing disturbed his rest. But, sleeping, he still subconsciously wandered. Voices talked. Men and women struggled. A young man took a long walk; south, toward the Orinoco. Here and there along that young man's way were small settlements, isolated huts of poor but hospitable mestizos, places where a white man could beg food and drink. But, avoiding them all, he trudged on, heading for empty distance. Somewhere out!

Out, as Dugan himself had dreamed only this afternoon. Out to hell-and-gone. So now, stiffly proud, dead. And now a harsh voice broke into the dreamy mix-up, rasping:

"*Crraa! Al infierno!* To hell with all, you—"

Dugan started up. Dull light was dawning eastward, pale stars fading westward. A parrot in a rickety little tree was talking tough. A horse, head raised but body lazy, lay close alongside. Another day.

Stretching, Dugan laughed:

"*Bueno*, big boy. That's telling 'em. And where do we go from here?"

Invigorated by safe sleep and more bananas, the bird soon showed him. Flying fast, it sped straight northeast. This time Dugan took a bearing with a pocket compass. When the flyer again vanished he leisurely followed.

Once he halted, struck by coincidence. Those raw feet of the unknown man back yonder—were they excoriated only by long travel over blistering earth? Again a parroted voice seemed to say:

"Huh, huh! Feet getting warm? Another touch of the iron, Zorro!"

For the moment the rider almost turned back to re-inspect those feet. Then he muttered:

"Zorro. Fox. You're the man I want to meet, Mr. Zorro—and your huh-huh boss."

Through the ensuing hours he moodily frowned. At length, far past siesta time, he let his horse enter a small palm-draped *morichal*, where must be water. It was empty of life. But there he found another death.

Near the scummy little spring lay a scattering of feathers. Green feathers, torn, and newly bloodstained; feathers strewn hither and thither in desperate, dodging fight. Then beside a palm trunk he detected a small dead parrot.

Mangled by talons and hooked beaks, it still bore on one wing-shoulder a few tattered red feathers signifying its royal name.

Dugan's dusty face reddened with wrath.

"Got him, hey, you dirty killers?" he grated. "By Judas, you'll pay!"

Teeth set, he glowered at something afar. Not the vindictive bird-gang which has killed this little lone adventurer; that was gone. Not even the imagined Zorro—a fox-faced torturer holding hot irons. Instead, a malignant thing as yet without face or shape, which maliciously chuckled as it somehow destroyed better lives than its own. Through long miles and hot hours the lone rider had developed toward that vaguely visioned demon a smoldering enmity which now flared into implacable hatred.

When the lethal heat-rays of mid-afternoon had somewhat lessened he rode on. Sundown was near when he approached an inhabited spot. A crooked line of low trees, a few thin cattle grazing half seen under leaf-cover, a yellowish blob amid the dull green betokened an *hato*; a poor little ranch on a shrunken creek.

As Dugan rode in, mongrel dogs rushed from a pole-and-palm hut, yelping challenge. A squatty brown man, frowzy with sleep, opened a flimsy door, then sturdily advanced. In his right fist a machete hung ready, and behind him a peak-faced woman peered warily out. His greeting was guardedly civil.

"*Buenas tardes*. What would you like, stranger?"

The stranger digested the voice, the humble home, the shrewish female face in the doorway. Then he rumbled:

"Information. Which way to Zorro, the Fox?"

The flat-nosed rancher drew back, mouth hardening; then stood his ground. His stubby left hand arose and pointed.

East-northeast, judged Dugan. He had been bearing a bit too far north.

"How far?"

The tight-lidded eyes glanced away at the setting sun, back at the questioner.

"Perhaps midnight," came strained answer. "That way!"

The left arm, stiff as a wooden road-marker, pointed on out.

"And what sort of place?"

Suspicion glinted under the drawn lids. No reply came until the horseman slid a hand to his gun-butt. Then, grudgingly:

"An *hacienda*."

"Thanks."

As the hard-looking stranger resumed

progress the brown fellow gradually re-laxed. And, watering his horse in the shal-low *caño*, the rider remarked:

"Tough territory, boy, when a lonesome squatter won't talk to a white man. But maybe we look pretty tough ourselves. And maybe—"

Rubbing his jaw, black with two days' unshaven bristles, he briefly smiled. And, once more out on the plain, he tilted his sombrero at a tougher angle.

* * * *

Night fell. Stars again blazed. In their wan light the shadowy traveler repeatedly checked his direction by compass. Once, stopping to breathe his mount and take a walk to stretch his own legs, he conclud-ed his half-spoken thought back yonder: "Maybe, old horse, this job's being laid out for us. Maybe, 'twas just as well that our lit-tle pal got knocked off. If he'd gone ahead and talked some more he might have tipped off Zorro and Company. Voices—"

His own voice died. And, moving on through the night, he spoke no more. With the whispering wind in his face and the slow clouds drifting dark on their mysterious voyages overhead, he felt an odd fatalism born of past wanderings. More than once, following an impulse and steered by appar-ently blind chance, he had seemed to mean-der as senselessly as the clouds; but, later, realized that some strange destiny seemed to have directed his course and planned the outcome.

About midnight his horse raised its head, sniffed, quietly snorted. Reins lax, sandaled feet nudging, the master silently urged him to find the right way. And, turning some-what more northerly, they presently entered a black mass of trees.

Through the thick darkness the animal cannily progressed, soon emerging into a starlit square bare of any growth. Hard-baked soil surrounded a hard-walled house, low but wide. Silent as a tomb, it also ema-nated the sinister repellence of a night-shrouded cemetery.

Sitting still, the night rider surveyed the place and absorbed its atmosphere. He had seen haciendas before now, by day and by dark; found hospitality at some, near-death at others. Outside all looked similar. Now, in the wan light of tonight and the reflection of past encounters, this one looked and felt deadly.

From the earth projected broad bumps; low-hacked stumps of ancient trees which long had given both shade and fruit to the dwellers here. Cut away, their denuded space now gave accurate aim to any gun-men now occupying the wilderness fort. Where were the old owners, who through generations of *llanos* life had been so re-spected that those slow-grown trees had grown stout?

Only the wind answered, sighing on into the emptiness of lost lives. And soon the outwardly callous but inwardly sensitive Macho drew rein backward, softly prompt-ing:

"Let's go, fellow. Hold everything till to-morrow."

They moved out downwind, as they had come. If any dogs lurked near, none had caught scent. And, a mile or two south, man and horse slept in a clump of cactus.

The sun was well up when they again approached. Slouchy, unkempt, with loose old clothes wrinkled but full cartridge belt drawn snug, the man traveled with apparent indifference to any watchers. Nearing the trees, he glimpsed something white which faded back and disappeared.

"Turn out the guard," he jeered. "Present arms. And then see what happens."

No guard and no guns, however, met him when he entered a short roadway, nor even when he crossed the plaza within. In-stead, the plaza was strangely empty of hu-man life. Only a dog, silent but menacing, stood watchful before a shut front door.

Huge, yellow, hostile, the dog was not

the usual small *llanos* cur but a powerful mastiff, heavy and strong enough to knock down and kill even an average horse. As for men—its cold eyes showed fixed study of the horseman, calculating chances. Dangerous as a lion, and more intelligent, it remained motionless while making up its mind.

In the thick walls, bulletproof shutters stood blank in narrow windows. In the outer grove nothing moved but the leaves soughing in morning wind. No peons, no horses, no hens, none of the right kind of daytime hacienda life was here. Yet the baked clay earth showed much pressure by feet. Outside the plains were cracked by dry-season heat. Here the dirt was smooth.

Insolently Dugan scanned the place; then walked his horse around the square-set walls, giving any hidden observers a chance to study him and his belt-gun. In Venezuela any such weapon was openly carried only by outlaws. Completing the circuit, he paused and asked the rigid mastiff:

"Are they all dead around here, big fellow? Hope you won't starve. I'd give you a feed, but I'm short of meat. So *adios*!"

He plodded northward, contemptuously giving his broad back to the house. The dog, digesting his tone and action, grew loose-muscled; then guardedly followed with heavy brow wrinkled and nostrils wide, breathing the stranger's back-blown scent.

In the northern sidewall a shutter standing slightly ajar swiftly opened. From it a white handkerchief fluttered in the breeze.

Through the outer trees the departing gunman slowly traveled, giving any unseen watchers more time for decision. No more time was needed.

"Halt!" commanded a voice.

CHAPTER III

Dugan halted. From behind a tree appeared a burly brown man with a rifle hanging loose in one fist. Behind other stout butts, other rifles faintly gleamed in set aim.

"*Quién es*?" demanded the challenger. "Who are you?"

"*Quién quiere*?" retorted Dugan. "Who wants to know?"

The guardsman studied the outrider's black-bristled jaw and big fist curled around revolver-butt. Wooden-faced, he then repeated:

"*Quién es*?"

"Well, if you have to know," drawled Dugan, "I'm called El Macho. And what do they call you?" The native's eyes briefly widened. His straw sombrero nodded downward. At that small signal the rifles behind the trees sank. "*Bien*. Come with me."

"Where to?" balked El Macho.

"The house."

"What for?"

The brown man scowled; then oddly smiled. Carefully he said:

"*Bienvenido, Señor*. You are welcome."

"Thanks. But I'm traveling. And if you think you can stop me, try it!"

Harsh as the untamable macaws on his back trail, his voice rasped rough threat. His heels nudged his horse, which stiffened for outward spring. But his reins drew back in covert restraint.

Eyes, boring into him, missed that left-hand back-drag. The stocky commander's mouth tightened. His head lifted. So did the guns flanking the truculent Macho.

"As you say," came cool reply. "We try it."

Dugan, glancing around at the newly menacing muzzles, snorted:

"Careful of your health, aren't you, hombre? Wouldn't take a chance at me alone.

What are you, anyway? Police?"

"*Cómo*? Police? Us?" The other snickered. "Hardly!"

"Or army?"

"Nor army. You are quite safe here, Macho."

"Grrump!" growled Dugan, visibly relaxing. "Then don't act like a gang of cops. I don't like 'em, see?"

"I see. Shall we go?"

With a dour grunt Dugan swung his horse back toward the plaza. So doing, he confronted the forgotten mastiff. Silently attentive, the big dog had stood two yards at rear. Now he turned and trotted houseward, long tail up and slowly wagging.

At that sign of canine friendliness the ambushed gunmen emerging behind Dugan stared and muttered in astonishment. Only their leader seemed to understand. Rifle down, he ambled contentedly after El Macho.

The front door now was open. Lounging in the portal, a slim man in whites narrowly eyed the returning mastiff, horseman, and rear guard. Yellow-skinned, sharp-nosed, thin-cheeked, thin-mouthed, he looked over Dugan like a wolf estimating prey.

"El Macho," quietly announced the guard leader.

The lounger yawned, straightened, and spoke the emptily polite old Spanish phrase:

"This house is at your service, stranger."

The voice was metallic. The undertone was a subtle sneer.

"Thanks!" came the sarcastic report. "Up and dressed, are you? All right, I'll come in, if you've got something to eat. Or have you? Yah-ha-ha!"

El Macho's hard bray brought no facial change. The wiry shape moved deliberately backward, paused, waited. Dugan, with another tough laugh, dismounted and swaggered in. The sharp-nosed man nodded sidewise.

In a shaded room another man sat alone at a table, eating. Gray-haired, gray-skinned,

sloppily dressed in soiled white shirt and baggy trousers, he mechanically chewed while he sized up the stranger. Soon he nodded backward in wordless command to enter.

Dugan lounged in, looked around, saw only bare walls, shuttered windows, and dark furniture. The gray man eyed the Northerner's hard jaw, heavyweight build, muscular legs and sandaled brown feet. His gaze lingered on the feet. Dugan, countering the look, noted a physical defect. Both the feet under the table were short, stubby, turned far inward. Clubfeet.

Then, swallowing his food at one gulp, the master of the house snarled:

"Take off your hat!"

"Says who?" demanded Dugan.

Silence. Thumbs over belt, the rough stranger drifted away from the open doorway at his back and leaned against a wall.

The clubfooted eater, with food sunk, now was hollow-faced. Hook-nosed, lank-cheeked, jawbones limned under skin seamed by deep downward lines, scantily bearded with recently unshaven whitish sprout, he hunched his round shoulders like a vulture. Then from the doorway came a deferential voice:

"*Señor*, this one is El Macho."

The commander of the outguard stood there, hat in one hand. Over the gray face flitted a strange change. A claw-like hand closed hard.

"Zorro!" snapped the whitish mouth.

The brown man stepped back. Into his place came the fox-faced yellow one, smirking.

"*Sí, Señor*. At your service."

"Why in hell didn't you say who this man was?"

Zorro cringed. "So sorry, *Señor.* I thought perhaps you had heard his name."

The clubfoot glared; then snapped: "*Malparto, vaya!* Get out!"

Zorro slunk away. Dugan hoarsely chuckled. Few Spanish epithets are more contemptuous than *malparto*.

"You spoke a true word there," he said. "And why do you keep a thing like that around here? It stinks."

The hunched shape grinned, showing a few scattered teeth.

"It has its uses," he evaded. Then, growing affable, "Come and eat, Macho."

"Oh, all right. Why not?"

Strolling forward, Dugan lifted a ponderous chair with one hand, put it down with back to a wall, and sat. The other man, observing both the easy strength and the habitual wariness against indoor backstabbers, grinned more widely. Then he struck a framed gong at his right.

A woman appeared. Dugan stared. Instead of a dumpy, dark-faced house-woman he saw a tall girl, pure Spanish. Black-browed but cream-skinned, coolly composed, simply but neatly dressed in a long white gown, she seemed mistress of the *rancho*. Yet she stood like a servant expecting orders.

"More food, woman!" grunted the club-foot. "And quick!"

She turned and was gone. Dugan, poker-faced, regarded the opposite wall. Its bare surface bore large rectangles of old paint, brighter than elsewhere; telltale marks of big portraits of bygone forefathers—now completely gone.

Gone where, and why? His random gaze sharpened. Such pictures were proudly treasured by legitimately descended owners. Now—

"What are you doing around here, El Macho?" the cripple asked.

"Me?" reacted the drifter. "Just cruising along. And what place is this?"

Answer was delayed. Elbows on table, the humped master once more surveyed the notorious Macho: man-killer who could smash antagonists down with bare hands—and, no doubt, could break them up more slowly if he would. A very handy man for certain kinds of work. In the cadaverous gray face grew a calculating light. The thin throat chuckled:

"Huh huh huh!"

Dugan tensed. There it was—the malignant tone and laugh which had come to him out of the air. Not only Zorro the Fox had been traced to his hole, but the diabolical creature which directed his cruelty.

Holding himself quiet, he strove for complete restraint of his fighting muscles. Word by word, step by step, the mystery of this place might be figured out. So advised one cool side of his mind. But in the other side—the hot side wherein burned memories of lost voices and dead souls on his back trail—a mangled bird and a tortured man clamored for vengeance.

Involuntarily his mouth hardened and his fists and feet moved. The sandaled feet scraped slightly back and the loose hands clenched. Into the hooded eyes across the table darted instant suspicion.

"A spy! So I thought, *Señor* Macho!"

The hunched body jerked back and the skinny right hand swooped down. A pistol sprang up and fired. It missed.

Dugan had leaped. That backward heave and down-snatch had been a second too slow. Swerving to the left of the treacherous host, El Macho dashed around the table-end and seized the gray neck. With a right-hand heave he yanked his antagonist up. With a sideswipe of the left fist he parried the next gunshot.

Writhing, kicking, vainly shooting again and again, the vulturous shape hissed and spat while its gun crashed out fire and noise. Dugan grasped the gun arm, forced the body against the table, and twisted with both hands. Bones gritted, crunched, and cracked. A queer screech sounded. The gun dropped to the floor.

Dugan's left hand rose and closed on the throat. Whirling the limp thing overhead, he flung it away to flop down and out, neck broken.

Another gunshot cracked. Beside the

corridor doorway projected a half-seen head, one eye gleaming over a leveled barrel which flashed again. Sudden shock smote Dugan's shirt, low down. Across his left side burned a streak of pain.

Again sidestepping, he drew and shot back. Three bullets gone, he ceased fire. The assassin's head vanished.

Gun up, he plunged out through the opening; then halted. On the corridor floor lay a yellow-faced, sharp-nosed sneak with eyes astonished and a short pistol gripped in one narrow paw. Right temple blown away, it now was nobody. It had been somebody named Zorro.

CHAPTER IV

The outer door was shut; so slyly closed and bolted that Dugan had not heard the movements. Glancing down-corridor, he saw a motionless shape and wheeled toward it.

Slowly his gun sank. Momentarily dark against the bright light of a doorway opening to a sunlit *patio*, the silent watcher was the white girl, standing petrified with a tray of food.

Snapping open his cylinder, he ejected empty shells, thumbed in fresh cartridges, holstered the gun; felt his left side, and dourly grinned. Zorro's bullet had only opened a stinging gash. Then, hot tide of fight ebbing, he looked at the dead men before and behind him and scolded himself:

"You damn fool, why did you give yourself away? Why didn't you stay deadpan till you knew what this is all about?"

His voice droned into glum silence. Then sounded another; low, vibrant, speaking English:

"One moment, sir!"

The girl was advancing. Tray still gripped in slender hands, she eyed Zorro, studied the broken-necked cripple beyond the doorway, and turned back toward the *patio*.

"Come, if you please," she bade. Dugan followed.

Under a veranda roof she set her tray on a small table. Entering another room, she returned, with two slim chairs. Dugan sat; poured strong coffee from a hot pot, and looked about.

Nobody else was there. Other doors in the square-set inner walls were closed. Inside, as outside, the *hacienda* seemed strangely deserted.

But now along the corridor sounded knocking at the front door; slow knocks with a gun-butt. The girl, listening, soon moved inward. Dugan arose and watched.

Tapping on the door, the girl received carefully spaced raps in return. She slid the bar. Sunshine blazed in and a male voice asked:

"You are safe, *Señorita*?"

"Perfectly, I think, José. But enter."

In walked the bulky guard-commander. He stopped, eyeing the dead Zorro; glanced into the room where lay the slain cripple; shot another look down-corridor at the dark shape of Dugan blocking the *patio* portal.

"Ah. I see," he purred. "Is there anything you desire, *Señorita*?"

His sombrero nodded toward the ominous Dugan. The girl hesitated. Something else interrupted.

The mastiff shouldered José aside. His big head looked anxiously up at the girl. Then, brow wrinkling, he sniffed. Suddenly he lunged past her to stare at the dead Zorro; then burst into furious barks.

Through a long moment his deep chest roared long-pent hate. All at once he stopped, muzzle up and twitching toward another smell. Abruptly he about-faced toward the room where lay the clubfoot. From him came a low growl, more deadly than his recent open-mouthed noise. Bristle-haired, stiff-legged, he stalked inward.

"*Perrito!*" spoke the girl. "*Aqui!* Here to me, little dog!"

Quiet but penetrating, the command reached through the thick skull. Slowing, the mastiff hesitated. Again she spoke, this time with a lilting uptone:

"*Perrito? Perrito?*"

Voice and sweetness were those once heard on Dugan's back trail.

The mastiff, years ago a *perrito* (puppy), now a huge brute, gave a final snarling snuffle and turned back to the coaxing woman. She walked away toward the *patio*.

Dugan moved back. As the girl passed him the dog stopped; smelled, then slouched along.

José lingered behind. Squatting, he drew the pistol from Zorro's hand; opened it, closed it, regarded spent shells on the floor, and tossed it outside. Rising, he sauntered into the master's room.

Grouped outside the front doorway, other slouch-hatted men awaited orders. Their commander soon reappeared. He spoke four words. At once four riflemen stepped in. The door swung half-shut.

"Hold it there, José!" warned Dugan.

José, without looking, motioned to his men. The exit reopened. The five strolled down the corridor.

In the *patio* José swung to his right and lounged against a wall, rifle loose. The four dummies obeyed the unspoken command, loafing likewise. The girl, standing straight against an outer pillar, contemplated all the men. At her feet the great dog lay mumbling in subsiding animosity toward things left behind. Dugan again sat, facing all, and drank his coffee.

Silence thickened. At length José volunteered: "This stranger—if you have not heard, *Señorita*—is one called El Macho. Very sudden in his actions, it is said. And it would seem so."

There he paused. The girl regarded El Macho—outwardly a ruffian who by blind chance had drifted in here, killed two men for no known reason, and now might be sent along. Sent where? And how?

Five riflemen stood apparently awaiting her verdict. Dugan smiled and chanted:

"*Perrito, perrito, Estas muy bonito!*"

His voice now was dulcet, with an upward lift. At the sound the mastiff cocked drooping ears. At the next words the dog arose with teeth bared.

"Huh huh huh! Feet getting warm? The iron, Zorro—"

The malicious voice stopped there. Then, in his natural tone, Dugan said:

"Thanks, folks. I only stopped here for a cup of coffee. Now I'll be traveling again. Unless there are objections."

Hands loose, he strolled toward the gunmen. "Any objections?" he pleasantly inquired.

They stood unmoved, watching the girl. She swiftly stepped forward, asking:

"Stranger, where did you hear those words?"

"Over the air, girl. José, I said I was traveling.

So—"

"Don't hurry," advised José.

The girl sprang at the departing outlander, grasping his left arm. As his muscles tensed she besought:

"No—no—do not hurry, friend! Where— Tell me— What brought you here?"

"Well, maybe a little bird." Quick light flooded her face.

"My little *lorito!* Where did you find him? And Ramón— Did you see Ramón?"

"Who might Ramón be?"

"My brother, sir! Tell me—is he safe?"

The dark eyes eagerly searched his. Then, as he regarded her in grave silence, she drew away, murmuring:

"Oh! He is—"

For a second she drooped. All at once she grew angry.

"Tell me!" she stormed, face now ablaze. "Tell me, or—*Caramba*, you who know so much— Too much, perhaps! Just what are you here for, and— *Válgame*, I can have you shot! I can—"

"A moment, *Señorita!*"

José, no longer deferential, broke in on

her incoherent wrath.

"You are not handling matters well," he sturdily continued. "This Macho is not to be threatened. And you may remember that he stopped here by your own signal. You spied him coming; and you waved the handkerchief to me when he was leaving. So we invited him in, instead of—"

The slight pause was sinister. Then:

"This Macho was attacked by both Satán and Zorro. Their guns prove it. And, *cra*, never have I seen so good work done by a man caught in a trap! But—"

Again he halted; then concluded:

"I say no more, *Señorita*—except that time may be short."

The last words seemed significant. The young woman's flush of rage receded, leaving her again cream-white. Formally she said:

"I apologize, sir." Dugan grinned.

"That's all right," he said.

"And if your boys feel like laying down their guns and smoking a *cigarrillo* maybe we'll all get together."

"An idea most excellent, Macho," accepted José.

Stooping, he laid his rifle flat. Rising, he drew a thin bag of tobacco and a thinner roll of bark wrappers. The four automatons beyond him followed the lead. Smoke floated out and up.

"Well, now," explained Dugan. "I was rambling down along the Orinoco. And why I was there is nobody's business. But then—"

Once more at ease, he told a concise story, the story of a desperate little bird, a dead man in a hammock, raw feet, and an idle drifter wondering why.

"I'm still wondering," he concluded. "But if you people wouldn't want to say—"

Yawning, he turned again toward the exit. José and his half-squad dropped their burned-out cigarettes. The girl drew a long sigh; then impulsively declared:

"The good God Himself must have guided you here, *amigo!* You have come like an avenging angel!"

"Thanks," dryly replied Dugan. "That's a new one. Some folks call me a son of the devil."

José chuckled.

"*Sí.* Especially in a fight," he remarked. "And that reminds me—you *muchachos* would be more useful outside. Let me know when you see— You know what."

The wordless quartet grasped their guns and shuffled away. Dugan quizzically eyed their foreman, who hinted:

"With your permission, *Señorita*—"

"*Sí,*" she agreed. "Tell him what he should know. I should be most lacking in gratitude if I withheld proper return to this *caballero.*"

The words were Castilian Spanish, the phrasing and pronunciation punctiliously correct. At Dugan's slight smile she flushed again.

"I regret, sir," she quickly added, "that I speak like a book—if you think so. But I have had no schooling except books—and the help of my father. I— Oh, what do you think of me, *Señor* Norteamericano?"

Hands clenched, she awaited sarcasm. None came. Instead he said:

"Well, I know you're no kitchen-mechanic. And if you haven't been anywhere yet, so much the better for you, maybe. The less you see of some schools the more you can be your real self. I've been in several—

and got out. Got kicked out! And I'm glad of it. Then I thought it was the end of the world. Now—*pfff!*

"Aside from that, I think you're a temperamental Spanish hellcat and maybe can fight like one. And I gather the idea from José here that things aren't finished around here yet. If there's any excitement due, I'm in no hurry."

His easy banter routed her momentary embarrassment.

"A hellcat, am I?" she laughed. "Hellcat! Ha ha ha! Perhaps that's true! And— Do you dislike hellcats, Macho?"

Her eyes sparkled, and her lithe body swung slightly forward, tantalizing. Then José coughed.

"As I was saying, *Señorita*—"

She frowned; then, glancing at the corridor, nodded.

"*Ahora*, it's this way, Macho," immediately pursued José. "This *hacienda* is that of *El Señor* Miguel Soto y Delgado. An old family. *El Señor* died half a year ago. God rest his soul!

"He left two children; Ramón, now gone, and Helena, now here. Then came one Soto, a legal relation. Very legal, Macho—if you get that. Politicians, lawyers, tax-greedy government vultures, all were behind this twist-footed, twist-brained desk-sitter. The—"

José tensed; stood with jaw shut, swallowing lurid words unfit for feminine ears. Then:

"You saw him, Macho. One named Soto. We called him Satán: the devil himself. He was. With his own feet only hoofs, he loved to torture the feet of real men. And— *Cra!* You know the rest."

He swung toward the corridor, listening, evidently uneasy.

"No, there's a lot I don't know," demurred Dugan. "Why would he act that way? And why did you stand for it? And—"

He nodded toward Helena. Why had she remained here, humbled, when some escape might be managed?

"He believed there was some treasure here," explained José. "An insane notion. He was *loco*. But he had the power, through some legal crook— and an armed gang to search and seize. Taxes, he said, had not been properly paid—and so on. Old pictures were taken down, walls were sounded, everything done—but nothing found. There was nothing to find.

"Servants were grilled until they ran away. Then they were overtaken and shot. You have been around, Macho; you know what can be done in the name of the law. We who were not so foolish as to run saved ourselves by seeming to be slavish servitors. Even the young *Señor* Ramón—he was not, God rest him, a fighter like the old Don Miguel—even Ramón endured indignity until Satán lost patience and burned him. His feet were not so badly burned as some before. He was given a day to think before a worse thing would be done.

"That night he disappeared. And you know the end of that.

"The *Señorita* Helena, though, was not harmed in any bodily way. We saw to that. Once I spoke plainly to Satán on that point, and he heeded. His way with her was to torture her pride with menial work and—"

Abruptly he turned doorward. There stood a shabby rifleman.

"Hah! *Qué pasa*, Tomas!" José grabbed his gun. "They come?"

"*Sí*," grunted the other. "From the west."

"West? They went north. Hah! And Ramón—poor lad—outguessed them by going south. They have swung about but not found him. And now, damn the dirty dogs—"

His teeth snapped like a steel trap. He took one step; then halted.

"Macho, this is not your affair," he asserted. "Stay in! And—if anything goes wrong—protect the *Señorita*."

The last words stopped Dugan's belligerent forward motion. Hiding within doors, with trouble looming outside, was not his habit. But now he shortly nodded.

"All right. Forget I was just a gentle angel from heaven. But roll your own, hombre. I'll stand by."

José leaped away. The flat-faced messenger had already gone. Dugan strode after the foreman and, shutting the front door, reached for the bar. Then broke a single hard bark.

The mastiff, recently quiescent, now was instinctively alive to outer danger. Lunging against the barrier, he pawed.

"Go get 'em, big boy!" chuckled Dugan, reopening. Perrito sprang out. The door closed and the bar slid.

Turning away, Dugan collided with Helena. Noiseless, forgotten, she now was close at hand, wide eyes teasingly innocent.

"What goes on, big man?" she softly inquired. "You're asking me?" he retorted. "You know more about this than I do."

"I? I know nothing, *Señor*. I am only a little *llanos* girl, and—" A hand rose and stroked his jaw. "I think, if you would shave, you would be quite handsome."

"Hell's bells!" he exploded. "Get out from under foot, will you? Go sit in the *patio!* I'm busy!"

Into the master's room he strode; the room where Satán lay like a misborn dead monkey. Heaving open a tight front shutter, he heard a mocking reply from the corridor: "As you say, *Señor!* I obey."

Outside he saw only the empty plaza and the brooding cordon of trees. But from somewhere near sounded a warning hiss:

"*Sssst!* Shut up!"

"Good advice," muttered the insider.

Moving the barrier almost tight, he glanced over his shoulder. Helena was gone.

Gloomy within, blank without, the *hacienda* waited under the sun.

Time dragged. Standing, waiting in thick silence, Dugan looked back at the broken Satán and fitted various pieces into a still broken puzzle. His own surprised survey of the white girl; the vulturous watch of the clubfooted schemer; the satanic idea that José, hitherto somewhat obstructive, now might be replaced by the more powerful, reputedly merciless Macho.

If skillfully baited by creamy beauty this black-jawed Northern tough might—

"That's what you thought, you lousy ape!" jarred Dugan. "But it's funny how things work out. And—"

His gun-hand dropped, clutched, held. His left moved the shutter an inch wider ajar. Outside sounded a dull thudding of tired horse hoofs.

CHAPTER V

Into the clearing trooped horsemen on drooping animals cruelly roweled by Spanish spurs; horsemen in semi-military uniforms, blouses open, with rifles slung awry in army scabbards. Under their sloppy sombreros their faces were dark. Their commander was black.

Dark brown Indians, flat-faced, brute-mouthed, were led by a coal-black Negro. Dugan, watching, grinned downward. No government men, these. Territorial hirelings, sent out by a *llanos* governor grasping all he could get by torture or death, and scheming to grab the Presidency of Venezuela next.

The same old picture. In this land where all shadings of white skin meant much, Presidential troopers should be led by a white man.

So the story of José added up right thus far. Now, outside, José quietly announced:

"*Bien 'sta.* All's well. You didn't find him, *Señor Capitán?*"

The black captain's cloudy eyes slid along the shut wall, then outward.

"Where's the guard?" he growled.

"Here. Perrito and I. The boys are on duty in the trees and reported your approach. But speak softly, *Señor Capitán.* The commandant is not to be disturbed just now."

"Hm!" A wicked smile flitted over the

black visage. "He was amused last night?"

"*Quién sabe*? It is not for me to know."

"*Bien*." Still crookedly smiling, the captain ordered, "Take my horse, *muchacho*!"

"*Mucho gusto*. A pleasure."

José stepped briskly forward. The black swung off and down. As he touched ground José purred:

"With my regards, *Capitán*—"

His rifle leaped to hip-level and fired.

Shot through the body, the troop leader doubled over, reeled, but kept his feet. Instantly José seized the horse's reins and kicked him in the belly. While astounded troopers sat momentarily petrified, the scared animal bolted across the plaza, José running with it in prodigious bounds.

"*Maldito!*" groaned the staggering black. "Kill—kill—"

Rifles sprang from scabbards and banged after José. A terrified half-scream told that the fleeing horse was hit. But a mocking yell testified that the human runner had escaped.

Then from the house-front rushed a tawny beast which snarled once and sprang like a *llanos* puma. Perrito, the mastiff, clenched his huge jaws in the crouched black man's neck. Shooting wild, the captain fell.

From the woods across the plaza broke a shout: "Now!"

The voice was that of José. Response was trigger-quick.

Flashes licked out from tree-trunks. Bullets whacked into flesh. Rapid reports hammered.

From right and left and ahead the lurking home-guard pumped sudden death into the bunched riders. Caught in the bare clearing which they themselves had made, semi-surrounded by ambushed enemies, blocked on one side by the wide front wall of the fort-like house, the trapped bloodhounds who had vainly hunted the young *Señor* Ramón had scant chance.

Leaderless, they reacted to attack in blundering confusion. Voices yelled, striving for command—but each order different. Horses reared, bumped others, threw their masters' rifles off hasty aim. Some men obeyed a random order to dismount and fight on foot. Some charged at the trees. Some about-faced to dash rearward—but met bullets. Turn whither they might, blunt .44 slugs knocked them down and out.

A stray bullet thumped into Dugan's shutter. The tough wood jumped back hard against his head. Dazed, he instinctively struck at it; then caught himself and wryly grinned. Fighting nothing—hiding like an old woman, while the boys' outside were—

"Grrrump!" he growled, striding to the barred door.

As he reached it another bullet thudded against it. Recklessly he yanked the bar and lunged out. He met no action.

The last shot had been fired. In the woods was ominous silence, broken only by irregular metallic clacks of breech-bolts relocking. Empty guns had paused for new loads.

But the work was finished. In the stumpy clearing nothing moved. Nothing but a red-jawed mastiff which, sated but still savage, arose from a sprawled black man-corpse and, licking chops, stalked away unhindered.

Elsewhere, the ground was littered with mingled bodies of men and horses, a few weakly struggling, others limp. Contortions soon ceased. Mercilessly efficient after long waiting, the executioners avenging many past crimes against this *hacienda* had wasted few bullets. Not a horseman nor a horse recently enforcing the rule of Satán and his politico-legal backers had won free to tell any tales.

Now again broke the exultant voice of José: "Forward, lads!"

From the tree-cover rushed wolfish shapes with guns up and yellowish faces fiercely agrin. No longer dumb slaves, but each a fighting man at last released, they swooped at their fallen enemies as a mop-up squad. Only a squad, plus José. Nine barefoot peons, who had just annihilated twenty-odd professional troopers and their mounts.

Dugan blinked. But then, multiplying the old-fashioned repeaters by their long magazine-loads and adding the advantages of pointblank range and trapped target, he sniffed and lounged against the door frame.

There, as the victors scrambled among the confused bodies, a hand closed on his shoulder.

"We have won, big man?" eagerly questioned Helena. "The tyrants are destroyed?"

"Looks that way."

"Thank God—and you, my brave savior!"

Her hand grasped harder, while her wide gaze burned into his. Dugan's lids narrowed. That grip was too strong, the reckless light in the flushed face too hot, for those of a girl who had obediently waited in the *patio*.

Seizing the hand, he smelled it. On it was the odor of gun oil.

As she tugged away he moved with her. Through the doorway both faded. Inside, he glanced left. There, opposite the master's room, was one similar—but with a shutter half-open and a rifle lying on the floor.

"So you took some shots yourself," he accused. Her flush deepened. Struggling with contrary emotions, she pulled back, came forward, stood hesitant. Then at Dugan's back sounded a harsh cough.

Turning, Dugan encountered the hostile gaze of José. Chest out, jaw clenched, brows down-drawn, the stocky home-guard glowered at the outlander holding the *Señorita* Helena. His rifle was gone, but each brown fist now held a military pistol gleaned outside; muzzles down, but—

For a second Dugan stared. Then, gauging the menace in the glittering eyes, he dropped the girl's wrists and slid a hand to his own gun-butt.

"Would you like to be traveling, Macho?" inquired José.

The jarring tone and ominous attitude roused reckless retort:

"So you're back again, General Nuisance? Just won the war, did you? And now you think I've got intentions on this lady? Well, so what? What's in your own mind, ugly-mug?"

The foreman's hands twitched, but stayed down. Then crackled another voice:

"José! Follow me!"

Blazing with inner fury, the *Señorita* Helena snapped the command in no sweet little-girl tone. José, hot with recent victory, lifted his chin defiantly. But then his face grew wooden.

"As you say, *Señorita*," he grudgingly acquiesced.

Stiffly he walked past Dugan. The girl, thin-lipped, said:

"*Señor* Macho, I request you to wait. I have something to say to this one."

"So have I. And I'll say it now. José, turn around here. That's right. Now listen: You're a big shot, you think. Awhile ago I thought so, too. But since I saw you shoot a man when he wasn't looking and run for cover behind a horse, I don't think you're so tough. If you were, why didn't you knock off Satán and Zorro and Company before I drifted in here? You had the guns and the gang. But you didn't have the guts. That's it. No real guts.

"And now you're the boss around here, are you? Maybe. I wouldn't know. But while the *Señorita* speaks her piece to you, you can leave your guns here. Drop 'em! Now!"

Holding his gaze, he shouldered the outer door shut and leaned against it, excluding other gunmen; then thinly smiled. Slowly José obeyed. His pistols clunked down on the floor.

"*Bueno!*" jeered El Macho. "Now about my getting out of here: That suits me, and the sooner the better. I'm no ranch mule, and nobody can tie me down. But anybody that tries to kick me out is liable to get a sudden shock. See?"

The impact of his hard words and bass rumble beat down the mestizo's smoldering self-importance. Watching him, Dugan did not see that his declared determination to go made Helena wince.

Then, wordless, the girl and her satellite walked away to the *patio*. Behind them the door closed.

Dugan slid the bar at the front door; eyed the dead Zorro; seized him, flung him into the room with Satán, shut that door also. Picking up the pistols dropped by José, he tossed them into the other room to fall near the emptied rifle. Once more he pulled a door tight. Alone in the dark corridor, he rolled a *cigarrillo* and smoked.

Time crept along. Outside, killers from ambush looted the dead, and black birds ghoulishly circled on long wings high in the hot blue. From the closed *patio* came no sound. At length, dropping his used-up cigarette, the waiter remarked:

"Just a little country girl, sweet as sugar. Ain't seen nothin' yet, big travelin' man. But you can shoot men in the back when they're busy, and step over a dead Zorro without knowing he's there. You forget 'em quick, Lady Cream-Puff, when they're dead ones. Yes, I'll be riding, as soon as—"

Abruptly the *patio* door reopened. José, wooden face oddly alight, padded rapidly up-corridor. Behind him glided Señorita Helena, head high, face cold; a Spanish queen in full command of her realm. To the lounging outlander she crisply ordered:

"Let my servant pass!"

Dugan stood impassive, lazily eye-ing both. José warily stopped beyond the Northerner's long fist-range. The girl, statuesque, waited behind him.

"As you please, *Señorita*," then drawled Dugan. "And I'll be going, too."

"If you wish, *Señor!*" she flashed.

Rigid, she waited while he unbarred the door and gestured José out. When the mestizo had passed he doffed his sombrero, swung it wide in exaggerated Spanish flourish of *adios*, and strode away.

CHAPTER VI

Stolidly José walked toward the woods, disregarding his gang of triumphant peons who, ready for more slaughter, wolfishly eyed El Macho and awaited only a sly signal. None came. At the mestizo's back El Macho swung easily along with hands loose but gaze fixed on the leader. One move out of turn, and—

José knew. Stepping high over the dead, he made straight for the woods.

As the two men reached the shade, the girl in the *hacienda* doorway sprang out— then caught herself. Looking at her peons, she drew back. Proudly white, she disappeared into the shadow of her dead house.

Within the grove, José led the way to a covert where Dugan's horse contentedly rested. Still wordless, he carefully saddled and loaded the animal, brought it forward, and stopped.

"As you see, *Señor* Macho," he then announced, "your horse has been given special attention. He was not put into the corral or made to find his own food. I have felt that you might be going.

"Now before you go, there is one matter to be mentioned. This *hacienda* lives to itself. It has no use for politicians or policemen or soldiers. On the other hand it has no use for revolutionists or outlaws or other bloodsuckers. In the law or out of the law, all they want is blood and gold. Either way, they always come in gangs.

"We have heard that El Macho is different. About this Macho there are many different stories, but they all agree that he also wants only to be let alone, like this *hacienda*—and tells no tales to the politicians or anyone else. So now— Adios y buen' suert'! Good fortune to you!"

Across his thick lips twisted a peculiar smile. Abruptly he jerked the horse forward into Dugan's grasp. As the Northerner's left hand closed on the reins he walked fast away.

"Say, wait a minute, hombre!" objected Dugan. "Maybe I've misunderstood you."

"Maybe you have, Macho," came brief reply. "You do sometimes make mistakes."

A sardonic chuckle, instantly repressed, floated back. Then José vanished amid the trees.

Dugan mounted and went. Out in the open, he drifted without conscious aim, yet again steering east, downriver, toward the far Atlantic Ocean where ships sailed for— where? Anywhere but here. Anywhere but North or South America; somewhere over the rim of the world, where—

Reaction had hit him hard. The strange air trail along which he had followed a winged voice had ended. The *hacienda* which he had happened to yank out of misery now had ushered him out with a snicker. So it seemed. And now the aftertaste of it all was sour.

But, hours later and leagues away, his grim mood changed. At another waterhole he paused for much belated lunch. Opening his food pack, he found something stealthily added by an expert saddler named José.

A canvas-wrapped sausage, tightly corded, was too hard and heavy to be mere meat. Loosed of its spiral winding, it became a bag. From it poured a compact mass of Venezuelan *morrocotas*: old-time gold coins, each worth about twenty dollars at old-time rates, and more today. Roughly, a thousand dollars.

Dazed, Dugan stared down at it; a small but potent heap of metal dropped on the starved dirt of the *llanos*, yellowly gleaming up with a mutely mocking echo of the farewell of José:

"You do sometimes make mistakes!" Rubbing his jaw, Dugan muttered:

"How the hell—"

Then, mind quickening, "Hm! Dumb Dugan, wake up! Old Clubfoot Satán was right. There's gold in them there walls, and the girl knew where it was, and now—"

Reddening, he flared:

"Now this is the payoff, hey, just to make double sure that the dirty damned tramp will keep his mouth shut? By Judas' Priest, I'll come back and make you eat this—and take it hot!"

He kicked the yellow dump. Coins scattered. With them jumped a hitherto unseen cube of white paper.

Scowling at it, he soon snatched it up. Neatly folded into many small squares, it opened into a sheet of precise script. Formally it stated:

Dear Sir:

We regret your departure from the house honored by your visit. We trust in God that our good fortune will soon return you to our humble home and—

Suddenly slashed out, the next bookish words were sunk in black ink. Bolder, the last ones read:

Adios—if you are afraid of
A HELLCAT

Dugan blinked as if slapped in the face. "Well, you little devil!" he muttered.

Crumpling the note, he walked out of the thin shade into the brown barrens, looking westward.

"You hellcat!" he softly said. "You've got plenty to give a man. And not only money. Not only a house and land and good tough dogs that'll stand by till—"

His musing voice paused; then continued:

"Till hell freezes over. And how it'll freeze, after you've got me under your thumb. Big fighting man from far away, romantic hero in the Spanish novels you've read, gets tamed down to just another house dog. And then if I don't jump when you snap the whip—"

Again he paused. In vivid memory he again saw José, respectful, then arrogant, then again reduced to subservience by tongue-lashing in a closed *patio*. "Just like that," concluded El Macho. "No, old brown boy, I won't cut you out of your job of running the rancho. Lady Cream-Puff hasn't much to learn about driving men— or shooting them. So, thanking you all very much for your kind attention, I'm not having any hellcats."

Ambling back to the gold, he scooped it up and retied the bag; ate, remounted, and asked his horse:

"Where were we going, old stumblebum, if anywhere?"

The animal turned south, heading again toward the huge yellow Rio Orinoco. Beyond that water-serpent still waited the mist-veiled mountains wherein ancient Indians with blowguns and poisoned darts killed white men at sight. Farther on lay the great green jungles of torrid backlands still unseen. So, leaving behind them the *llanos hacienda* where tame security would end roving adventure, the two drifters faded away into dreamy distance. Footloose and free.

✗

HERITAGE
by Arthur T. Hillman

Now the poet was old, and he knew that his days on Earth were numbered. So when he heard a soft knock at the door and glimpsed his tall, gray visitor, he knew him.

They went out together and down the narrow street, threading their way through busy, unheeding crowds. Death talked pleasantly, and the poet was content to listen.

"There is my companion for tomorrow." Death nodded towards a bent old man on the opposite side. "And yonder..." a skeletal finger pointed at a young girl, face pinched with want and toil, who peered into a grimy shop window, "my tryst with her is but three days off."

The poet pursed his lips grimly, but said nothing.

Now they had passed through the town and were out in the open oountry. And lo, as they journeyed amid the tall grass of a meadow, a youth passed them. His little curls were crowned with laurel and his face was fair and frank to see. A tiny piping voice rose in sweet notes of gladness.

Death scowled visibly and averted his eyes, and the poet smiled gently.

"There goes one you will never accompany, " he said. "There goes my child."

And the twain wended their way, while the infant song skipped and danoed and laughed at the bees and the nodding flowers.

✗

F.O.B. VENUS

by Nelson S. Bond

Something had gone a little haywire with my bug, and I had just repaired it and was CQ-ing on the 20 band when the door opened and Captain Hanson walked in.

Naturally, I was surprised. We were only four hours out of the Venus H-layer, and I hadn't expected any visitors; least of all the skipper. But he plunked himself down in the best chair and said, "Sparks, look at me! What do you see?"

That gave me a jolt. Even the best of them make the old dipsy-doo once in a while, but I never thought I'd live to see the day when Captain Hanson went space nutty. He'd been with the Corporation, man and boy, for more than thirty years now, and had never spent a day in dry-dock.

I reached behind me cautiously and said in as soothing a voice as I could muster, "Why, I see a very nice man, Captain. Now, just you sit quiet for a minute. I've got to—"

"Stop bein' a damned fool, Sparks!" said the skipper wearily, "An' put down that monkey-wrench! I'm not slippin' my gravs—yet. I'm just askin' you a simple question. What do you see?"

I said, "Is it facts you're after, Cap, or am I allowed poetic license? If it's facts, I see a swell, slightly gray-haired guy in his middle fifties who's been through the mill, knows space like a book, and—"

"Wrong.'" said Hanson. "Sparks, all radiomen are dumb. I guess that's why they're radiomen. What you see before you is a broken man. A man sadly buffeted by Fate and the dread clutch of circumstances. Not to mention meddlesome vice-presidents."

This time I got it.

"Biggs?" I said.

"Yes, Sparks. Biggs. Now tell me, man to man, what did I ever do to deserve Biggs?"

He had me there. Being the skipper of the *Saturn* is not what I'd call an easy job under the best of conditions. The *Saturn* is the oldest space-lugger still doing active duty on Corporation runs. She was built 'way back there before the turn of the centu-

ry. For the past ten or twelve years, she had been on freight service, having been judged unfit for passenger duty by the SSCB— Space Safety Control Board.

To make matters worse, while we were taking on cargo at Sun City spaceport, the skipper had been called into the company offices. When he came out again, he had this Biggs in tow.

Biggs was tall. Biggs was lanky and gangly and all the other adjectives you can think of that mean a guy's Adam's-apple sticks out. He was overflowing at the mouth with a great big grin, and he was as dumb as they make 'em. He had his Third Mate's papers and was entitled to be known as "Mister" Biggs—the "Mister" being a nice camouflage for his real name, Lancelot.

But—Biggs was the nephew of crusty old Prendergast Biggs, first vice-president of the Corporation. So there was nothing the skipper could do but gulp and say, "Very good!" when they assigned Biggs to the *Saturn*.

There was nothing to prevent him from hoping Biggs would stumble over his suitcases and bust his scrawny neck—but Biggs didn't do it. He was awkward enough to stumble, but lucky enough to fall on a cushion if he did!

I said gently, "What's he up to now, Captain?"

"What isn't he up to?" groaned the skipper. "First, he said he could handle the gravs when we broke out of Venus' clutch. So—"

"Oh!" I said, "*He* did that, did he?"

"Stop rubbin' your head an' feelin' sorry for yourself," said Hanson. "You got off lucky. Chief Garrity is nursin' two black eyes. One of the wipers has a busted arm. Everybody on the ship went floatin' off to the ceiling, same as you did."

"Anything else?" I asked.

"*Everything* else!" snorted Hanson. "While we were all scramblin' around in midair, Biggs made a grab for the hand-controls. He got the manual deflector by mistake. Todd has just finished shapin' the course revision. We're point-oh-seven degrees off course now; almost three hundred thousand miles! We've got to up revs and waste fuel to get back, or we'll report in to Earth a day late. And you know what that means!"

Sure, I knew what that meant. Cap on the carpet before the Board; the rest of us sitting around chewing our fingernails, wondering whether they'd yank the *Saturn* off the Venus run.

"Well, what are you going to do about him?" I asked.

"What can I do?"

"There's always the airlock," I suggested. "Nobody would ever blame you."

"This ain't no time to be funny, Sparks!" complained the skipper. "This is a serious problem. We've got a valuable cargo of *mekel*-root and *clab*-beans to take into New York. But if that guy messes up our flight any more—"

He shook his head dolefully. I scratched mine. Then I got a brilliant idea.

"Cargo!" I said. "There's your answer, Captain!"

"I'm listenin'," said Hanson.

"Put Biggs in charge of the cargo. That way he'll be down in the hold throughout the trip. He won't be up in the control turret to bother you. And there's nothing he can do down there that'll hurt anybody."

"But that's the supercargo's job," frowned the skipper. "Biggs knows that."

"Sure. But Harkness will play along with you. Tell him to let on he's sick. Give him a vacation for this trip. He deserves it, anyway. Then it's logical enough to put Biggs on special duty below."

The skipper grinned.

"Sparks, I take it back what I said about radiomen. I think you got somethin' there!"

"Then you'll do it?"

"Immediately," said Hanson, rising, "if not sooner!"

* * * *

So that was that. That night my relief came on duty, and I went down to the mess hall to eat whatever I could stomach of Slops' slumgullion. First person I met up with was Mr. Lancelot Biggs himself.

"Hello, Sparks," he said.

"Hello, yourself," I answered. "What are you doing at this mess? Thought you ate at the skipper's hour?"

"I did until now," he grinned. "Harkness was taken ill this afternoon, and the Skipper put me on emergency duty in his place."

"Is that so?" I said, looking as surprised as possible. "Well, that's quite a job. Lot of responsibility, you know. That cargo's valuable."

I had to grin at the way his lean face sobered.

"I realize that, Sparks. I'm devoting a lot of thought to the job, too. You know, I'm a bit of an experimenter, and it seems to me—"

One of the mess boys brought on my chow then, and I didn't listen to the rest of his chatter. Which was a sad mistake. If I had listened, I would have been able to warn Captain Hanson that trouble was on the way.

I think it was about the third day out that I began to smell those smells. Yes, I know it was the third day, because I'd just contacted Joe Marlowe on Lunar Three, giving him declination and cruising speed of the *Saturn*. I thought it was funny, but guessed it would go away. It didn't. It got worse. Finally, on the fifth day, I decided to do something.

There's nothing like meeting trouble halfway. I was just on my way from the radio room to the control turret when I bumped smack into Captain Hanson. It was a head on collision, but the Skipper's "Oof!" took longer than mine, so I got to talk first.

"Listen here!" I yelled, "I've had about as much of this rickety old tub as I'm going to stand. If you can't put a stop to those stinks Slops makes in the galley—"

Hanson gave me a look that would wilt lettuce.

"I don't want no trouble with you, Sparks!" was his comeback. "I been smellin' those smells, too. That's what I was aimin' to ask *you* about. Have you been foolin' around with some of them chemical experiments of your'n?"

"I have not," I informed him loftily. "And besides, while chemicals may stink sometimes, they don't ever give out a smell like the butt of an overripe cabbage. Except perhaps some of the sulphur compounds." Then I stared at him. "I'm not kidding. I think those smells are coming up out of the galley."

The skipper groaned softly.

"Trouble. Nothin' but trouble. It ain't enough I'm supposed to shuttle this barge between Earth an' Mars. Now I got smells to worry about, too. Well, come on! Let's look!"

We went down to the galley. Slops was stirring something in a bowl. I took one look and shuddered. Tapioca—again. And don't tell me you're not supposed to stir tapioca. I know it. Tell Slops.

Then the skipper loosed his blast.

"Okay, Slops," he snarled. "We give up. Where'd you hide it?"

Slops looked puzzled.

"Hide what? I didn't hide nothin'. What is this, a game?"

"Sure," I chimed in. "It's called Sniff-the-Atmosphere. You play it by pressing your thumb and forefinger to your nostrils. Then you try to guess what died."

"Quiet, Sparks!" roared the skipper. Then, to the cook. "Well, Slops?"

Slops shrugged.

"I ain't done nothin'," he protested. "I ain't hid nothin', and I ain't smelled nothin'. Now I got a meal on the fire. Go 'way and leave me alone."

The skipper looked at me, and I stared back at him. Both of us realized the same thing at the same time. Slops wasn't lying. The smell *wasn't* as bad here as it had been updeck.

Hanson scratched his head. He said, suspiciously, "Sparks, are you sure you ain't been mixin' chemicals?"

"I'll swear it," I told him, "on a pile of logbooks. That smell came from— Hey! What else beside the galley lies beneath my room and the control turret?"

"I'm a cook," said Slops, still stirring the tapioca, "not a blueprint. Don't ask me."

"Shut up!" snapped Captain Hanson. "He ain't askin' you. Let's see, Sparks. There's the storage closet...the reservoir...the refrigeration tanks, and the—" His eyes widened suddenly; fearfully. "Sparks!" he husked.

"Yes?"

"The vegetable hold!"

Man, that was it! The minute he said it, I knew. The vegetable hold—and Biggs in charge!

We hightailed it for the nearest ramp. The minute we turned down the corridor, the smell got worse. Hanson blasted down the aisle like a rogue asteroid, with me trailing along behind. We hit the door, rammed it open—

Biggs was in there. The darned fool was standing in there dressed in a bulger, calmly spraying the bins of *mekel*-rool and *clab* with a hose!

He turned as we entered and his eyes lighted behind the quartzite. His audiophone clacked pleasantly. "Hello!" he said. "Is there anything wrong?"

"Anything wrong!" bellowed Captain Hanson. "He asks if there's anything wrong! That—that suit! And that hose—" The skipper's face was turning purple. "And this heat!"

"I turned off the refrigerating unit," said Biggs pleasantly. "You see, I had a theory that since the climate of Venus is warm and moist, it would be better for the cargo if I attempted to simulate its normal conditions of growth. So I—"

"And the suit?" roared Hanson. "Why the bulger?"

Biggs moved his hands deprecatingly.

"Why, possible infection, you know. I didn't want to expose the vegetables to any organisms—"

"Infect...moisture...heat..." Captain Hanson gave up. He buried his face in his hands. "Tell him, Sparks! Tell him what he's doing!"

I said, "Listen, Biggs—your theory is no good. *Clab* and *mekel* have to be kept in a cool, dry atmosphere or they rot. As a matter of fact, they are rotten! That's why the captain and I came down here—to investigate the smell. If you weren't wearing a bulger, you'd notice it yourself."

"Smell?" said Biggs. "Why, now, come to think of it, I have noticed a curious odor about the ship from time to time. But I thought it was rats!"

Rats! On a space ship! Imagine!

That was the last straw for Hanson. He'd been trying, and trying hard. But now he exploded.

"Biggs!" he roared, "You've ruined this cargo! Now you're relieved from your command! But before you report to your quarters, I want every bit of this mess cleaned up. And I mean every last bit, understand? Junk it! Clear it out!"

Biggs faltered, "B-but, Captain, I only tried to—"

"You heard me!"

The skipper wheeled, fiery with wrath, and strode to the doorway. I hurried after him. I whispered in his ear, "Take it easy, Captain. He's the vice-president's nephew. Maybe you ought to go slow!"

"Slow?" groaned the skipper. "A fifty thousand dollar cargo ruined—and you tell me to go slow? I'll see that idiotic son-of-a-space-wrangler fryin' in chaos. I'll blast him out of space if I'm blacklisted for it!"

I said nothing more. What was there to say? Fifty thousand bucks worth of cargo rotting in the hold. The Board would love that!

* * * *

That was all until the next morning. The next morning I was on the bridge when Captain Hanson had a visitor: Garrity, the Chief Engineer. Garrity never came to the bridge. So I knew, the minute I saw him, that something was vitally wrong.

It was. Garrity's first words made that clear. He glared at the skipper accusingly from eyes that were still faintly purpled.

"Captain Hanson," he exploded. "Would you be so kind as to tell me where I can find my Forenzi jars?"

Hanson said, "Forenzi jars? What are you talking about, Chief?"

"You'll be knowing what a Forenzi jar is, no doubt?" said Garrity caustically. "'Tis a lead container for battery solution. Yesterday there were thirty of them in the storeroom. Today there are only a half dozen left!"

Hanson said pettishly, "Now, Chief, be kind enough to conduct your own search for the jars. I don't know anything about them. If you can't watch your own equipment, don't complain to me about it!"

"I'm complaining to you, sir," said the Chief, "for the verra simple reason that 'twas one of your men who removed them from the locker. Your third mate, Mister Biggs!"

"Biggs!" said Hanson. "Biggs!" His face reddened. He walked to the intercommunciation unit, jabbed the button that connected with Biggs' quarters. "Mr. Biggs?" he yelped, "Chief Garrity is up here in the turret asking about twenty-four lead containers that disappeared strangely from his equipment locker. Do you know anything about—"

The diaphragm clacked an answer. Hanson started. His eyes bulged. He yelled, "What?"

Again some metallic buzzing. This time Hanson didn't try to answer. He tottered away from the 'phone.

"G-Garrity," be faltered, "will you be needin' the Forenzis before we make port?"

"Well, 'tis not exactly *vital*—" admitted Garrity.

"But—why?"

Hanson made a weak gesture.

"Because they're—out there!"

"What?" I said. "Outside the ship? How come? Why?"

Hanson's eyes were haunted.

"Biggs," he said in a hollow voice, "thought they were garbage cans! He used them to dispose of the rotten cargo!"

* * * *

Well, there wasn't any danger of the Forenzis getting lost, anyway. But do you know I even had to point that out to Mr. Biggs? Yes. That night I got a personal message for him, and I took it down to his cabin. Being confined to quarters, he was lonely. He looked so abject that I felt sorry for him and lingered to talk for a while.

"I guess you think I'm a frightful dummy, Sparks," he said ruefully. "And I know Captain Hanson thinks so. But—this is my first flight, you know. And nobody ever told me what to use for garbage pails—"

"Look, Biggs," I told him, "there's no need for garbage pails in space. You can't just dump things out the airlock and expect to get rid of them."

"But Captain Hanson said to junk the spoiled vegetables."

"Junk. Not dump! They should have been thrown into the incinerator. You see, anything tossed out of the *Saturn* in free space just follows along with the ship." I grinned. "I'd hate to be one of the spaceport attendants on Earth when the *Saturn* comes in surrounded by twenty-four lead satellites full of garbage."

He picked me up on that one quick as a flash.

"But—but they won't be with us when we land, Sparks. As soon as we hit Earth's atmosphere, the friction will destroy the Forenzis and their contents."

I whistled softly.

"By golly, you're right. I clean forgot about that, and Hanson was so sore, he forgot it, too. That means we have to get those containers back into the ship before we hit the tropo, or we're going to lose a couple hundred bucks worth of equipment."

Biggs said meekly, "I—I'll be glad to go out and reclaim them, Sparks. Can you fix it up with the skipper?"

"I'll try," I told him.

* * * *

So the next day I told Hanson about it. The captain yanked his lower lip thoughtfully and agreed.

"Let him do it. That's better than giving him a free ride to Earth. And maybe he'll slip into the rocket blasts."

I passed the order on to Biggs, then went back to the radio room. Joe Marlowe was calling me from Lunar Three. And what he had to say drove all other thoughts from my mind. His message came right from Corporation headquarters.

"Please report," it said, "exact amount and probable value of cargo. Must have immediate reply."

I shot through an O.K. and passed the message up to the skipper. Then, my curiosity aroused, I contacted Joe on our private conversation band and asked him how come and why. He answered cautiously.

"Stock market taking nosedive in New York, Bert," he told me. "Corp. bonds fading. Need this cargo badly."

Boy, there was bad news! It was a private message, but I figured the Old Man ought to know it. So when he came in, I passed it along. He stared at me.

"Hell's bells, Sparks! Then in that case, I can't send this!"

"This" was the message he had intended to relay: It said, succinctly, "Cargo ruined. Value zero."

"If you do," I told him, "we'll all be

studying the want ads as soon as we hit port. Stock markets are screwy. This can't be a bad panic, or a fifty thousand buck cargo wouldn't be that important. But if the Corporation's under suspicion, and they learn the *Saturn*'s cargo is worthless—"

"What will we do then?"

"Stall," I suggested. "Maybe by the time we get in, the situation will be cleared up."

So we framed a message that wouldn't upset the apple cart too soon. It said, "Value of cargo estimated at Sun City spaceport as $50,000." And that was true enough...

* * * *

Biggs, with his unerring faculty for selecting the wrong moment, chose this time to come bouncing into my radio room. He had taken off his quartsite headpiece, but he was still wearing his bulger, and its deflated folds hung around him like the poorly draped carcass of a Venusian mammoth.

He said, "Hey, Sparks, have you got a book on energy and radiation?"

"Help yourself," I said, pointing to my bookcase. "Why, what's the sudden excitement?"

"I've been thinking," he began, "that maybe—"

Captain Hanson let out a blat like an angry lion.

"Mister Biggs! I thought you were reclaiming those Forenzi jars?"

"Yes, sir. I was. I mean—I am. But—"

"Never mind the 'buts'! Get back to work!"

"Y-yes, sir!" Biggs saluted meekly; tossed me a grateful glance. "Thanks, Sparks. I've got an idea, and if I'm right—"

"Get out, Biggs!" roared the skipper.

"Yes, sir." Biggs backed out hastily. He was thumbing the pages as he disappeared. Hanson yanked his lower lip angrily.

"The Corporation goes bust. The *Saturn* goes under the hammer. We're all out of jobs. And that—that insane young whippersnapper wants to play school!"

"He seemed mighty excited about something," I said.

"He'll be worse than that," promised the skipper, "if he doesn't get those jars back on board."

* * * *

All this, to get Biblical about it, took place on the seventh day. The *Saturn* is a ten-day freighter. So we had three more days of headaches before us till we slipped into New York Spaceport.

They were three days of headaches, too. The skipper and I spent most of our time hanging over the radio, watching the progress of the stock market slump in New York. We hoped the situation would ease up so that our coming in with a zero cargo wouldn't make any difference—but no such luck. Somehow the rumor had gotten around that the *Saturn*'s cargo would not be of sufficient value to keep the Corporation in the blue. And the Wall Street wolves were closing in, getting ready to snap if the rumor proved true.

In the meantime, our stupid friend, Biggs, was taking a hell of a long time to reclaim those Forenzis. It's really not a hard job, you know. All he had to do was slip out through the airlock, throw a grapple around each jar, and bring them in.

But he seemed to be as awkward at this as at every other job he had ever attempted. On an off-period, I went down to watch him once. I found he'd thrown grapples around the jars, but had not brought a single one into the airlock yet.

I told him, "You'd better get a wiggle on, Biggs. We hit the tropo tomorrow. If those things get into the atmosphere, you'll be able to pour them into the airlock."

"I know," he said abstractedly, "but I'm not quite ready to— Sparks, according to that book you lent me, cosmic rays go down to Angstrom units."

"That's right," I told him.

"That means they are more than ten times

as intense as gamma rays."

"Right again. Why? What's the pay-off?"

"That's what I'm trying to find out," he said strangely. He finished tying a loop around one of the jars, then pushed himself free and toward the airlock.

"You want me to help you drag 'em in now?" I asked.

"No thanks, Sparks. I think we'll leave them out till tomorrow," he said.

"But Captain Hanson—" I began.

"Tomorrow."

"After all, I'm just a radioman," I said with a shrug. "It's your funeral," I said.

* * * *

He got them inside the next day. I saw them lying in the corridor beside the airlock, covered with a strip of tarpaulin. And he got them in just in time, too, for about an hour later we hit the Heaviside layer.

We set out our Ampie and eased through all right. From there on. it was just an easy coast to Earth. We threw out our lug-sails—the retractable metal fins which give "space luggers" their name—and put on the power brakes. In a couple of hours we were settling into our hangar off New York spaceport.

I closed out my key and locked the radio room.

There was nothing more I could do now. So I went up to the control turret and found Captain Hanson gnawing the fingernail of his index finger down to the second joint.

"Well, Captain?" I said.

"Any late news, Sparks?" he demanded anxiously. I shook my head.

"Only bad news. The Board's sending over their appraisers immediately."

He said wearily, "Well, we did our best. If it hadn't been for that crazy Biggs, we'd still have our cargo. But as it is—"

"I wonder if International Stratoplanes need any radio operators?" I said gloomily.

We were grounded now. As we walked down the corridor the motors went off, and

I could hear the hiss of the airlock opening. We reached the port just as the committee entered. Doc Challenger was there, and Col. Brophy, and old Prendergast Biggs himself. I knew, then, that things were in a bad state, or all the big bugs would not have come out.

Challenger stepped forward, beaming.

"Happy landing. Captain!" he chortled. "I need not tell you how glad we are you came in safely. We've been experiencing bad times in New York, sir, bad times! But everything's all right now."

Hanson said, "Yes, sir. But I've got something to tell you, sir—"

"Later, Captain, later! First we must take up this cargo question. Approximately $50,000 worth of *mekel* and *clab*—is that right? We have our appraisers here. If your estimate is right, the Corporation will weather this—er—mild storm."

Hanson coughed nervously. He hedged.

"Well, now, you see—about that there cargo—" You never saw three faces lose their smiles so suddenly. There was stony silence for a minute. Then Col. Brophy said in a deep voice, "Captain Hanson, there's nothing wrong in your estimate of the cargo's value, is there?"

"No, sir. I mean the estimate was right, but—"

It was right here that young Lancelot Biggs interrupted.

"Excuse me, gentlemen," he said, "but I don't quite understand. Is it important that we land a cargo of *clab* and *mekel*?"

Captain Hanson whirled on him.

"Biggs!" he snapped sternly. Then he turned to old Prendergast Biggs. "Sir," he said, "I've delayed telling this as long as possible. But now I must tell you. This precious nephew of yours—"

The old man smiled fatuously.

"Yes, yes, Captain Hanson. A fine lad, isn't he? What was it you were starting to say, Lancelot?"

I grabbed Hanson's arm. I thought he was going to blow his tubes and hit somebody right then and there. But before he got a chance, Lancelot Biggs was talking again. To the Captain.

"Captain Hanson," he said seriously, "I wish you'd told me this before. I didn't realize that our cargo was so important—"

Then he turned to the committee.

"I hope you will not be surprised to learn, gentlemen, that our cargo is not vegetable. At the last minute, Captain Hanson decided to make a change—" Hanson's face turned white. He squawked, "What! Are you trying to shift the blame to—"

Biggs' voice drowned out his protest.

"—and so, gentlemen, we have placed the cargo right here for your inspection. Look!" With a swift motion he tore the tarpaulin off the Forenzi jars. I looked—and gulped! They were the same jars, all right. Only different! They were no longer a dull, whitish metal. They were a glinting copper color! Biggs patted one of them affectionately.

"Ask your appraisers to estimate the value of these, gentlemen. I think they'll find their value to be approximately a quarter of a million dollars. These are—pure gold!"

It's a good thing I was holding on to Captain Hanson's arm. For just as the committee was exclaiming, "Excellent! Excellent trading, Captain Hanson!" the skipper's nerves gave out. He collapsed like a punctured bulger. I remember shouting. "Water! Water, somebody!" Then I passed out, too!

* * * *

Afterward, the three of us were alone in the turret. And Hanson was asking. "But how, Biggs? I don't get it at all? How in blazes did it happen?"

Biggs blushed and looked uncomfortable.

"Why, it's pretty obvious when you come to analyze it, Captain. I can't understand how it is that no one ever discovered it before, in twenty years of space travel. But perhaps it's because ships and bulgers

are made of permalloy instead of lead. Or it may be that some enzyme secreted by the rotten vegetables acted as a catalyst. Lab workers will have to study that."

"You're still not telling us what happened."

"Don't you know? It was transmutation, induced in the lead Forenzi jars by the action of cosmic rays."

Captain Hanson said in an awed tone. "Exposure to cosmic rays done that?"

"Yes. Artificial transmutations were caused 'way back in the early 20th Century through bombardment with gamma rays. And cosmic rays are more than ten times as short as gammas.

"I began to suspect something strange was happening to the Forenzi jars when I first went out to gather them in. Their color had changed slightly, and their exterior was rather more granular. That's why I came in to borrow Spark's book on radiation. What I saw convinced me that the lead was being transmuted; was then in the mesolead stage, approximately an isotope of thallium.

"I decided to wait and see if the transmutation would continue—"

Hanson wiped his hand across his forehead.

"Suppose there'd been more time? And suppose'n the transmutation had gone on a step farther? What then?"

"Well, now, there's an interesting question. The next element down the ladder is platinum. It's quite possible that—"

"Wait a minute," interrupted the skipper. "Did you say platinum?"

"Yes. Why?"

"Nothin'. That is, nothin' much."

The skipper rose and strode to the intercommunicating phone.

"Ross?" he yelled. "Listen—I want you to get this crate ready to roll again. We're takin' off for Venus first thing in the mornin'. An', hey, Ross! Send to the warehouse for about five—no, make it six—dozen Forenzi jars. Yeah. Forenzi jars, I said.

"And Ross—get the biggest ones they got! The Corporation ain't found it out yet, but we're goin' into the transmutin' business. And Mister Biggs comes aboard as First Mate!"

THE WEAKLING
by Robert E. Howard

I died in sin and forthwith went to Hell;
I made myself at home upon the coals
Where seas of flame break on the cinder shoals.
Till Satan came and said with angry yell,
"You there—divulge what route by which you fell."
"I spent my youth among the flowing bowls,
"Wasted my life with women of dark souls,
"Died brothel-fighting—drunk on muscatel."

Said he, "My friend, you've been directed wrong:
"You've naught to recommend you for our feasts—
"Like factory owners, brokers, elders, priests;
"The air for you! This place is for the strong!"
Then as I pondered, minded to rebel,
He laughed and forthwith kicked me out of Hell.

NIGHT-FEAR
by Frank Belknap Long

In the big house, upstairs, a child was sobbing. Dr. Brannon could hear the sobs from the foot of the stairs, and his nearsighted eyes grew troubled. It was more than he could understand. Johnny wasn't a maladjusted youngster, starved for sympathy and affection; he was a perfectly normal seven-year-old, fond of games and well-liked by his playmates. A self-reliant, confident lad, even if he did have a way of smiling which made him seem wise beyond his years, at times.

Dr. Brannon tried hard to swallow his fear as he climbed the stairs. For the first time in ten years he felt really old—weary and baffled and old. He found himself thinking of Johnny's pretty young mother, and how hard she had tried to spare her son the loneliness and dread which had cast a shadow on her own childhood.

Even unto the third generation, he thought, and for an instant bitterness tightened his lips and drove the gentleness from his eyes. Why should a child playing with other children in the warm, bright sunlight feel a sudden, terrifying sense of insecurity? What could have darkened the sunlight for him and undermined his confidence in himself?

Dr. Brannon glanced nervously at his watch. Try as he might, he could not rid his mind of the alarming hour-old memory of a laughing, healthy child eclipsed by a little worn-looking white-faced stranger with tormented eyes and tear-stained cheeks.

Psychologists were always harping on the almost-miraculous sanity of childhood, its freedom from morbidity, its joyous acceptance of life as a shining, untarnished coin. How blind they were not to realize that children were at the mercy of night fears—great, shadowy-winged creatures which could inflict cruel wounds, and go flapping off into the darkness, leaving their small, terrified victims in full flight from reality on a plane incomprehensible to adults.

It is always a trying moment when an elderly physician must win the confidence of a young patient by absolutely untried methods. Dr. Brannon could still hear himself asking, "What frightened you, Johnny? Did you talk it over with the other children? Is that why you're so frightened?"

He might as well have saved his breath. Johnny hadn't wanted sympathy of a wheezing, red-faced old fool of a doctor.

The door of Johnny's room was ajar. Dr. Brannon could hear Johnny's mother moving about and making a difficult situation worse by talking to her son as if he were still a tot of three with a stubborn streak, and a bad case of sulks.

With an impatient grimace, he stepped into the room, and shut the door quickly behind him. "Well, Johnny, how do you feel now?" he asked. "Don't you think we'd better have another little talk—man to man?"

Johnny's mother ceased rearranging the pillows at her son's back and straightened with a sigh that was half a sob, the bedside lamp casting a circle of radiance about her pale hair.

"I'm sure he'll talk to me now," Dr. Brannon said, conscious of a faint irritation with the woman for being so beautiful seven years after the death of her husband. Somehow the mother of an ailing child who was not a little worn-looking grated obscurely on his sense of propriety.

In utter silence he drew up a chair, sat

down and looked at the lad on the bed over the top of his spectacles. He saw Johnny's face as a misty oval, the eyes darkly shining.

He coughed and adjusted his glasses. Seeing Johnny's face clearly, he felt a curious helplessness which his reason could not justify. Surely Johnny wasn't beyond help; he wasn't physically ill, or running a fever. His mother had perhaps unwisely put him to bed, and pulled down the shades, leaving him for a full hour in deep darkness. Naturally he would be blinking now, and confused, and resentful. He couldn't possibly be as tormented as he looked, as inwardly beyond hope of rescue.

Dr. Brannon hitched his chair nearer to the bed, and the smile that came to his face was slow and friendly. "If you were away at school I could understand your not wanting to talk about it," he said. "Strangers might not know what a brave lad you really are. But I *know*, Johnny. Surely you can talk freely to an old friend in your own home!"

For an instant Johnny drew back as if in secret pain. Then, abruptly, he leaned forward, his eyes accusing, his hands tightly clenched. "This *isn't* my home!" he said, and his voice seemed no longer the voice of a child, but that of some aging wanderer, shaken by despair and wretchedness.

Dr. Brannon stared for a long moment into the bewildered, angry eyes in shocked disbelief. Then his lips tightened, and he said in a voice that was almost a whisper: "So you've found that out at last, lad!"

Johnny's mother straightened as if stung by a hornet. "How *could* he find out?" she breathed. "None of the other children knew."

"How did you find out, Johnny?" Dr. Brannon asked.

Johnny shook his head, then looked away quickly.

"All right, Johnny," Dr. Brannon said, gently. "Keep it to yourself, if you wish."

He turned around to face Johnny's mother. "You can't keep secrets from some youngsters," he said. "You just can't, that's all. It's as great a folly as trying to hide a jam pot on a high shelf. Most likely the other children knew just enough to enable him to put two and two together."

Dr. Brannon took his spectacles and blew upon them. "Children's minds are tricky. When a lad like Johnny puts two and two together he'll come up with a figure that cuts across all mathematical boundaries. Not four, mind you, but a figure that cuts much closer to the truth."

Johnny's mother sat down on the side of the bed, put her arm around him and kissed him. "Johnny—" she whispered.

Dr. Brannon's eyes had a glint that might have been compassion or amusement—or both. "Your mother's here, Johnny," he said. "Doesn't that make it your home?"

"No, it doesn't."

"You're afraid, lad—is that it? For the first time in your life, you feel lost and afraid and alone?"

There was a quick, answering look of torment in Johnny's eyes.

Good lad, Dr. Brannon thought. *Someday, Johnny, you'll answer all the well-meant questions fearlessly. It's the only way we can give and receive help in the loneliness and the darkness.*

Dr. Brannon pushed back his chair, and stood up. "I'm going to prove to you that you have a home, Johnny," he said. "There's something you've got to face, and we're going to face it together."

At the door he paused to speak to Johnny's mother. "Get him ready," he said. "I'll be back in twenty minutes."

* * * *

When Dr. Brannon returned Johnny was ready. If Dr. Brannon had moved wearily before he now seemed to bear the weight of the world on his shoulders. "All right, lad," he said. "We may as well get going."

Dr. Brannon took Johnny by the hand, and together they descended the stairs of the big, silent house, moving slowly and awkwardly. Then out across a sun-drenched playroom they went, and down a long sloping corridor with shining walls.

Doors opened at their approach with an eerie droning, and closed noiselessly behind them. Five doors with winking lights, and then they were in another corridor which was almost a tunnel, and a cold wind seemed to blow in upon them.

At the end of the corridor they halted, and Dr. Brannon said, "You were born here, Johnny. For all the years of your life, this has been your home. A good home, Johnny, a home to be proud of. I was not born here, but the sunlight up above is as warm and bright as the sunlight I knew as a child."

"It's not real sunlight," Johnny said.

"No, of course not; but it's just as healthful. You see, lad, even now we who should be strong and self-reliant sometimes become frightened. We let ourselves become frightened, and it is very foolish." Dr. Brannon pressed Johnny's hand. "We thought we could protect you from the cold and the dark—to keep you from feeling lost and afraid for the few happy years before eight. We of an old generation had a less secure childhood."

Dr. Brannon scratched his ear. "I'm afraid we were not too successful; you were too smart for us. Youngsters really know how to cut corners to get at the truth, and when they do—" He smiled. "There's a fine kettle of fish to unboil, lad!"

Dr. Brannon tightened his grip on Johnny's hand. "So now for the first time you'll see your home as it really is. I'll tell you how it became your home, and you'll be proud—you'll be so very proud of the men who gave their lives to make it your home— you'll forget to be afraid.

"Now remember what I told you. That spacesuit is heavy and weighs you down. But away from the station's artificial gravity, you'll be as spry as a harvest mouse in a field of summer corn."

Dr. Brannon pressed a button and there was a steady, humming sound.

Dr. Brannon said slowly, "Now put on your oxygen-helmet, lad. That's right; just let it settle gently on your shoulders, the way your father did when the Earth was forever behind him, and he walked from the rocket with the courage of a true pioneer."

For a moment Dr. Brannon seemed to grow in stature, as if the bracing of his shoulders had added a cubit to his height. Then the airlock swung open, and the man and the boy walked forward together, and emerged hand in hand on the cold, dark surface of the moon.   ✗

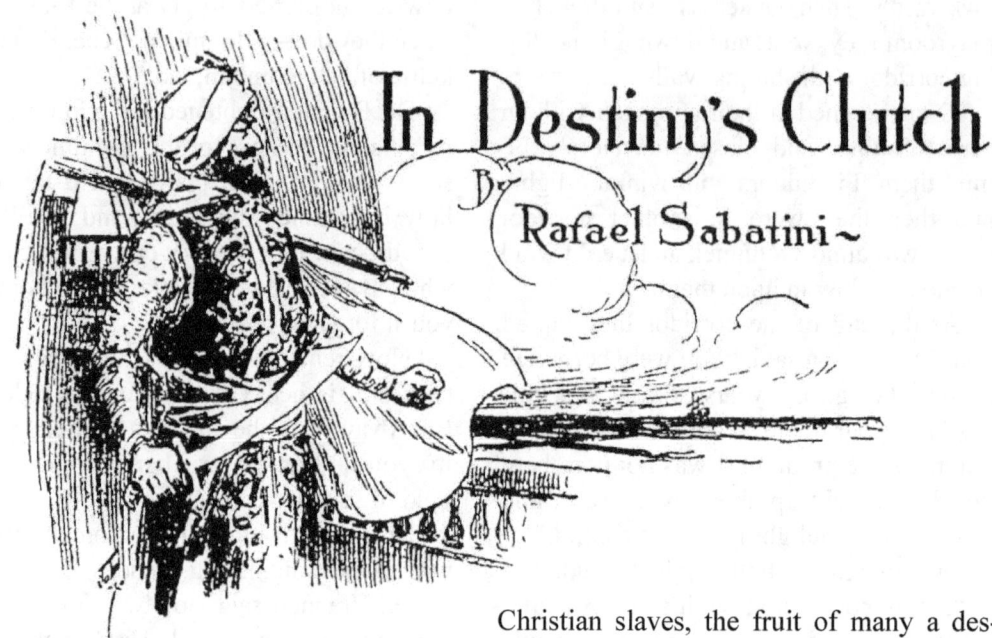

In Destiny's Clutch

By Rafael Sabatini

CHAPTER I

Corsair of the Seas

Ordinarily Dragut-Reis—who was dubbed by the Faithful "The Drawn Sword of Islam"—loved Christians as the fox loves geese. But in that fateful summer of 1550 his feelings toward them acquired a far deeper malignancy; they developed into a direct and personal hatred that for intensity was second only to the hatred which the Christians bore Dragut. The allied Christian forces under the direction of their emperor had smoked him out of his stronghold at Mehedia; they had seized that splendid city and were in the act of razing it to the ground as the neighboring Carthage had been razed of old.

Dragut reckoned up his losses with a gloomy and vengeful mind. He had lost his city, and from the eminence of a budding Basha in the act of founding a kingdom and perhaps a dynasty, he had been cast down once more to be a wanderer upon the seas. He had lost three thousand men, and among them the very flower of his redoubtable corsairs; he had lost some twelve thousand Christian slaves, the fruit of many a desperate raid; he had lost his lieutenant and nephew Hisar, who was even now a captive in the hands of his inveterate enemy, Andrea Doria. All this had he lost, and he was naturally embittered.

Yet Dragut was not the man to waste his days in brooding over what was done. Yesterday and today are but pledges in the hands of destiny. He returned thanks to Allah the Compassionate, the So-Merciful, that he was still alive and free upon the seas with three galleases, twelve galleys, and five brigantines, wherewith to set about making good his losses, and he bent his energetic, resourceful knavish mind to the matter of ways and means.

Meanwhile he had been warned by the Sultan of Constantinople that the Emperor Charles, not content with the mischief he had already done him, had, in letters to the Grand Signior, avowed his intent to pursue to the death "the pirate Dragut, a corsair odious to both God and man." He knew, moreover, that the emperor had intrusted this task to the greatest seaman of the day, to the terrible admiral of Genoa, Andrea Doria, and the Genoese was already at sea upon his quest.

Now once already had Dragut been captured by the navy of Genoa, and for four years, which he cared but little to remember, he had toiled at an oar on board the galley of Giannetino Doria, the admiral's nephew. He had known exposure to cold and heat; he had been broiled by the sun and frozen by the rain; he had known aching muscles, hunger, and thirst, and the sores begotten of the oarsman's bench, and his shoulders were still a crisscross of scars where the bos'n's whip had lashed him to revive his flagging energies.

All this had he known, and he was not minded to renew the acquaintance. It behooved him therefore to make ready fittingly to receive the admiral when he should appear. And by way of replenishing his coffers at once, venting a little of his vengeful heat, and marking his contempt for Christian pursuers, he had made a sudden swoop upon the southwestern coast of Sicily.

Beginning at Gergenti, Dragut carried his raid as far north as Marsala, leaving ruin and desolation behind him. At the end of a week he stood off to sea again, with the spoils of six townships and some three thousand picked captives of both sexes. He would teach the infidel Christian emperor to allude to him as "the pirate Dragut, a corsair odious to both God and man"— he would so, by the beard of the Prophet!

He put the captives aboard one of the galleys in charge of his lieutenant, Othmani, and dispatched them straight to Algeria to be sold there in the slave market. With the proceeds Othmani was to lay down fresh keels. Until these should be ready to reenforce his little fleet, Dragut judged it well to avoid encounters with the Genoese admiral, and with this intent he steered a southward course along the coast toward Tripoli.

Toward evening of the day on which Othmani's galley set out alone for Algiers, a fresh breeze sprang up from the north, and blew into the corsair's range of vision a tiny brown-sailed felucca as it might have blown a leaf of autumn. It was hawk-eyed Dragut himself, who, lounging on the high deck of his galley, first sighted this tiny craft.

He pointed it out to Biretta, the renegade Calabrian gunner who was near him. "In the name of Allah," quoth Dragut, "what walnut shell is this that comes so furiously after us?"

Biretta, a massive, sallow fellow, laughed. "The fury is not hers, but of the wind," said he. "She goes where'er it bloweth her. She'll be an Italian craft."

"Then the wind that blows her is the wind of destiny. Haply she'll have news of Italy." Dragut turned on his heel, and gave an order to a turbaned officer on the gangway below.

Instantly the brazen note of a trumpet rang out clear above the creak and dip of oars. As instantly the rowers came to rest, and from the side of each galley six and twenty massive yellow oars stood out, their wet blades glistening in the evening sunlight.

Thus the Moslem fleet waited, rocking gently on the little swell that had arisen, its quality advertised by the red and white ensign displaying a blue crescent that floated from the masthead of Dragut's own galley.

CHAPTER II

Winds of Destiny.

On came the tiny brown-sailed felucca, helplessly driven by what Dragut accounted the winds of destiny. At closer quarters they saw indications of the desperate effort that was being made aboard her to put her about. But they were lubberly fellows who had charge of her, and Dragut was content to wait. At last, when she was in danger of being blown past them, he crossed to meet her. As the long prow ran alongside of her grappling hooks were deftly flung to seize her at mast and gunwale, and but for these she must have been swept away by the oars of the galley.

From the prow Dragut himself, a tall and handsome figure in his gold-embroidered scarlet surcoat that descended to his knees, his snow-white turban heightening the swarthiness of his hawk face with its square-cut black beard, stood to challenge the crew of the felucca.

There were aboard of her six scared knaves, something between lackeys and seamen, whom the corsair's black eyes passed contemptuously over. He addressed himself to a couple who were seated in the stern sheets—a tall and very elegant young gentleman, obviously Italian, and a girl upon whose white, golden-headed loveliness the corsair's bold eyes glowed pleasurably.

"Who are you?" he demanded haughtily in Italian.

The young man answered for the twain, very composedly, as though it were a matter of everyday life with him to be held in the grappling hooks of a Barbary pirate. "My name is Ottavio Brancaleone. I am from Genoa on my way to Spain."

"To Spain?" quoth Dragut, and laughed. "You steer an odd course for Spain, or do you look to find it in Egypt?"

"We have lost our rudder," the gentleman explained, "and were at the mercy of the wind."

"I hope you find it has been merciful," said Dragut, leering at the girl, who shrank nearer to her companion, fear staring out of her blue eyes. "And your companion, sir, who is she?"

"My—my sister."

"Had you told me different you had been the first Christian I ever knew to speak the truth," said Dragut amiably. "Well, well, it's plain you're not to be trusted to sail a boat of your own. Best come aboard and see if you and your fellows can do better at an oar."

"I'll not trespass on your hospitality," said Brancaleone, with that amazing coolness of his.

"You shall earn it, I promise you," the corsair reassured him. "So come aboard. I am Dragut-Reis."

It pleased his vanity to notice that his name was not without disconcerting effect upon that smooth young gentleman. In the end there was a short, sharp tussle. Dragut flung a half score of his corsairs into the felucca to capture her voyagers, and one of them was stabbed by Brancaleone ere they overpowered him.

The prize proved far less insignificant than at first the corsair had imagined. For in addition to the slaves he had acquired, and the girl, who was fit to grace a sultan's harem, he found a great chest of newly minted ducats that it took six men to heave aboard the galley, and a beautifully chiseled gold coffer, full of gems of price. He found something more. On the inside of this coffer's lid was engraved its owner's name—Amelia Francesca Doria.

Dragut snapped down the lid with a prayer of thanks to Allah the One, and strode into the cabin where the girl was confined. "Madonna Amelia," said he.

She looked up instantly. Obviously it was her name, and the casket was her own.

"Will you tell me what is your kinship with the admiral?" Dragut asked.

"I am his granddaughter, sir," she answered, "and be sure that he will avenge terribly upon you any wrong that is done to me."

Dragut smiled. "We are old friends, the admiral and I," said he, and went out again. A mighty Nubian bearing a torch—for night had now descended—lighted him to the galley's waist, where about her mainmast lay huddled the seven pinioned prisoners.

With the curved toe of his scarlet slipper the corsair touched Messer Brancaleone. "Tell me, dog," Dragut commanded, "all that you know of Messer Andrea Doria."

"That is soon told," answered Brancaleone. "I know nothing, nor want to."

"You lie, as was to be expected," said

Dragut. "For one thing, you know his granddaughter."

Brancaleone blinked and recovered. "True, and several others of his family. But I conceived your question to concern his movements. I know that he is upon the seas, that he is seeking you, that he has sworn to take you alive, and that when he does—as I pray he will—he will so deal with you that you shall implore them of their Christian charity to hang you."

"And that is all you know?" quoth Dragut, entirely unruffled. "You did not peradventure sight his fleet as you were sailing?"

"I did not."

"Do you think that with a match between your fingers you might remember?"

"I might invent," replied the Italian; "but I doubt it. I have told you the truth, Messer Dragut. Torture could but gain you falsehood."

Dragut looked searchingly into that comely young face, then turned away as if satisfied. But as he was departing Messer Brancaleone called him back. And when he spoke now the Italian's tone and manner were entirely changed. His imperturbability, real or assumed, had all departed. Anxiety amounting almost to terror sounded in his voice.

"What fate do you reserve for Madonna Amelia?" he asked.

Dragut looked down at the man's pale face, and smiled a little. He had no particular rancor against his prisoner. On the whole he was inclining to admiration for the fellow's almost philosophic courage. At the same time there was no room for sentiment in the heart of the corsair. He was quite pitiless.

"Our lord the sublime Suleyman," said he, entirely without malice, "is as keen a judge of beauty as any man living. I account the girl to be a worthy gift even to the exalted of Allah; so I shall keep her safe against my next voyage to Constantinople."

And then Brancaleone's little lingering self-possession left him utterly. From his writhing lips came a stream of vituperation, which continued even after the Nubian had struck him a blow upon the mouth and Dragut had taken his departure.

CHAPTER III

When the Galleys Came.

Next day a slave on Dragut's galley having been taken ill at his oar, the wretch was unshackled and heaved overboard, and Brancaleone, stripped to the skin, was chained in the fellow's empty place. There were seven men to each oar, and Brancaleon's six companions were all Christians and all white—or had been before exposure had tanned them to the color of mahogany. Of these, three were Italians, two Spaniards, and one Frenchman. All were grimy and unkempt, and it was with a shudder that the delicately nurtured Genoese gentleman wondered if he were destined to become as they.

Up and down the gangway between the rowers' benches walked two Moslem bos'ns, armed with long whips of bullock hide, and it was not long ere one of them, considering that Brancaleone was not putting his share of effort into his task, sent that cruel lash to raise a burning wheal upon his tender flesh.

He was sparingly fed with his half-brutalized companions upon dried dates and figs, and he was given a little tepid water to drink when he thirsted. He slept in his shackles on the rowers' bench, which was but some four feet wide, and despite the sheepskins with which the bench was padded it was not long before the friction of his movements began to chafe and blister his flesh.

In the scorching noontide of the second day he collapsed fainting upon his oar. He was unshackled and dragged out upon the gangway. There a bucket of water was flung over him. It revived him, and the too-swift-healing action of the salt upon his seared flesh was a burning agony to him. He was put back to his oar again with a warning that if he permitted himself the luxury of swooning a second time he would be given the entire ocean in which to revive.

On the third day they sighted land, and toward evening the galleys threaded their way one by one through the shoals of the Boca de Cantara into the spacious lagoon on the northeast side of the Island of Jerbah, and there came to rest. It was Dragut's intent to lie snug in that remote retreat until Othmani should be ready with the reenforcements that were to enable the corsair to take the seas once more against the admiral of Genoa.

But it would seem that already the admiral was closer upon his heels than he had supposed, and that trackless as are the ocean ways, yet Andrea Doria had by some mysterious means contrived to gather information as he came that had kept him upon the invisible spoor of his quarry.

There was not a doubt that the folk on that ravaged Sicilian seaboard would be eager to inform the redoubtable admiral of the direction in which the Moslem galleys had faded out of sight. Perhaps even that empty felucca left tossing upon the tideless sea had served as an index to the way the corsairs had taken, and perhaps from the mainland, from Monastir, or one of the other cities now in Christian hands, a glimpse of Dragut's fleet had been caught, and Doria had been warned.

Be that as it may, not a week had Dragut been moored at Terbah when one fine morning brought a group of friendly islanders with the astounding news that a fleet of galleys was descending upon the island from the north.

The news took Dragut ashore in a hurry with a group of officers and from the narrow spur of land at the mouth of the harbor he surveyed the advancing ships. What already he had more than suspected became

absolute certainty. Two and twenty royal galleys were steering straight for the Boca de Cantara, the foremost flying Andrea Doria's own ensign.

Back to his fleet went Dragut for cannon and slaves, and so feverishly did they toil under the lash of his venomous tongue and of his bos'ns' whips, that within an hour he had erected a battery at the harbor mouth and fired a salute straight into the Genoese as they were in the very act of dropping anchor. Thereupon the galleys of Doria stood off out of range, and hung there, well content to wait, knowing that the fox was trapped, that the sword of Islam was likely to be sheathed at last, and that all that was now required on their part was patience.

Forthwith the jubilant Doria sent word to the emperor that he held Dragut fast, and he dispatched messengers to the viceroys of Sicily and Naples asking for reinforcements with which, if necessary, to force the issue. He meant this time to leave nothing to chance.

Dragut on his side employed the time in fortifying the Boca de Cantara. A fort arose there, growing visibly under the eyes of the Genoese, and provoking the amusement of that fierce veteran Doria. Sooner or later Dragut must decide to come forth from his bottle-necked refuge, and the longer he deferred it the more overwhelming would be the numbers assembled to destroy him.

CHAPTER IV

"Betide What May"

Ever since Giannetino Doria had surprised him on the road of Goialatta off the coast of Corsica, on that famous occasion when he was made prisoner, had Dragut found himself in so desperately tight a corner. He sat on the deck of his galley, muttering imprecations against the Genoese with that astounding and far-reaching fluency in which the Moslem is without rival upon earth. He pronounced authoritatively upon the shamelessness of Doria's mother, and the inevitably shameful destiny of his daughters. He called perfervidly upon Allah to rot the bones and destroy the house of his archenemy, and he foretold how dogs would of a certainty desecrate the admiral's grave. Then, seeing that Allah remained disdainfully aloof, he rose up one day in a mighty passion, and summoned his officers.

"This skulking here will not avail us," he blazed at them, as if it were by their contriving that he was trapped. "By delay we but increase our peril. What is written is written. Allah has bound the fate of each man about his neck. Betide what may, tonight we take to the open sea."

"And by morning you'll have found the bottom of it." drawled a voice from one of the oars.

Dragut, who was standing on the gangway between the rowers' benches, whipped around with a snarl upon the speaker. He found himself gazing into the languid eyes of Messer Brancaleone. The rest of the last few days had restored the Italian's vigor, and certain thoughts that he had lately been indulging had restored his courage.

"Are you weary of life?" wondered the corsair. "Shall I have you hanged before we go to meet your friends out yonder?"

"To do one or the other," said Brancaleone, "would be to render absolute the conviction which has been growing upon me during this week past."

"And what may that be?"

"That you're a dull fellow when all is said, Messer Dragut. Hang me, and you hang the only man in all your fleet who can show you the way out of this trap."

Dragut stared between anger and amazement. "You can show me a way out of this trap?" he echoed. "What way may that be?"

"Strike off my fetters, restore me my garments, and give me proper food, and I will discuss it with you."

Dragut glowered at him. "We have a shorter way to make men speak," he said.

Brancaleone smiled and shook his head. "You think so? Another of your delusions."

It was odd what a power of conviction dwelt in his imperturbable tones. The corsair issued an order, and turned away. A half hour later, Messer Brancaleone, nourished, washed, and clothed, looking once more like the elegant Italian gentleman who had first been hoisted aboard the galley, stepped on to the deck, where Dragut-Reis awaited him in some impatience.

Seated cross-legged upon a gorgeous silken divan that was wrought in green and blue and gold, the handsome corsair combed his square black beard with fretful fingers. Behind him, stark-naked save for his white loin cloth, stood his gigantic Nubian, his body oiled until it shone like ebony, armed with a great curved scimitar.

"Now, sir," growled Dragut, "what is this precious plan of yours—briefly?" His tone was contemptuous.

"You begin where we should end," said the imperturbable Genoese. "I owe you no favors Messer Dragut, and I bear you no affection that I should make you a free gift of your life and liberty. My eyes have seen something to which yours are blind, and my brain has conceived something of which yours is quite incapable. These things, sir, are for sale. Before I part with them we must agree upon the price."

Dragut stared from under scowling brows.

He could scarce believe that the world held so much impudence. "And what price do you suggest?" he snarled, by way of humoring the Genoese.

"Why, as to that, since I offer you life and liberty, it is but natural that I should claim my own life and liberty in return, and similarly the liberty of Madonna Amelia and of my servants whom you captured; also it is but natural that I should require the restoration of the money and jewels you have taken from us, and since you have deprived us of our felucca, it is no more than proper that you should equip us with a vessel in which to pursue the journey which you interrupted.

"Considering the time we have lost in consequence of this interruption," Brancaleone went on, "it is but just that you should make this good as far as possible by presenting me with a craft that is capable of the utmost speed. I will accept a galley of six and twenty oars, manned by a proper complement of Christian slaves."

"And is that all?" roared Dragut.

"No," said Brancaleone quietly. "That is but the restitution due to me. We come now to the price of the service I am to render you. When you were Giannetino Doria's prisoner, Barbarossa paid for you, as all the world knows, a ransom of three thousand ducats. I will be more reasonable."

"Will you so?" snorted Dragut. "By the splendor of Allah, you'll need to be."

"I will accept one thousand ducats."

"May Allah blot thee out, thou impudent son of shame!" cried the corsair, filled with fury.

"You compel me to raise the price to fifteen hundred ducats," said Brancaleone smoothly. "I must be compensated for abuse since I cannot take satisfaction for it as between one Christian gentleman and another."

It was good for Dragut that his feelings suddenly soared to an intensity beyond expression, else might the price have been raised even beyond the famous ransom that Barbarossa had paid. Mutely he stood glowering, clenching and unclenching his hands; than he half turned to his Nubian swordsman. "Ali—" he began.

Brancaleone once more cut in. "Ah, wait," said he. "I pray you calm yourself. Remember how you stand, and that Andrea Doria holds you trapped. Do nothing that will destroy your only chance. Time enough to call in Ali and have my head hacked off when I have failed."

That speech arrested Dragut's anger in full flow. He wheeled upon the Genoese once more. "You accept that alternative?"

Brancaleone smiled with almost pitying amusement. "Why not? I have no slightest fear of failure. I can show you how to win clear of this trap and make the admiral the laughingstock of the world."

"Speak, then; let me know your plan!" cried Dragut fiercely.

"If I do so before you have agreed to my terms, then I shall have nothing left to sell."

Angrily Dragut turned aside, and strode to the taffrail. He looked across the shimmering blue water to the fortifications at the harbor mouth; with the eyes of his imagination he looked beyond at the fleet of Genoa riding out yonder in patient conviction that it held its prey.

The price that Brancaleone asked was outrageous—a galley and some two hundred Christian slaves to row it and fifteen hundred ducats. In all it amounted to fully as much as the ransom that Barbarossa had paid for him, yet Dragut must pay it, or fall into the power of his Christian foes. He came to reflect that he would pay it gladly enough to be out of this tight corner.

He came about again. He spoke of torture once more, but in a half-hearted sort of way; for he did not himself believe that it would be effective with a man of Brancaleone's temper.

Brancaleone laughed at the threat, and shrugged his shoulders. "You may as profitably hang me, Messer Dragut," he said, "for your infidel barbarities will but seal my lips for all time."

"We might torture the woman," said Dragut the ingenious.

Brancaleone, on the words, turned white to the lips; but it was the pallor of bitter, heart-searing resolve, not the pallor of such fear as Dragut had hoped to awaken. He advanced a step, his imperturbability all gone, and he sent his words into the face of the corsair with the fierceness of a cornered wild cat.

"Attempt it," said he, "and as God's my

witness I leave you to your fate at the hands of Genoa—ay, though my heart should burst with the pain of my silence. I am a man, Messer Dragut; never doubt it."

"I do not," said Dragut, his piercing black eyes upon that set white face. "I agree to your terms. Show me a way out of Doria's clutches, and you shall have all that you have asked for."

CHAPTER V
Really Simple

Trembling still from his recent emotion, Brancaleone hoarsely bade the corsair call up his officers and repeat his words before them. "And you shall make oath upon this matter," he added. "Men say of you that you are a faithful Moslem. I mean to put it to the test."

Dragut, now all eagerness to know what plan was stirring in his prisoner's brain, unable to brook further suspense in this affair, called up his officers, and before them all, taking Allah to witness, he made oath upon the beard of the Prophet that if Brancaleone could show him deliverance, he on his side would recompense the Genoese to the extent demanded.

Thereafter Dragut and Brancaleone went ashore, with no other attendant but the Nubian swordsman. It was the Genoese who led the way, not toward the fort, as Dragut had expected, but in the opposite direction. Arrived at the northernmost curve of that almost circular lagoon, where the ground was swampy. Brancaleone paused. He pointed across a strip of shallow land, that was no more than a half mile or so in width, to the blue-green sea beyond. Part of this territory was swamp, and part sand; vegetation there was of the scantiest; some clumps of reeds, an odd date palm, its crest rustling slightly in the breeze, and nothing else.

"It is really very simple," said the Italian. "Yonder lies your way."

As he spoke, a red-legged stork rose from the edge of the marsh, and went circling overhead. Dragut's face was purple with rage. He deemed that this smooth fellow had brought him there to make mock of him.

"Are my galleys winged like that stork, thou fool?" he answered passionately. "Or are they wheeled like chariots that I can sail them over dry land."

Brancaleone looked at him in stupefaction. "I protest," said he, "that for a man of your reputation for shrewdness, you fill me with amazement. I said you were a dull fellow. I little dreamed how dull. Nay, now, suppress your rage. Truth is a very healing draft, and you have need of it. I compute now that aboard your ships there will be, including slaves, some three thousand men. No doubt you could press another thousand from the island into your service. How long would it take four thousand men to dig a channel deep enough to float your shallow galleys through that strip of land?"

Dragut's fierce eyes flickered as though he had been menaced with a blow. "By Allah!" he ejaculated, and gripped his beard. "By the splendor of Allah!"

"In a week the thing were easily done," Brancaleone resumed, "and meanwhile your fort will hold the admiral in play and mask your labors. Then, one dark night, you slip through this channel, and stand away to the south, so that by sunrise you shall have vanished beyond the sky line, leaving the admiral to guard an empty trap."

Dragut laughed aloud, in almost childlike glee, and otherwise signified his delight by the vehemence with which he testified to the unity of Allah. Suddenly he checked, and his eyes narrowed as they rested upon Brancaleone. "'Tis a scurvy trick you play your lady's grandsire!" said he.

The Genoese shrugged and, smiled deprecatingly. "Every man for himself, Messer Dragut. We understand each other, I think. 'Tis not for love of you I do this thing."

"I would it were," said the corsair, with

an odd sincerity, and thereafter, as they returned to the galleys, it was seen that Dragut's arm was about the shoulders of the infidel, and that he spoke with him as with a brother.

The fact is that Dragut, fired with admiration of Brancaleone's resourcefulness, was cast down at the thought that so fine a spirit should of necessity be destined to go down to the pit. He spoke to him now of the glories of Islam, and of the future that must await a gentleman of his endowments in the ranks of the Moslem; he had of a sudden conceived so great an affection for him that he was filled with the desire to convert him to the true faith. But this was a matter in which Brancaleone was politely obdurate, and Dragut had not the time to devote to the conversation, greatly as he desired it. There was the matter of that canal to engage him.

Brancaleone's instructions were diligently carried out. Daily the fort at the Boca de Cantara would belch forth shot at the Genoese navy, which stood well out of range. To the admiral this was but the barking of a dog that dared not come within biting reach, and the waste of ammunition roused his contempt of that pirate Dragut whom he held at his mercy.

There came a day, however, when the fort was silent; it was followed by another day of silence, in the evening of which one of the admiral's officers suggested that all might not be well. Doria agreed with him.

"All is not at all well with that dog Dragut." Andrea Doria laughed in his white beard. "He wants us within range of his guns. The ruse is a little too obvious."

And so the great Genoese fleet remained carefully out of range of the empty fort, what time Dragut himself was some scores of miles away, speeding as fast as his slaves could row for the archipelago and the safety of the Dardanelles. In the words of the Spanish historian, Marmol, who has chronicled the event—although many of the details here recorded escaped his knowledge—

"Dragut left Messer Andrea Doria 'with the dog to hold.'"

Brancaleone accompanied the Moslem fleet at first, though now aboard the galley which Dragut had given him in accordance with their agreement, and with him sailed the lovely Amelia Francesca Doria, his chest of gold, the jewels, and the fifteen hundred ducats that Dragut, grimly stifling his reluctance, had paid the Genoese.

On the second day of their voyage, the corsair was able to replace the vessel granted to Brancaleone. They met a royal galley from Naples, manned by Spaniards, and rowed by Moslem slaves. She was speeding to Andrea Doria with news that the viceroy was sending reenforcements. There was a sharp, short fight, and Messer Dragut added her to his fleet, liberating the Moslem slaves, and replacing them by the Spaniards who had manned the vessel.

Some hours later, Messer Brancaleone and the corsair captain parted company with many expressions of mutual good will, and the Genoese put about and steered a northwesterly course for the coast of Spain.

CHAPTER VI
That Impudent Genoese

It was some months ere Dragut learned the true inwardness of Messer Brancaleone's conduct. He had the story from a Genoese captive, captain of a carack which the corsair scuttled in the Straits of Messina. The fellow's name chanced to be Brancaleone, upon learning which Dragut inquired if he were kin to one Ottavio Brancaleone, who had gone to Spain with the admiral's granddaughter.

"He is my cousin," the man answered.

And Dragut now learned that in the teeth of the opposition of the whole Doria family, the irrepressible Brancaleone had carried off Madonna Amelia. The admiral had news of it as he was putting to sea, and it was in pursuit not only of Dragut, but also of the runaways, that he had come south so far as Jerbah, having reason more than to suspect that they were aboard one of Dragut's galleys. The admiral had sworn to hang Brancaleone from his yardarm ere he returned to port, and his bitterness at the trick Dragut had played him was increased by the reflection that Brancaleone, too, had got clear away.

Dragut was very thoughtful when he heard that story. "And to think," said he, "that I paid that unconscionable dog fifteen hundred ducats and gave him my best galley manned by two hundred Christian slaves for rendering himself as great a service as ever he was rendering me!"

He bore no malice, however. On the contrary, his admiration grew for that impudent Genoese, the only Christian who had ever bested Dragut in a bargain, and if he had a regret it was that so shrewd a spirit should abide in the body of an infidel. "In the service of Islam," he was wont to say, "such a man as Brancaleone might have gone far indeed. But Allah is all-knowing."

QUEST
by **Wanita Norris**

Mankind will search and seek and never rest
Until it has fulfilled the age-old quest
Of setting foot on new unsullied land
Wher'er jungle dense or bleak and icy strand.

Now Man has turned his eyes toward the skies
For in them he has sensed adventure lies
And planets that ere once beyond his key
Now echo to the ringing tread of men

Then many wonder lie before his gaze
And each new find will mankind's knowledge raise,
For Man will always seek the unknown shore
And shall search for adventure evermore.

THE HAUNTED LANDSCAPE

by Greye La Spina

Only once in my life did I experience contact with the supernatural, and the incident is still inexplicable, looked at from the materialistic standpoint. It happened in connection with the death of a close friend of mine, Jack Lindsay, the artist.

Jack was possessed of a stubbornly determined nature; he never gave up anything once begun, no matter how difficult the circumstances in connection with it. He was especially determined in regard to his painting; he often remarked, with a touch of quite natural melancholy in character with the observation, that death alone would stop him from reaching the highest point in his artistic career before he was thirty. He was about twenty-seven when he said that.

In discussing Jack's dogged grit with a common friend, Doctor Wilmott, the latter said: "If Jack lives to be forty he will already have become famous." When I replied that Jack had declared it his intention to make a name for himself by the time he was thirty, our friend assented thoughtfully. "I believe he will make the attempt," he granted; "but he has no time to lose."

The last time I saw Jack was just before he went away on one of his frequent sketching trips. When he mentioned his itinerary, I found he was passing within a few miles of a city where a cousin of mine was living, and I penciled a few words of informal introduction on the reverse of one of my cards, which, however, as afterward transpired, he never presented. He left me, apparently in high spirits, and although I heard nothing from him for a couple of months, I thought nothing of it because he was a notoriously poor correspondent.

Then I received a notice that shocked me to the soul. The police of a certain small town had found a dead body, presumably his, in the woods, where it had lain for weeks. Their supposition was that the young artist had taken his own life, as there were no marks of violence upon the body, and apparently nothing had been removed from the pockets. My card had served to identify him. His sketching paraphernalia in its entirety had been located at the home of a farmer of the neighborhood, Pete Grimstead, one of those "poor but honest" countrymen in which America abounds.

The farmer declared that several weeks back the artist had stopped at the house for something to eat; that after lunch he asked permission to leave his sketching outfit, as he wished to take a stroll through the woods without it. Grimstead had put the things into the "front room," which, as anyone who is at all acquainted with country people knows, is rarely used by them. Naturally they had forgotten all about the things until the hue and cry was made upon the discovery of the artist's body, when they had immediately notified the police and given up the dead man's effects.

Both the farmer and his wife had declared that they were glad to get rid of the things. Asked why, they said they didn't know, but they felt there was something queer about them. And they did seem relieved to have the last vestige of the unfortunate man's visit removed from their house.

I did not like the idea of Jack's having committed suicide on the verge of a promising career; it was quite out of character with what I knew of him. But Grimstead and his wife were well regarded in their vicinity, and there seemed no reason to suspect that anything other than suicide or an accident of some kind had happened to poor Jack. However, the thought clung to me and persisted in obtruding itself the rest of the day when I was back at the country hotel, that there was much more back of the affair than appeared on the surface. The coroner persisted in his belief that it was a case of suicide, although I begged him to let it go down on the records as death by accident.

You know how it is when you suddenly feel an antipathy to a person without the slightest foundation for your feelings. Well, I simply "felt" that Grimstead and his wife knew more about Jack's tragic death than they had related, and the more I thought it over the more strongly was I convinced in my intuition. There was something I didn't like about the hanging head of the farmer; something shifty in the wife's eyes and unpleasant in the constant restless rubbing and twisting of her thin, gnarled hands. I determined to ferret out the secret hidden back of their apparently simple story.

Jack's effects were turned over to me, in lieu of relatives, and I put them in my room at the hotel. That night I set up the easel and put the landscape on it; I wanted to look at my friend's last piece of work while I strove to untangle the threads of thought which threatened to become hopelessly knotted. I lit my pipe and sat back comfortably, reflecting sadly on poor Jack's sudden and tragic death, the while my eyes took in the salient features of the landscape before me.

It was a carelessly executed bit of work, quite unfinished as yet on the right-hand side. The left side showed a bit of country with woods beyond and plowed fields toward the center. At the right appeared the roughly sketched-in outlines of a house. And it was upon this house that my attention became fixed as I smoked and reflected. Perhaps I grew drowsy; perhaps it was a case of auto-suggestion; perhaps it was the powerful will of my friend projected no one

knows how. Whatever it was, the longer I looked at that house the clearer the outlines grew. Such is the magic of the imagination that it seemed to me that an invisible brush was working over the house, dashing in a bit of color here, a touch there, until the whole house stood out clearly before my eyes.

I realized that I was hardly normal; that my long reflection on my friend's death had resulted in my becoming half drowsy, half languid; but I dreamily contemplated the picture, watching it come up, as it were, under my intent gaze, from a mere sketch into a finished piece of work. All that I saw I attributed to the vivid working of an over-stimulated imagination, but at last something happened in that picture which by no means could have been attributed to imagination. A light sprang up within the house and shone through one of the windows!

II

I rubbed my eyes, leaned forward, taking my pipe from my lips, and looked intently, incredulously. There was no mistake about it; there was an actual flicker of light from behind one of the half-closed shutters of a window toward the rear of the house. I pinched myself vigorously and felt the pain with waking nerves, but the light did not fade away; it shone steadily on.

I whipped the picture from the easel and turned it over. It was an ordinary canvas, such as Jack had always used. A cold chill began to play down my spinal column as I returned the picture to the easel. I realized that there was in truth something unearthly about my friend's landscape; the farmer and his wife had been correct in their assertions that there was something supernatural and queer about it. I did not blame them for wishing to be rid of such a strange and unusual painting.

As for myself, I felt certain that there was something more than appeared upon the surface of this supernatural manifestation. I held myself rigidly alert, watching that strange and weird lighting of a painted landscape. I was aware that there was a Presence in the room with me and that there was something, some message, which it desired to impart; but while I held myself open for the intuitional reception of such a message, I could not restrain the cold shiver that went over me at the realization of the propinquity of the discarnate, although I realized that my old friend could mean no harm to me.

I kept my eyes upon that mysteriously lighted window. As I watched, suddenly the door of the house seemed to open, and the light from within streamed out along the path before it. Simultaneously a shadow fell across the shaft of light, projected by moving figures within, and there appeared in the doorway a dark mass that, as it issued, could be distinguished as three figures. I strained my eyes to see the better. Good heavens, it was the figures of a man and a woman, carrying between them the limp body of another human being! As the significance of this flashed through my mind, they stopped on the threshold to close the door, shutting out the stream of light from the path. But as they passed the lighted window, where the path wound past it to the front gate, I saw, outlined against it in a broken but unmistakably familiar silhouette, the face of the honest farmer who had last seen my poor friend alive!

In my excitement I cried aloud. "You shall have justice, Jack!" I exclaimed.

The light in the window faded slowly away, but the outlines of the house remained, as did all the color work invisible hands had brushed in before my startled eyes. And the painting remained as it is today, a finished picture, the last gift of my dead friend to me.

I sat back, filled with unutterable awe at what I had witnessed. I knew that my friend had not died by his own hand; nor had he fallen and injured himself mortally in the woods. I knew that he had been foully done to death by hands which I could, and would,

identify. I cannot say that I was afraid during the period of that marvelous manifestation; no, it was fury I felt that my friend must lie under the accusation of suicide when he had in reality been the victim of a sordid crime. I knew that he had come back to me to justify himself and to point out his murderers. I determined that they should be brought to justice. But how?

III.

The rest of the night I sat smoking pipe after pipe, going over all the circumstances of Jack's death as they had been presented to me by the police and by Grimstead and his wife. There was no flaw in the story of the latter couple; it was probable enough for the country constables to credit it readily. They had known Pete Grimstead and his wife for years, and had never seen anything to their discredit, save that they were poor and had a hard struggle for existence.

But—poverty is frequently the motive for crime. Yet what could have tempted them to kill a poor artist, who certainly had not carried on his person more than a few dollars? And the small amount found upon his body might have been all in his possession at that time. What else could he have shown them that they might have envied? His watch? It was a dollar watch, the fob a knotted black silk cord. Nothing tempting about that. Moreover, it had been found upon his body. His cuff links? Plain white buttons.

The body had been fully clothed when found. Stop! I did not remember having seen his hat. There had been no hat, and Jack had always worn—it was his only extravagance—a superfine Panama. His hat! Perhaps here was the clew to the mystery. It was not until dawn that I finally retired to sleep brokenly, sure in my heart that I had found a clew that would eventually unfold the motive and the mystery of the crime. It could not be that my poor friend had been murdered, at the threshold of a promising career, for the sake of a Panama hat! But that the hat was closely connected with the real story of his death I was fully persuaded. I was filled with impotent fury, but I determined to get a good sleep and then to make a visit to Pete Grimstead's farm. I did not wish to present myself there with my brain stupid after a sleepless night.

It was late that afternoon when I walked up the path to the house I had seen pictured so strangely in poor friend's last painting. I had asked the local constable to drive me out, and I recognized it immediately as the scene of the crime. He sat waiting outside in the wagon until I should have completed my questioning. I felt as though I were in a dream as I stood upon the threshold from which I had seen, the night before, that guilty pair issuing. I knocked strongly.

It was the woman who answered. She opened the door slowly, and, as it appeared to me, cautiously. When she saw who it was she uttered a single choked exclamation, and shut the door sharply in my face. I heard her hurried footsteps retreating in the hall, and then the sound of her voice calling her husband from the back door.

I kept up an occasional sharp knocking. The constable, who had not seen the door opened, called out that I'd better go to the back door, so I stepped down to the path. As I turned the corner I saw the woman on the doorstep, her face absolutely gray in the soft afternoon light, her eyes straining anxiously toward the barn, from whence came the gruff call of her husband. When she heard my footsteps she turned abruptly, threw out her hands as if to ward off something, made as though to reenter the house, and crumpled up in a heap on the door stone.

I stood rooted to the spot, torn by conflicting emotions. She was a woman, an elderly woman, and I should have gone to her assistance. She was a woman—but perhaps her hands had been stained in the blood of my dearest friend! I stood coldly aloof, awaiting events.

It was her husband who lifted her from the ground, shooting a vindictive glance at me as he bent over her. I could see that he had been suffering mentally; yet I felt nothing but fierce pleasure at the sight. He was a murderer, and it was meet that he should experience mental torture until such time as he suffered the legal punishment that was his just due.

He carried the limp form into the house and laid her down on a horsehair sofa in the front room. I followed him. The chill of that room penetrated my bones with a horrid suggestion of what had taken place there so short a time ago. He turned upon me with a sudden bracing of his shoulders and a tossing back of his head that reminded me against my will of a gallant stag driven at bay.

"Well, what do you want?" he asked, with such hopelessness in his tones that I could have felt pity for him in his plight had I not steeled my heart for what I had to do.

"I want to ask you a few more questions about the—the manner of my friend's death," I replied tensely, bending a piercing gaze upon him.

He took an involuntary step backward against the sofa where lay the unconscious partner of his guilt. The movement displaced a crudely decorated sofa pillow, one of two propped against either arm of the sofa. It slipped, and would have gone to the floor had he not thrown himself upon it with a desperate effort that seemed out of all proportion to the trifling incident.

"Well," he shot at me, but in an agitated manner, "what is it you want to know?"

He remained before the sofa, his attitude that of one who hides a secret or protects something helpless. Flashing through my mind came the subconscious memory of a glint of white under the pillow. With a quick movement I sprang to the sofa, and although the farmer flung himself simultaneously against me he was too late. I pulled the cushion away with determined hand and disclosed—Jack Lindsay's Panama hat!

IV.

I looked at Grimstead with stern accusation. He regarded me with horror written large upon his weather-beaten countenance. His eyes were stricken; his shoulders, so courageously braced back a moment since in an assumption of innocence, sank in and stooped over. He was the very picture of confounded guilt.

Stepping to the door, I hallooed to the constable, who clambered out, secured the horse, and came hurrying up the path. Wordlessly I pointed to the hanging head of the guilty man and to the Panama hat, crushed up against the arm of the sofa. The officer stood with dropped jaw and straining eyes.

From the sofa came the moaning cry of the woman. "Tell them the truth, Pete! Oh, I told you it would have been better to have told it in the beginning! Such things are always found out."

The constable looked horror-stricken at me, and I looked triumphantly back at him. I had located the murderer when no one had so much as suspected a murder; I had vindicated my poor friend from the charge of suicide, under which his noble spirit had been unable to rest in peace.

The woman's voice went on weakly. "He came in here to get something to eat," she wailed. "We gave him his lunch. When he got up to go he put his hands suddenly to his heart, opened his mouth as if he were going to speak, and then fell right down on the floor. He was dead! Oh, believe it or not, he was dead! We didn't lay a hand on him. But he was dead, in our house, and we were afraid. We are poor. We were afraid of what people might think, because that very morning Pete plowed up the bag of coins he had lost thirty years ago. We wouldn't dare spend it. We were afraid we'd be accused of killing and robbing!" Her voice rose in a shrieking crescendo of agony: "Oh, believe it or not, it is true—every word I'm telling you is God's own truth!"

Her husband threw himself down beside her, hiding his face in his toil-worn hands.

"What did you do then?" I managed to ask, my head whirling.

Grimstead lifted a defiant face. "I don't suppose you will believe us," he said shortly and without bitterness, "but what my wife says is quite true. After he dropped and we found he was dead, we talked it over. We were afraid of what people might think. We decided to carry his body away to a distance and say he had left here for a walk and had never returned. I wish now," he added dejectedly, "that we had come out with the truth in the beginning. I suppose it looks worse for us now than it would've looked then."

The constable's eyes questioned me appealingly.

I touched the Panama hat. "And this?" I questioned.

"It fell off when we were carrying him away," said Grimstead dully. "We found it on the path when we came back, and we didn't dare go out there with it, so we hid it here."

"Why didn't you burn it?" queried the constable, astonished that this incriminating evidence should have been left in such a conspicuous hiding place.

Grimstead shrugged his shoulders. "We weren't guilty of anything. Why should we burn it? We never thought anyone would come looking here. We'd have given it up with the other things, only it might have looked queer if we'd had his hat."

He looked directly at my companion then. "Well, why don't you arrest me?" he demanded.

Again the constable and I exchanged glances. By common consent we stepped out of the chilling atmosphere of the room into the soft light of summer afternoon.

"I must tell you," said the constable, "that I remember hearing, when I was a young fellow, that Pete Grimstead had the money ready to pay off the mortgage on his farm and lost it somewhere as he was plowing his fields. Hunt as he might, he could never lay hands on it again. There's never been anything against the Grimsteads, in all the time I can remember, except that they are poor and hard working, and that isn't really a crime. Of course, sir, if you feel that you want to go further in the matter," his voice died away, and his eyes questioned mine.

I thought hard and fast. Perhaps, after all, my poor friend's spirit had come to me not to bring murderers to justice, but merely to vindicate his own reputation, he who had always intended to fight it out to the end, he who had determined to become famous before death cut short his career. As I came to this conclusion I felt a lightness of heart that convinced me I had arrived at the correct significance of Jack's manifestation.

At the expression on my face the man drew a long sigh of relief.

"I'm glad you aren't going to pile up troubles for them." He jerked his thumb toward the house. "I'm sure the story is just as they told it. Did your friend ever mention his having any heart trouble, now?"

Into my mind flashed Doctor Wilmott's words. "If he lives to be forty he will be a famous man," he had said.

As I recollected more or less distinctly, there had been a faint accentuation upon the word "lives."

"I believe they've told us the truth," I said heartily, meeting the other man's eyes frankly. "The only thing I want now is to have the record of suicide cleared up positively once and for all. I'm sure it can be done without implicating those poor unhappy people further."

The constable stepped to the door. "Better give me that hat," he suggested, his cheerful, matter-of-fact voice affecting both the stricken man and his wife with sudden hope. "I'm sure you don't want to be reminded of the affair any longer," and he put out his hand for the Panama, which he passed on to me. Then he stretched out his right hand wordlessly to Grimstead.

The farmer took it wonderingly, his expression incredulous. So much had he suffered from his own fears for weeks that he could hardly believe the matter entirely cleared up. Not so Mrs. Grimstead. With happy tears streaming down her cheeks, she said brokenly: "God bless you both for believing us!"

The records in town were changed when the constable returned, so that my unfortunate friend was no longer charged with suicide; his death was entered as heart failure. But no mention was made of the Grimsteads. The story they had given in the beginning stood in the records as true; only the constable, the coroner, and myself knew the real facts.

Upon my return to my home city I satisfied myself that Doctor Wilmott had indeed accented the word "lives"; he had examined Jack, and had told him that only with the utmost care could he expect to live longer than five or six years and that even this time might be cut short without a moment's notice.

As for the haunted landscape, it hangs on the walls of my room, one of the best examples of my dead friend's masterly art. There seems to be nothing mysterious about it now, for although I have often sat late, smoking, watching the half-closed shutters of the house, never again have I seen light streaming from the windows upon the pathway before the door.

THREE A.M.

by Walt Klein

The clocks are all awry
this hour of the secret
night—the slender hands
all aimless; the terrible, slender
hands all fingering
a different cipher, and the stars
all reeling in their orbits.
  O time! time! time!

Time and death have vanished
this enchanted moment, forgotten,
lost in the endless
corridors of mind. But who—
who will know tomorrow
of this moment fleeing, lost?
  Wailing, wailing, wailing...

The pendulum, rasping, drops,
the door springs open,
and a tinny voice shrieks:
  "Cuckoo! Cuckoo! Cuckoo!

Coin of the Dead

By Lemuel L. DeBra

We sat in a booth of the Hang Far Low, my good friend Chan Yin Do and I, munching Shensi almonds and rice cakes and sipping a most fragrant Dragonbeard tea. From the street below, the main avenue of San Francisco's Chinatown, came the weird strains of a Chinese orchestra; and I knew that the funeral procession, the services of which we had witnessed, was passing. When we could no longer hear the discordant wail of the flageolets nor the jarring clang of cymbals, Chan Yin Do put his tiny bowl aside, smacked his lips with satisfaction and answered the question I had put to him.

"Yes, it is quite true that in some parts of China it was once the custom to bury sums of money with the dead; and although many of those tombs have been looted by you foreigners, there yet remains much treasure in the old graves of the Middle Kingdom."

I refilled our bowls with the steaming Dragonbeard, and passed the cigarettes to Chan Yin Do.

"Why do you say all the looting was done by foreigners?" I inquired politely. "You know many of the younger Chinese have abandoned the superstitions of the older generation. I believe I read once that in a certain province, I have forgotten just where, revolutionists planned to finance their movement by robbing the graves of that 'coin of the dead.'"

Chan Yin Do nodded, and an odd look came into his slant, black eyes. With a long, polished nail he flicked the ash from his cigarette, and as he raised his arm the flowing sleeve of his satin blouse fell back and disclosed a bracelet of finest Yunnan jade.

"That would be very wicked and foolish," he said. "The money could not be recovered without disturbing the bones of the buried; and, as anyone knows, great misfortune would befall the one who did such a sacrilegious act; and, what is still worse, evil spirits would pursue and bring ill luck to the family of the one whose bones were disturbed, even though many generations had intervened. Only when the bones of one's ancestors lie in peace can one have a propitious fung shui."

To this, I made no reply. We sat a moment in silence.

"Still, it has been done," Chan Yin Do admitted, finally. "Once there was in San Francisco a young man of the family of Lee, named Wah Sin, who, because he had gone to an American school, thought he was very smart and that the older Chinese were very foolish. One time he read in your books about the ancient custom of burying money with the dead in China; and, remembering how he had seen such things in his childhood, he went back to the Middle Kingdom to rob the graves. He thought he would very easily become a wealthy man. And he—he found—"

Chan Yin Do hesitated. I summoned a waiter and directed him to fetch more tea and cigarettes; and while Chan Yin Do, with noisy relish, sipped at the steaming tea, I waited in silence. I wanted to hear what happened to Lee Wah Sin when he defied the religious beliefs of his people and went back to his native land to steal that "coin of the dead."

Presently Chan Yin Do lighted another cigarette. Then he began:

* * * *

Lee Wah Sin was the son of a fishmonger whose stall was on Clay Street and who was a very honest and industrious merchant. Old Lee wanted his son to learn the fish and shrimp business, which is quite profitable when one knows how to evade the foolish laws of the foreign devils; but the boy was very unfilial and disobedient, as are so many of the younger generation.

"My stomach rebels at the sight of your filthy shop!" he told his father one day. "When I see you coming home for evening rice with a noisome gunnysack about your middle and fish-scales on your slippers and a basket of fish-heads on your arm, I am ashamed to admit to my fine friends that that smelly old man is my honorable father."

"But one must do something," spoke up his mother who hoped in her heart that the boy would become almost anything save a cleaner of fish and a sheller of shrimps.

"Yes," agreed Lee Wah Sin, "that is quite true. So I shall go to an American school and learn the wisdom of the fan quai; and then I shall earn money easily like old Soo Hoo Nam Art who, because his stomach is big with wisdom, does nothing but cut pieces from the fan quai newspapers and then write them in our language for the Chinese Daily World."

Old Lee was very angry because of his son's perverseness; and he would have given the boy a sound beating with bamboo, which he richly deserved. But the boy was very strong and willful, and the old father had lost his strength from much opium-smoking, and a strange disease which many fish-cleaners get had attacked his eyes and made him almost blind. So while old Lee sputtered angrily, Wah Sin left the house and went whistling down the street to play billiards.

One day when Lee Wah Sin had learned so much from the American books that he had almost forgotten his "Thousand-Word Classics" and the other things his old Chinese tutor had taught him, he picked up a foreign-devil book that told about Chinese customs. The writers of those foolish books think our customs very strange; but, as anyone should know, they are not strange at all. Lee Wah Sin thought the book very amusing indeed; for he had come to think that he was very smart and he laughed at the things the old Chinese do.

In the book, he read how the old Chinese always have a geomancer select the burial ground so that the evil spirits will not molest the dead; how we do not build houses or go on journeys unless the geomancers agree that the time is propitious; how we worship our ancestors who have gone, instead of giving all to the new generation which is here; and he read about many other customs which my people in the Middle Kingdom have followed faithfully for four thousand years and more, but which you white foreign devils, because you are so young, and hence very ignorant, think quite foolish.

And among those customs which Lee Wah Sin read about in the book was the one of burying money with our dead. It reminded him, as I have told you, of how, when he was a child in the Middle Kingdom, he had often seen sums of money placed on the altar with the ceremonial meats and buried with the dead.

"Now, instead of burying that money with those who are dead and, therefore, know nothing, how much better if it were given to the young men and young women for fine clothes," reasoned Lee Wah Sin. "Haie, I wish I had some of it! There must be quite a fortune in those old burial grounds! There are many, many millions of people in the Middle Kingdom; but the number that walk the earth is but a handful compared with the number of those who lie in the ground. If I could get even a part of that 'spirit money' that lies with those crumbling bones, I would be very rich."

So in the days that followed, Lee Wah Sin thought much about the money that lay in the moldy graves of his ancestors; but he said nothing about the plan that was taking shape in his scheming heart.

It was several moons later that the great opportunity came to Lee Wah Sin. An American importing company wanted a Chinese youth with an English education to go to Canton for them to act as buyer. Lee Wah Sin lacked much of having completed his education, but he could speak English with a very glib tongue. He obtained the position, and sailed on the first steamer.

He had been in Canton only a month when he asked permission to visit his father's people who lived in the interior on the Si-kiang to the west of Canton. His employers did not like to let him go; but Lee Wah Sin was very obstinate, and on that same day he obtained passage on a ho-tau that was leaving for the upriver villages.

Since he thought he was a very shrewd fellow, Lee Wah Sin dressed now like his own people; and he pretended to be one of them, although all the time he was laughing at them and at their customs.

* * * *

In the months that had passed since Lee Wah Sin first thought of going to China to steal the money that had been buried with the dead, he had made a definite plan. He remembered that, many years before, he had seen his father's elder brother laid away with the ceremonial meats and quite a sum of money. So Wah Sin had planned to go first to their native village and steal the money from his uncle's tomb. If this venture proved successful, it would give him capital and confidence to continue his undertaking.

"If I find only a few strings of copper cash in each grave, I shall soon become a rich man as riches go in China," thought Lee Wah Sin to himself as he sat on the deck of the ho-tau, listening to the chanting song of the boatmen.

Thus it was that when Lee Wah Sin arrived at the village of the Lees, he sought someone who could tell him of the family of Lee; and so he came that morning to my father's house, for the villagers told him that at the house of Chan he could obtain food and lodging and could learn about his own people. My father was a very old man, and he remembered the father of Wah Sin very well. When he learned that old Lee had prospered in the land of the white foreign devils and that the son had a well-filled purse, my father took him in and charged him only a trifle more than was the custom.

So Lee Wah Sin stayed with us, spending his time wandering around the village and into the fields. He visited many of the family of Lee; but he soon learned that they were much more interested in the money in his purse than in him.

Then one day Lee Wah Sin said to one of the family of Lee:

"On the morrow I must begin my journey back to Canton. I have already told you how I promised my honorable father that I would visit the burial ground of the Lees and make sure that the sepulcher of my father's father and of my father's elder brother has not been disturbed by marauding hands. So today I ask that you go with me and point out the place where lie the bones of my honorable uncle and grandfather, that I may keep the promise I have given."

Now the Lees thought this a very generous and filial thing; so, for a small sum, one of them guided Lee Wah Sin through the pulse fields to the low, rocky hills where, for many generations, those of the family of Lee had been interred. It was a very propitious spot, high, and free from dampness. The graves were dug in the sides of the soft rock; and, after the coffin, with the ceremonial meats and the "spirit money" had been placed therein, the opening had been closed with rocks and sealed with clay from the river. Lee Wah Sin was very loud in his praises of the Lees for the way they had cared for the burial ground of their ancestors; but, secretly, he was thinking how easy it would be to find the place at night and to break into the sepulcher of his uncle.

We thought nothing of it that evening, my father and I, when Lee Wah Sin, as was his custom, went out shortly after dark, saying he would walk by the river; nor did we suspect anything unusual when he returned somewhat late and went directly to bed without speaking to anyone. It was not until morning rice that we knew something was wrong. Lee Wah Sin did not arise and eat with us. When my father went to call him, he found Lee Wah Sin still in bed, very green in his face, and moaning with pain. Seeing that one of Lee Wah Sin's arms was badly swollen, my father examined it. The arm was broken.

"How did this happen, Lee Wah Sin?" demanded my father. "Why did you not tell me last night?"

"I—I fell over the riverbank onto the rocks," Lee Wah Sin replied. "I did not tell you because I was not sure it was broken."

"That was very foolish," my father scolded him. "Surely you must have known it was broken. Now the arm is badly swollen; and it will be much more difficult to mend."

So my father sent me quickly to Lung Nim's to buy some Leung-Tsoy-Suen Tit-Dar Yeuk Tsau, which, as anyone knows, is a very wonderful remedy when one's bones are broken; and he called in old Doctor Ng Poon Gee who, since it was seven o'clock when he arrived, gave Lee Wah Sin seven large pills and put seven healing plasters on his broken arm. I heard my father and Doctor Ng Poon Gee talking in low voices where Lee Wah Sin could not hear them. They said something I could not quite understand; but it was about the length of Lee Wah Sin's purse and the length of time he would probably be ill.

* * * *

Instead of being well the next day, Lee Wah Sin was much worse. He had a very bad fever, and he talked foolish words and would not eat. My father shook his head, and Doctor Ng Poon Gee shook his head; and they agreed that Lee Wah Sin must have done something very wicked indeed.

Then one day, when Lee Wah Sin had been sick a long time, although his fever had been cured with a medicine my father made of two kinds of serpents, a buffalo's foot, ginseng and rice spirits, a Lee man came to our door and asked for my father. I remember the Lee man spoke very angrily:

"Aih-yah, bad luck has fallen upon the family of Lee. The riverbank on which we have had our hoghouse for many seasons has caved in, and we have lost three hogs.

A strange disease has attacked our ducks, and nine have already died. At the same time, a son was born to one of the wives of Lee Gow; but, although the child was taken quickly to the river and washed, an evil spirit stopped its nostrils, and the child died."

"Ts, ts! What misfortune!" sympathized my father. "Have you made the propitiatory offerings?"

"We have," replied the Lee man; "but, as you very well know, such misfortunes could come only from a bad fung shui. So we sent one of the family of Lee to our burial ground to see if, perchance, water which mildews the bones had seeped into the graves; or, what would be much worse, to learn if any enemy had disturbed the bones of our ancestors."

"Haie, that would be a terrible thing!" exclaimed my father, drawing away from the Lee man, and looking about him fearfully. "What did you find?"

"We found," cried the Lee man, fiercely, "that someone has broken into a sepulcher of the Lees and scattered the bones. It must have been done at night, for the opening had been very poorly closed, as though the one who did it worked in darkness. Now, as you very well know, distinguished and venerable Chan, there is no one in the village who would do such a wicked thing. We believe it was done by our cousin, Lee Wah Sin, who has forgotten the good his father taught him and remembers only the evil he has learned in the land of the white foreign devils. Only a few days ago, Lee Wah Sin had Lee Gum's boy show him the way to the very grave that has been disturbed. We know that Lee Wah Sin was staying under your roof, but we have heard that he has not been seen for several days. Is not his flight sufficient proof of his guilt? So I have come to you, honorable Chan, to ask if you know whence Lee Wah Sin has fled."

When the Lee man had finished speaking, my father, as was his custom, smoked a pipe in silence. Then, blowing the ashes from the bowl, he shook his head sadly, and clicked his tongue.

"Ts, ts! What misfortune!" he exclaimed. "I am very sorry for you; but I do not know if I can help you. Perhaps by tomorrow this time I may have news for you. Yes, on reflection, I am sure that if I had a few handfuls of cash to hire errand boys, I could have some very good gossip for you tomorrow."

So the Lee man gave my father the money. And when the Lee man had gone, I said:

"Honorable father, I wish you would permit me to earn a few of those cash. And if you need another errand boy, I could get Wong Sam for you."

My father frowned at me. "You are very stupid, Yin Do," he said.

Then he put the whole of the cash into his own purse, and went into the room where lay Lee Wah Sin. Wondering why my father had thought me stupid, I sat down close by the door and listened. And almost at once I heard Lee Wah Sin exclaim:

"Oh, distinguished and excellent Chan, surely your liver is large with benevolence! I heard what the Lee man said; and I know how you have protected me. But, sir, it is true, all true, what the Lee man said. I have had much time to meditate while lying here; and I know now that I have been very foolish and wicked. What can I do, sir? How can I escape the righteous wrath of the Lees?"

My father was silent a long time. I could hear the sputtering of his long pipe, and I could hear him blowing the ashes from the bowl.

"It is a very difficult matter," he said at length. "Perhaps I can help you; but first tell me: Why did you do this terrible thing?"

Then Lee Wah Sin told my father the whole story, as I have told it to you. He told my father how he had read in the book of the "spirit money" that lay in the graves of China, and how he had planned to rob those graves.

* * * *

So I went back that night to the grave of my father's elder brother," said Lee Wah Sin, "and with a stout spade I opened the sepulcher. With my flashlight, which I brought with me from San Francisco, I searched around the coffin on the rocky floor; but I could not find the money I sought. Then, finally, I turned the coffin over, and there I saw many coins.

"I gathered the coins and put them in a bag I had brought for the purpose; and, as I gathered them, I thought what a foolish custom it is to bury money with the dead, and what a foolish belief it is that any harm will come of taking that 'spirit money.'

"I was still picking up coins when a strange thing happened. My flashlight, for no reason that I knew, went out.

"And then, while I knelt there in the darkness, I heard the rattle of a stone outside the grave. Thinking that someone had discovered me, I hastened out. It was very bright with starlight. There was no sound. There was nothing that I could see that could have caused that stone to move.

"But that was not all. As I looked down at the willows by the riverbank I saw a most terrible sight, and I heard a fearful sound. Those willows, honorable Chan, were tossing and swaying; and I heard a noise like the sobbing and moaning of winter winds through dead branches. Yet there was no wind!

"I began to feel very strange; and my stomach grew cold. It seemed that the air all about me was moving with the angry spirits of the Lees. I looked back into that dark grave; and a great fear took hold of me. I dared not enter that sepulcher again.

"So I hastily covered the opening; then, with the spade in one hand and the sack of 'spirit money' in the other. I walked my way in great haste and in fear. There were noises all about me; yet I could see no one. The tall grass of the foothills billowed like an angry sea; yet there was no wind.

"I started to run; and it was then I fell. I stumbled; yet the path was smooth and there was no reason why I should have stumbled; and I fell over the riverbank to the rocks below. I knew my arm was broken, but I was afraid to tell you.

"Yes, I have been very foolish and wicked," concluded Lee Wah Sin. "While the fever was on me, I had visions of the wrong I have done. The old Chinese are right: The bones of one's ancestors must not be disturbed. It is because I have done this wicked thing that misfortune has fallen upon the Lees. It is because of my evil deed that I have been lying here ill. I have been punished; and it is proper that I should have been punished. So I ask you, venerable Chan, what can I do? If the Lee men find me here, they will surely slay me."

I was very glad when Lee Wah Sin finished his story, for it seemed that the room had become very cold and dark, and I was trembling with fear. While I debated whether to run from the house into the sunshine, my father spoke:

"Ts, ts! What a wicked thing you have done! Yes, the Lee men will surely slay you. That is the law. And it is right."

There was silence then, for about the time it takes to drink a cup of tea; then my father said:

"It would help some, perhaps, if the 'spirit money' could be restored to the grave of the Lee man."

"Ah, I have it all here," spoke up Lee Wah Sin, eagerly. "It is all here in this bag by the grass-seed pillow. I have not touched it. I have not even dared to look at it. Could you, sir scholar, take it back for me?"

"It would be very dangerous," my father objected. "A Lee man might observe me and think that I was the one who had stolen the money. Besides, the spirits would be angry with me if I even so much as touched the string that binds the sack."

"Yes, that is true. But I will pay you well.

I will pay you anything you ask."

"Haie, I could not accept money for such a thing!" exclaimed my father, haughtily. "It would be sacrilegious. Still, on reflection, I think there would be no harm in giving me a sum of money to buy offerings, for I shall have to propitiate the spirits."

"I will do that, gladly."

"Then it would be well to give the Lees a good present of money so they can rebuild the hoghouse that has fallen, buy more hogs and ducks, and pay the expenses of burying the child that died."

"I will do that, too, sir," agreed Lee Wah Sin. "How much would you suggest?"

My father meditated a moment.

"Count what money you have," he said, finally. "First, pay me what is owing for your keep. Then set aside enough for your passage back to Canton. Divide the remainder into two parts: one-half for the Lees; and the other half to be used by me in making sacrifices."

For a time, Lee Wah Sin did not answer. Then he spoke very quietly: "But, honorable Chan, that will leave me nothing." "You will need nothing. You will be in Canton where you have a good position."

"Alas," cried Lee Wah Sin, "I no longer have even a position. I told my employers that I might engage in other business, and that if I did not return at a specified time, they could secure someone in my place. The appointed time for my return has passed while I lay here ill."

"Well, you will at least have your life, and that is more than you will have if the Lees discover you. On reflection, I am half a mind to turn you over to the Lees, for by helping you I am incurring the anger of the gods, and there is no profit in it for me."

"Oh, I will pay, I will pay!" cried Lee Wah Sin. "Do not turn me over to the Lee men!"

"Then it is settled," said my father. "A ho-tau leaves at sunrise for Canton. I will hide you in the rice fields below the village; and when the ho-tau passes, you can swim out and go aboard. Now count out the money as I have directed; for the longer you wait, the angrier the spirits will be."

So Lee Wah Sin took his purse and divided the money as my father had told him. Then my father said:

"Now give me what is owing me for your keep." And Lee Wah Sin gave it to him. Then my father said:

"Now, of the remainder, give me the half that I am to use in making propitiatory offerings for the sin you have done." And this, also, was given to my father. Then my father said:

"Now give me the other half that I may send it at once to the Lees before they learn you are here and take both your life and your money." And this, Lee Wah Sin did also, thanking my father for his generous help and wise counsel.

"Now," said my father, "since I have the money in hand with which to buy the sacrificial offerings, the spirits know of my good intentions; therefore, you may now give me the bag of money you took from the grave of your father's elder brother."

Lee Wah Sin lost no time in taking the bag from beneath the grass-seed pillow and handing it to my father.

For a time, neither made speech; and I heard only the sputtering of my father's pipe, and the hissing of his breath as he blew the ashes from the bowl. Then at length he spoke; and I thought his talk was very strange and startling.

"Haie!" he chuckled. "You are indeed a fool, Lee Wah Sin. Your head is as empty as your purse. You have a little learning; but you have not learned enough. You were right about the money buried in our graves; and yet you were wrong. What do you think is the value of this money you found beneath the bones of your uncle?"

"Why, I did not take time to count it," replied Lee Wah Sin; "but there are several silver coins in addition to many copper cash. I would say the value is at least five thousand cash."

My father laughed uproariously. He shook the bag of jingling coins.

"It is worth about two hundred cash!"

Lee Wah Sin uttered a great cry, and he spoke words that were very strange to me although I have since heard foreign devil teamsters use the same words in speaking to their lazy horses.

"Let me explain," said my father. "It is true that we used to bury sums of good money with the bodies of our dead. But one time the word went about from village to village that there was to be a revolution, and that the revolution was to be financed by opening the graves and recovering this 'spirit money.' Whereupon the people reasoned that to have the graves of their ancestors profaned and to be robbed at the same time was too much; so they went quickly to all the graves and recovered the money themselves. Then they went to the gold and silver merchants and had worthless pieces of metal struck off in imitation of the real money; and they put these worthless counterfeits in the graves. Since then they use these imitations, a whole sack of which costs no more than two hundred copper cash; in some places they use merely little round pieces of paper. It is all the same to the spirits of the dead.

"So, Lee Wah Sin, you see now why you are a fool. The money that was buried with your uncle was long ago recovered by the Lees. All you got is this bag of worthless metal." And again my father laughed and shook the jingling sack.

* * * *

Afterward I learned that when my father finished speaking, Lee Wah Sin looked at him a long time; then, with a groan like that of one who is dying, or wishes to die, Lee Wah Sin turned his face to the wall.

Presently my father came out. I remember he carried in one hand the good money Lee Wah Sin had given him; and in the other hand he had the sack of "spirit money" which Lee Wah Sin had stolen. I saw him put the good money into a bag and hide it in his blouse. Then he looked long and thoughtfully at the sack of "spirit money" which he had placed on the table.

I saw my father reach out a hand to take hold of the string that was around the neck of the sack; I saw him suddenly draw back his hand, and I heard his breath hiss between his lips. Then, after awhile, he seized the cords in his trembling hands and untied the bag; and as he peered into the sack, a startled look came over his face and his hands shook so that the sack slipped from his fingers and fell, jingling, to the table.

The room, it seemed to me, had again become very dark and cold; and I was trembling with fear for I knew my father had done a very profane and dangerous thing. I turned and fled out of the house into the sunshine by the bamboo fence.

I was there by the fence, wondering at the things I had seen and heard, when my father came to me and said:

"Go quickly with these two hundred cash to Gow Li. Tell him I desire to purchase 'spirit money' with the whole sum."

So I did as my father told me.

The next day when the Lee man called, my father said:

"I find that what you have told me regarding Lee Wah Sin is correct. He has gone. He did not go at the time you thought, but that has nothing to do with the matter. He left my house at night and hid in the rice fields below the village until morning, when he swam out and boarded a ho-tau for Canton."

"Then, venerable Chan, we can do nothing," cried the Lee man.

"It is a foolish man who is hasty in speech," retorted my father. "Listen well to what I have to tell you: Before he left, Lee

Wah Sin gave a bag of money to my keeping. Undoubtedly, he repented of his sin and desired to make amends. Tonight, go to the grave that has been disturbed. Do not take a light, but in darkness cast this 'spirit money' into the sepulcher of the Lee man whose bones have been molested. Then quickly close the grave and seal it. If you do faithfully what I have said, your fung shui will become propitious and the evil spirits will no longer pursue the family of Lee."

Then, while the Lee man could not speak for joy, my father took from beneath his blouse a sack of jingling coins; and the Lee man thanked my father in a loud voice, and walked his way in haste.

I spoke up quickly:

"Honorable father, you have made a grievous mistake! You did not give the Lee man the sack of 'spirit money' that Lee Wah Sin took from his uncle's grave; you gave him the one I bought of Gow Li for the two hundred copper cash!"

My father jumped. He turned quickly and closed the door.

"Haie, you are a fool!" he cried fiercely. "Hold your tongue until you have learned wisdom!" And he scowled at me so horribly that I said no more, knowing that I must be very stupid, indeed; for, of a truth, I was about to tell my father, also, that he had forgotten to give the Lee man the money Lee Wah Sin had left to pay for the hoghouse that fell, the hogs and ducks that were lost, and the expense of burying the child that died because of Lee Wah Sin's wicked deed.

My father went to his great bamboo chair by the table, and sat down. From his stocking he took his long, tasseled pipe; and for a time there was silence save for the sputtering of the pipe and the hissing of my father's breath as he blew the ashes from the bowl. Finally he spoke to me, more kindly:

"My son, I perceive that you are observant. That is an excellent trait. If I had not been observant I would not have noticed that the sack of 'spirit money' which Lee Wah Sin took from the grave of his uncle was all good money. That was true what I told him about the people recovering the good money that had been buried with the dead; but I recalled afterward that the Lees used to quarrel about that very thing, accusing one of not bringing back all the money they were sure had been put in the grave of a Lee. Lee Wah Sin, being more greedy than religious, searched more carefully, and found a sack of good money worth perhaps five thousand cash. Since the Lees have forgotten all about the money, I can keep it without any loss to them.

"Observe then, how it is more profitable to do good than to do evil!" my father concluded. "I could have given Lee Wah Sin over to the Lee family, and they would have slain him and would have divided his money amongst themselves, which would have been of little benefit to them because there are so many Lees. So I chose to do good. I restored the fung shui of the Lees. I saved the life of Lee Wah Sin. And, out of it, I have made a nice profit."

Again I refilled our bowls with the steaming Dragonbeard.

"And Lee Wah Sin?" I inquired. "What became of him?"

Chan Yin Do looked at me, and I was sure I saw a smile lurking in the depths of his long, black eyes.

"Haie!" he exclaimed softly. "That was a very good lesson for Lee Wah Sin. He fled from China and returned to San Francisco as soon as possible. He found that during his absence his father had died. Since Lee Wah Sin had given up his schooling before it could be of any real use to him, he took over his father's fish market. He is a very old man now, and they speak of him as one who observes faithfully all the old Chinese customs. If you should stand by the Restaurant of the Fragrant Flower near the hour of evening rice you will see an old man come slowly up Clay Street. He wears a noisome gunnysack about his middle; there are fish-scales on his slippers and a basket of smelly fish-heads on his arm. That, my son, is Lee Wah Sin."

THE SEA AT EVENING
by Andrew Duane

It was in the purple evening, as the moon rose on the sand,
When I heard the restless waters calling me across the land;
And I left the moors and meadows and the forests stretching free,
Left the wind-swept fields behind me, and went down to meet the sea.

How the surges roared to meet me, soared to meet me as I came!
And it seemed that they were calling clearer, chorusing my name.
With the moonlight on them glowing like the luster in a pearl
And the sapphire dwelling in their depths, I saw the waves uncurl
As they spread their crystal fingers, carving figures in the sand—
That the sea had known and bounded, tales from every distant shore;
And I knew that the enchantment would be with me evermore,
That the restless roll and refluence would shackle me apart,
For the sea was in my spirit, and its song was in my heart.

THE PHANTOM HEARSE

by Mary Fortune

Many of my readers will have observed that many "Corner" shops, whatever their location, are known by the names of their owners.

The one I am going to introduce you to was literally a corner shop, and the individuality of the man who kept it had obscured the very name of the street. You never heard hip shop called the corner shop; it was "Jones's" or "Old Jones's," and the corner at which it stood was, and is, "Jones's Corner."

I introduce Jones and his place of business to you on one sunny afternoon in March, when Lumsden, the new "bobby," was airing his dignity in taking a survey of this particular part of a beat that was quite new to him. Indeed, all beats were new to the young man, who had only just been "called in," though his name had been on the list of applicants for police employment for a good while. Lumsden was an especially raw recruit, and as full of an idea of his own importance as raw police recruits generally are.

He was standing on the pavement engaged in a condescending conversation with a sharp-looking resident named Jack Turner, a man of forty, perhaps, and of a small, wiry build. Turnder had been relating to Lumsden a legend of the neighbourhood, about which the policeman was disposed to air his superior knowledge.

"And do you tell me, now, that there are live people hereabouts so ignorant as to believe that kind of a yarn?" he asked, with a smile that puffed his fat cheeks out till they met the collar of his jumper.

"Plenty of 'em; why a man can't help believin' what he sees with his own eyes."

"And have you seen it?"

"Yes, I have, and many more 'n me; but if you want to hear all about it just ask old Jones—he knows the story from the beginning."

Perhaps Lumsden would not have condescended to exhibit his curiosity to old Jones or anyone else if he had not been provided with a convenient excuse. He was standing in front of Turner's door, and the corner shop was obliquely opposite when a man came to the door of old Jones's shop and, with his face turned back, indulged in some pretty strong language that was apparently addressed to old Jones himself.

"Who is that?" asked Lumsden of his new acquaintance.

"It's a chap that lives down the lane behind here. Jerry Swipes they calls him; him and old Jones are always having rows."

"What about?"

"Goodness knows. Jerry is in the old man's debt I fancy, and it's hard to get any money out of Swipes."

"Jerry Swipes? Is that the man's real names?"

"Blest if I can tell you, but it *may* be a nickname, for he is a regular swipe and no mistake."

While Lumsden had been gaining this information, Jerry—a tall, slouching figure, with a sandy face and a long, sharp nose—had been roaring his uncomplimentary remarks to old Jones, who now came to the door of his shop with a red and anygry face, as Swipes edged up the street toward the lane.

"Don't let me catch you inside my shop again!" shouted the old man, as he shook his fist after Jerry; "as sure as I do, I'll give you in charge! You're nothing but a sneaking thief—that's what you are!"

"I'll ram them words down your old throat one o' these days!" shrieked Jerry, as he reached the end of his lane. "Police, is it? By gar, it'll be police with yourself first! You'll give me a glass of whiskey next time I call? Eh, old man!" and the dirty unkempt-looking mortal disappeared into the mouth of the unsavory right-of-way.

Old Jones's vituperation stopped as suddenly as Jerry disappeared, and such a look of fear came into the twinkling eyes under his penthouse, ragged eyebrows that even Lumsden observed it, and Turned had to turn away his face to hide the grin of enjoyment that over-spread his parchment-tried visage; but he controlled himself to remark ere he entered his door—

"Now is your time to go and ask old Jones about the phantom funeral, and you will be sure to hear all about this quarrel with Jerry."

Lumsden took the hint, and marching across the narrow street, was at "Jones's" almost as soon as the old man had got behind his counter again.

"Jones" has all the characteristics of a thriving corner shop, with a little extra dirt and untidiness into the bargain. It was so small that the counter on two sides left but little space for the use of customers, that small space behind further curtailed by "stock" in the form of boxes of soap, bags of potatoes, rice, oatmeal and sugar. The narrow shelves were laden with fly-marked packages, and boxes and bottles of great variety; and the space that ought to be empty under the ceiling was hung with brooms, brushes, clothes lines, and tinware the original brightness of which was dimmed by age and smoke. Into this confined emporium Constable Lumsden stepped, meeting old Jones suspicious eyes as that worthy very unceremoniously resumed his usual seat behind the counter, placed his spectacles astride his nose, and with a sharp rustle shook out the morning paper on his knee.

"Good day to you," said the young policeman as he looked curiously around him.

"Good day it is; what can I serve you with?"

"Serve? Oh, nothing. I heard some strong language at your door just now and came in to see what it was all about."

Old Jones gave his paper an angry rustle as he answered—"If you come in here to know what's the matter every time I get cheek from a customer you'll not be able to do much in the other parts of your beat."

"The cheek wasn't all on the customer's side this time. I heard you calling the man a thief, and in the open street. That's something in my line, you'll allow?"

"And so he is a thief," cried old Jones angrily; "he's the biggest loafer in Melbourne. He only comes near the shop when he wants to shake a plug of tobacco or a pipe."

"What did he shake today?"

"When I want to lay a charge against him, I'll take it up to the sergeant," said old Jones, expecting that it would shut up the officious young trap. But it had very little effect on Constable Lumsden, who was, fortunately for himself, not very thin-skinned.

"Ah! Two might play at visiting the sergeant. If Jerry Swipes went up himself, he has a very good charge against you, and me for a witness. It's again' the laws to call a man a thief in the open street."

"I can prove it."

"If you could prove it twice over, all the same the law won't allow you to do it; and I'd advise you to give him that glass of whiskey he seems to expect from you the next time you get the chance."

At this second allusion to the whiskey, old Jones once more grew white under Lumsden's observing eyes, and his knobby, hard hands shook so that they rustled the paper he held. Seeing this repeated agitation at the allusion to spirits, Lumsden took it into his head that drink was sold "on the sly" at Jones's, and he determined to keep a close watch on the place in future.

The old man made no immediate reply to Lumsden's advice about the treatment of his enemy, Jerry. He was considering within himself that it would, perhaps, be better for his own interests that he should take a different tone with the new police man. The independent sharpness of Lumsden was a new experience at the Corner, the last man on the beat having been an old, steady-going policeman who duly considered Mr. Jones's status in the neighbourhood, and was friendly accordingly. Old Jones would have liked to twist the impertinent young constable's neck, but he tried to do the amiable instead—a very difficult matter for the crusty old man.

"The fact is my temper's wore out with them sort of customers," he said with a sigh at his amiability. "It's a very low neighbourhood, especially down Long's Lane, and it's getting lower every day. They get a few things from you, then they get into your books somehow, in spite of you, and they wind up with dropping in to steal when they think your back's turned."

"A bad business," returned Lumsden, but without the least intonation of sympathy. "What does that fellow you were jawing to do for a living?"

"Jerry Swipes? Ah! He'd be a puzzled to tell you. He hires a truck, and pretends to attend to the markets and that. I've heard of him rag and bottle gathering, but it's all a blind."

"You've been a long time in the neighbourhood, I suppose?" asked Lumsden, as failing anything else in view, he took a pinch out of the oatmeal bag and began to munch it.

"I've been nigh on thirty year in this house and this shop, and if anyone knows the neighbourhood I ought to."

"Ye-es, I suppose so," was the slow and evidently absent reply; "and that reminds me; I've been told some ridiculous yarn about the ghost of a hearse that appears about here. Can you tell me anything about

it?"

"There's nothing ridiculous about it, young man; it's only too true that the Phantom Funeral, as people have got to call it, is often seen in S—— and O—— street. I've seen it often, and I know how it began. There isn't a man in C—— can tell you as much as I can about it."

Old Jones's air had quite undergone a change when his favourite topic came to be dwelt on; the paper was cast aside, and he rose from the old arm-chair. He took off his old, greasy felt hat, and ran his fingers through his stubbly grey hair until it stood nearly straight up, and then he replaced the hat and "ahem"ed as he looked inquiringly towards Lumsden.

"I'd like to hear the story," said the latter, as he looked out of the door to see there was no "duty" staring him in the face, and then leaned easily against the heap of bags, as he listened to old Jones.

"It's getting on for twelve years ago now since that hearse was first seen, and people always said it was because Sam Brown was carried out of No 9 in the dead of the night and taken to the morgue, without common decency, in a dray. Sam was murdered or

committed suicide—it was never actually decided which—and from that day to this the hearse haunts the place as a sort of revenge on the neighbours that they didn't pay more respect to his remains."

"But that's trash," said Lumsden. "How

could a dead man set a hearse to haunt a neighbourhood? I don't believe a word of it."

"I've heard a many say that, as grew white to hear the hearse mentioned within less than a year after," returned old Jones solemnly. "It's the scoffers as see it, and it's not lucky to see it."

"Not lucky?"

"No. If a man sees it—as you may when you're on night duty—the best thing he can do is to turn his back and walk away from it. There has never been a man foolhardy enough to watch it but he died within the year."

"But you've seen it, you say?"

"Aye, by chance. One night a woman was very bad down Long's Lane there, and she wasn't expected to live over the night. I got quite nervous like, and couldn't sleep. It was a bright moonlight, and about two o clock in the morning I saw a slow shadow cross the blind of my window there. Before I had time to think, I was out on the floor and had the curtain

in my hand, for I thought it was the 'Phantom Hearse.' It was. I saw it for a moment moving slowly past, and I dropped the blind quick, and got into bed again."

"What was it like?" asked Lumsden.

"Like a plain, low, box-hearse, all black and with one black horse in it. Sometimes there is a driver, and sometimes a man in black walks at the horse's head. It makes no sound, and is like a dream."

"By George, I'd make a nightmare of it!" cried the young trap. "Do you mean to tell me that no man has ever had the courage to walk up to the thing and grip it?"

"No man has ever been foolhardy enough to go straight to his deathbed that way," was the serious answer.

But the unbelieving policeman laughed aloud as he raised himself and went toward the door, saying lightly—

"Well, here's one man that'll take the first chance of *feeling* what that ghostly machine is made of, at all events. Good gracious! To think people believe such yarns as that!"

As soon as Lumsden had left the shop, Jones's face fell, and he muttered uneasily to himself as he stood by the counter, with his hands upon it, and an anxious look in his scowling face. He was not at any time a pleasant picture, that old Jones of the corner shop, but he looked absolutely repellant as he stood muttering to himself, with his ragged eyebrows almost met in an anxious scowl.

A few minutes later the old man, dashing the old greasy hat under the counter, began to divest himself of his rag of a coat, leaving the shop by the back as he did so. He went through a very slovenly kitchen, and to the verandah at the back of it, where an old, meanly-attired woman was washing in a wooden tub that seemed almost as old as herself. She looked up with a frightened air as Jones shouted at her—

"Margery!"

"Yes, master."

"Leave that washing and get on a clean apron. I'm going out; you'll have to mind the shop."

"Yes, master," and the thin, trembling

arms were being hastily wiped in her wet apron as she was hurrying away.

"Stop. I want to speak to you."

She stopped instantly, and humbly turned an apparently vacant face towards him.

"You've got to watch that boy—that's *your* business, you know. Don't *you* go trying to serve, or you'll poison someone, but keep your eyes *sharp* on Con. You hear?"

It would be queer if she didn't hear, for the man was roaring at the top of his voice, and at every emphasized word the poor old creature jumped.

"I hear. I'll watch him well."

"I'll leave nothing in the till; and *mind*, see that there's something in it when I come back. Give *no credit*. Do you hear?"

"Yes, master. I'll let nothing go without the money."

"And *count* it before you let the things go out of your hands."

"Yes, master."

While Jones had been giving these instructions, he had been making a pretence of a wash in the old woman's tub from pure suds, and when he dismissed her with a nod, he seized a grimy old towel and rubbed his face with it. It seemed as if Jones was in an awful hurry, for he had not finished with the towel when he had crossed the littered yard, and was giving some more orders to a sharp-looking boy of about thirteen who had been occupied in washing bottles in a dilapidated shed.

"Con!"

"Yes, sir."

"I'm going out for an hour or so, and the old woman is to mind the shop; *you* keep your eye on her."

"Yes, sir."

"Let her sit in the chair and count the money. Do you serve, and mind don't give *one penny of credit*!"

"Very well, sir."

"And watch the old woman well; see that she doesn't get slipping a penny now and

then into some corner of her gown. I've known her do it afore."

"I'll watch her close, sir."

"That's right. And see you keep account of every penny's worth you let go."

"I'll be very careful, sir."

* * * *

Ten minutes afterwards, old Jones was scuttling away down the street pretty easy in his mind, because he had put in practice his favourite receipt for keeping people honest. "Set one to watch the other!" he would say, "that's the way to do it! You don't want no detectives if you set one to watch the other!"

Very few would have recognised the two happy faces that beamed behind old Jones's counter that afternoon to be those of the stupid, hopeless-looking old woman who was previously slopping grimy rags at the back, and the half-discontented one of the boy who had listened with such outward respect to a master he both disliked and despised.

The old woman, who was no other than old Jones' lawful wife, sat in Jones' chair stiffly and upright, with her hands folded on a clean white apron and a broad-bordered, starched muslin cap on her unsteady head. Her withered old face was beaming with pride and delight, and with an air of dignity that was pitiful when one knew its short lived nature. The one happiness of poor old Mrs. Jones was in being permitted to play at keeping shop, for it was only play after all, Con doing in reality whatever was necessary in the small sales. Con was very busy just now wiping down the counter and "tidying up things a bit," as he was wont to call it when speaking to Mrs. Jones.

"Isn't this fine!" cried the gratified old creature with a child's unreasoning delight. "If the master would go away oftener and let us keep shop, Con, wouldn't it be nice?"

"It would," answered the boy with some decision, "but no sich luck. Some old men die, but the likes of *him* never dies."

"I wish he would die," Mrs. Jones said

in a deep whisper to the lad. "I'm allays a wishing it. If he did there would be no one to knock me about, and I would sit in the shop allays. I wish that dead hearse would stop right under his window some night, I do!"

"Did you ever see the dead hearse, Mrs. Jones?" questioned the boy as he ceased his rubbing at the counter and looked at the old woman curiously.

"I did," she replied with an energetic nod that set her wide cap frills bobbing. "I seen it one night last March. The master he woke me up to see it. It was passing the window, and stopped opposite Grinder's. Mrs. Grinder, she died next day but one. That's the reason I wouldn't never sleep in that front room again; and, besides, the master he was allays a-knockin' me about for snorin'. I don't snore. *He* does."

"Aye! Jones wanted to get you out of his room, missis, and he wasn't short of an excuse. *I* know!"

This unexpected remark was made by no other than Jerry Swipes, whose lanky figure had entered the shop unobserved in the deep interest attached to the "dead hearse," as poor old Mrs. Jones called it. Con stared at the man, but Mrs. Jones was on her dignity and bridling asked what business it was of Jerry Swipes?

"None, missis, none whatsomever, only no man as is a man likes to see a lawful wife med a slave of and beat when another woman—but it's none of my business. Con, hand me a threepenny plug and a pipe."

"You don't know what you're talking of, Jerry Swipes!" cried Mrs. Jones with angry suspicion. "It was my own doin's as made me go to sleep in the back room."

"Was it? Oh, then, maybe you knows what Jones does of a night since you left. If ye doesn't, jest watch him, and you'll see, that's all."

Listening open mouthed to these strange words of the disreputable customer, Con had mechanically laid the required articles on the counter. In an instant the tobacco and pipe were transferred to Jerry's pocket, and his ragged ulster wrapped over them.

"Put 'em down, me boy," he said with a leer as he made for the door. "Me credit's always good with Mr. Jones. Yes, missis, that's what *I* say—watch him an you'll know."

"Oh, Mrs. Jones, he's never paid for 'em!" cried Con. "The master'll kill us!"

"Watch him an' you'll know," murmured the old woman, on whom Jerry's words appeared to have made a strange impression. She was staring at the door out of which Jerry had just passed, with her brows bent together, and a queer, thoughtful look in her faded eyes that puzzled the boy.

"Please. Mrs. Jones," reiterated Con, "that Swipes took the pipe and baccy without paying for it. What'll we do? The master'll kill us.

"Watch him and you'll know," again murmured the completely absorbed old woman; "and it's true. He used to go somewheres at night. I've missed him."

Fortunately for Con's peace of mind at this moment, there entered two legitimate customers who put a few shillings in the till, and distracted Mrs. Jones's thoughts again. It was painful even to the boy to see her pluming herself in the chair, and feeling so proud and happy, when it was so certain that at the first sound of her master's harsh voice she would drop into the cringing, half-stupid slave, who seemed to have no idea beyond the avoidance, by unselfish service, of the kicks and thumps the brute was in the habit of bestowing on her whenever he wanted some object to explode his temper on.

* * * *

By this time Constable Lumsden had worked 'round his beat and was in the vicinity of "Jones's Corner" again. As he was about to pass the door, he looked in and, seeing only the boy and the half idiotic face of an old woman behind the counter, he changed his mind and entered. Mrs. Jones bridled immediately. The poor old creature had a very exaggerated idea of a policeman's importance, and, being a woman, was not, perhaps, insensible to the young chap's ruddy and healthy looking face. Con was not so sure of Lumsden. He had a town boy's detestation of all bobbies, big and little, young and old, and would just as soon have seen a big brown snake wandering into the shop as that young man in blue.

"Is Jones at home?" asked Lumsden.

"No, sir, he's gone out on business. This is Mrs. Jones."

"Yes," she nodded proudly as she smoothed down the white apron with both trembling hands. "I'm keeping shop. I'd like to keep shop every day."

"Would you?" Lumsden asked, with a suspicious look into the childish looking face, for the constable was not quite sure whether she was laughing at him or was in reality half-witted. But he was soon at his ease, for it was impossible to doubt the want of intellect so plainly pictured in the vacant, withered features. "I suppose, now, you sell everything here?"

"Yes," she answered proudly, "everythink."

"I was just wishing for a glass of something," Lumsden said, in a low tone, as he glanced towards the quiet street. "There's no one about; I'll take a glass of spirits, please," and he quietly laid a shilling on the counter.

"Oh, we don't keep no drink here, sir," quickly returned Con, as he pushed back the shilling, for which the unconscious old woman's hand was already outstretched.

"I wasn't talking to you," snapped the constable. "Are you Jones's son?"

"No, sir, I'm only hired; but I've been with them a good while."

"You're too precious sharp," Lumsden said, with a frown that he believed suffi-

cient to overcome the sharpest youngster in the city. "Missis, can't you sell me a glass of something?"

"The master takes a glass often," she mumbled, "but he never gives me none. I

don't know where he keeps his bottle; s'pect it's in the front room. Master allays locks the front room when he goes out."

"Hum, give me sixpen' worth of lollies, boy;" and the discontened constable pushed back the shilling on which the old woman's eyes were fixed greedily. Con weighed the lollies and was graciously presented with some of them for his own use.

"Did you ever see this ghost of a hearse that haunts this neighbourhood?" asked

Lumsden of the lad, as he decided that the old woman was not worth talking to.

"No, sir, *I* never did, but Mrs. Jones has seen it. Haven't you, Mrs. Jones?"

"Seen the dead hearse? I should think so. Ha! There's allays someone dies when that comes. I wish 'twould stop right *there* tonight," and she pointed a shaky finger straight out of the shop door to the empty street, on which the afternoon sun was shining warmly. And then as if the subject brought back to her memory Jerry Swipes' words, she repeated them to herself, with her brows again tangled into a thoughtful frown—"Jest you watch him, and you'll see."

"What is she muttering?"

"Oh, nothing of any consequence, sir; she's talking to herself half the time."

"Um! A little queer, eh?"

"A little, sir."

"Did you never see the old chap sell a glass now?" asked the clever new policeman; and Con's naturally rosy face grew crimson.

If there is one thing more despised than another by even the lowest Melbourne lad, it is an informer. In this case, Con had nothing to tell, but it insulted him that it should be supposed possible that he *would* tell, even if he knew anything.

Lumsden saw the boy's increase of colour, and it increased his suspicions.

"No," Con answered—without the 'sir' this time, you will observe—"nor I never see no spirits of any kind about, even for Mr. Jones's own drinkin'. If he keeps any, it must be, as Mrs. Jones says, in his own room, that's mostly always locked."

The mention of her name aroused the old woman from an unusual absorption in thought, and she repeated over and over again—

"Yes, Con, in his own room; allays in his own room."

In a very discontented mood, Lumsden strolled out to the pavement again, munch-ing his lollies as he went; and it so happened that Jerry Swipes at that moment appeared at the corner of the lane, and after a sharp look up and down the empty street, beckoned to the policeman. Lumsden was inclined to stand on his dignity, and let the drunken-looking fellow come over to him if he wanted him; but all at once he remembered that this was the man old Jones had been abusing, and thinking of the probability of retaliation, he put his dignity in his pocket with the lollies and crossed the narrow street.

"Just come down here a few steps, constable; I want to speak to ye."

Lumsden followed the speaker a few yards and then stopped. The lane was most uninviting to all senses, and two or three red-faced, loud-voiced women were in front of some old wooden cottages farther down, gossiping amid the noise of screaming babies and quarrelling children.

"If you have anything private to say, there's no need of going any farther—there's nothing but a dead wall here."

"It's the fence of Turner's woodyard," returned Jerry, "and I guess you're right. We can speak low, and besides, there's no one in the yard—I saw Turner go out five minutes ago."

"Well, what is your business?"

"Are you game now to go halves in an informin' business?" asked Jerry, cunningly, in reply so this question.

"Informin'? Is it about old Jones?" was the sharp return.

"The very man."

"By Jove, I suspected it!" cried Lumsden, as he stooped and slapped his leg in thorough enjoyment. "Game? I should think so!" And then a sharp suspicion crossed his mind, and made Lumsden look steadily into the bloated face with the sharp nose. "If you are on the look-out for a reward, how is it you don't try to keep it all to yourself?" he asked.

"D'ye think I'd ever get it if I hadn't

someone decent to back me up?" Jerry asked cunningly. "I couldn't take him in single-handed. I'd want help—and if I was the respectablest in Melbourne, there wouldn't be a conviction without the worm."

"Without the worm? What do you mean? What are talking about?"

"I'm talking about a *still*—didn't you know it afore?"

The low whistle that gave expression to Lumsden's surprise so prolonged that Jerry cut it short with a, "Hush."

"I thought it was sly grog-selling," he exclaimed. "I noticed the effect your mention of the glass of whiskey had on Jones a while ago, and I thought it was sly grog-selling. But a still! By Jove! Are you sure, man?"

"As sure as that there fence is made o wood," was the answer, as Swipes put his hand on Turner's fence; "an' now just wait a minnit till I see if Turner's back."

He stepped on a stone as he was speaking, and craned his neck in an examination of the wood-yard.

"No, he's not at home yet, for the back door's shut an' the barrow's not there. Come now, let us settle about it. It must be done tonight, for I gave him a good many hints today, an he may be frightened."

"He's gone out," said Lumsden.

"Yes, and I am afraid he's gone to try and get rid of the plant somehow, for he must have customers for the spirits somewhere, and they're bound to help him. The best thing that you and I can do is to go up to the sergeant at once, and lay our claim to reward."

There was a little more talk about it, and when it was over, they separated so as to avoid suspicion—appointing, however, a time when they were to meet at the police office in the presence of the sergeant.

* * * *

Old Jones came home very shortly after in one of his humours. At the first glimpse of his face in the doorway all brightness fell from that of the poor old wife, who hobbled to the back, leaving Con to face "the master;" and Con did with more confidence than usual for there was some money in till, and he had some news to tell Jones that might make him think less of Jerry having outwitted him in the matter of the pipe and tobacco.

"Well! Everything at sixes and sevens, I suppose?" Jones asked with a furious look around the shop. The man *wanted* something to swear at, for his blood was boiling within him.

"No, sir. Everything's all right in the shop; only—" the boy hastened to add, ere Jones had time to explode—"that young bobby's been here, sir."

"Again! What the deuce did he want?"

"I'm afraid he was after no good, master," replied Con, as he shook his head sagely. "He tried to get a glass of spirits out of the mistress and me; actually put the money on the counter for it."

"What!"

"Yes, indeed, sir. He gammoned that he knew drink was sold here, but when he could get nothing out of us he bought sixpen' worth of lollies and went away."

Jones absolutely turned grey with apprehension as he stared at the boy.

"You are sure you didn't tell the villain anything?"

"I had nothing to tell him, sir."

"That's true, Con—of course, you had nothing to tell him. You may go out and finish them bottles now."

Jones fell into his old arm-chair behind the counter dumbfounded. He felt that he was caught in a trap and didn't know where to seek help. He had taken off his best hat, and held the old one in his hands, looking at it in a queer, bewildered way, when a man entered with an active step. It was Turner, the small, sharp, dark man that kept the wood-yard.

"How many hundred of wood will I bring

you over, Jones?" he asked as he bent over toward the old man with a strange grin on his face.

"Not one!" shouted old Jones, as the blood rushed into face, and his eyes flashed under their overhanging brows. He had got someone to vent his rage on at last. "Not one; and I'll never take another from you—you swindling rascal. The last was green messmate."

"Hush, hush, Jones! You have no idea what a mess you're in. I've come to give you a bit of neighbourly help, for both Jerry Swipes and the new bobby'll be down on you in a brace of shakes."

"Jerry Swipes! The new bobby! Oh, curse them."

But even as the words fell from his lips, they trembled, and he put on his old hat in a hopeless way very unusual with him.

"Yes and there's no time to waste. Jerry has been watching you by nights, it seems, and he's found out all about the still. He's told Lumsden, and they've gone up to the sergeant and are agreeing to share the reward for informing between them."

"Oh, Lord, what'll I do?" groaned the old man.

"That's what I'm come to tell you. I have the horse ready in the cart and the wood in it. I'm going to bring it into the yard, and you'll pack all your whiskey into it, as well as the whole still, if we can manage it, and I'll drive 'em off before the informers come."

"Where will you take 'em?" Jones asked doubtfully.

"Where they'll be safe. Never you mind so long as they don't get 'em *here*."

"But what are you doin' it for? I never was friends with you, Bill Turner. What are you so willin' to do this for?"

"No! You old screw, you never *was* friends with me, I don't owe you so much as a thank-you for one neighbourly act. What am I a-doin of it for? What a darned fool you are to ask! I'm a-doing it for what I can make out of it, of course! Do you think I'm a fool to do it for nothing? I'll save you a fifty-pound fine and the loss of your stock, never fear, but I'll ask for my pay when the job's done!"

Strange to say this assertion, though it touched the weakest part of old Jones (the region of his pocket), convinced him of Turner's sincerity, and before many minutes had elapsed the woodman's cart was in the old storekeeper's yard. Jones sent Con and Mrs. Jones into the shop while a new load was packed into the bottom of the conveyance and covered with a layer of wood that made all, as Turner declared, look quite natural.

Few could have guessed in what a state of excitement old Jones had lately been, had they looked into the shop after Turner's departure and seen him, spectacles on nose, apparently absorbed in the paper; at least, Jerry Swipes didn't guess it when he entered with a wicked grin on his dirty visage, and with Constable Lumsden at his heels.

"I hope I don't intrude, Mister Jones," sneered Jerry, who had evidently managed an extra glass somewhere. "Allow me to introduce me friend, Constable Lumsden."

"Stash that!" cried Lumsden angrily, as he pushed Jerry out of his way very unceremoniously and advanced to the counter. "I'm here on duty, Jones. We have received information that you are carrying on a sort of private distillery here in contravention to the laws, and we're here to search the premises."

"Search and be hanged to you!" was the very unexpected reply; "but by the heavens above me, if that drunken thief comes inside my private premises—I'll brain him, so help me !"

"Will you?" retorted the pot-valiant Swipes. "Maybe two could play at that game; though if it comes to brains it's very little you'd have to let out. Stand back, Lumsden, and let me blacken that old villain's eyes."

"If you don't keep quiet, Swipes, I'll put you out myself," was all the comfort the angry man got from his unwilling companion, who went on to Jones—

"You may as well let us in peacefully, Jones. There's two constables in the back yard by this time, and there's no earthly use offering any resistance."

"I'm offering no resistance; didn't I tell you to search? There's the door open; but I say again, if that informer crosses that threshold, I'll fell him."

"Oh, I'm an informer, eh? D'ye hear that, Lumsden? By George, the old fool is giving himself away. It seems there's something to inform on, eh?"

"Hold your jaw, Swipes. You had better go 'round to the back; there's no use having any unnecessary row." And the young policeman went behind the counter to the door that old Jones was still holding open with shaking hands.

Jerry, finding himself in a minority, did as Lumsden had suggested, and went 'round to the yard, cursing Jones all the way. Jones immediately shut the shop door and barred it behind him, going out then after the young policeman to see what disturbance they would make among his household gods.

That part of the household gods represented by poor Mrs. Jones was in such a state of bewildered surprise at the advent of two strange men in blue entering her slovenly kitchen that the entrance of another from the shop-way added nothing to her confusion. Lumsden, as befitting the fact that he was co-informer, took the lead in what followed, his first action being to proceed towards Jones own bedroom and order it to be opened.

"My information is that the door of a cellar opens in a closet of this room," he said importantly, "and that in that cellar is the still."

Without a word Jones unlocked the door and flung it open. At this moment Jerry Swipes, fortified by the presence of so many policemen, advanced to push his way into Jones's room; and, without another word of warning, the old man who had been a pugilist in his young days lifted his fist and struck Swipes so heavily between the eyes that the half-drunk man fell to the floor almost as if he had been shot.

"I had a right to do it!" cried Jones. "I warned him! I put no hindrance in the way of the police, but that man I'll not let cross my threshold! Clear out o' this, or I'll let you have it double!"

Jerry, who was picking himself up with difficulty, turned to go, but as he did, he uttered a threat that was remembered against him afterwards.

"Do you see them?" he asked, pointing to the drops of blood on the floor. "You drew 'em from my face, but by heaven, I'll let every drop out of your heart for 'em," and he staggered blindly out to the yard.

It is unnecessary to enter into particulars of the unsuccessful search made by the constables of Jones's cellar and premises generally—there was nothing whatever incriminating discovered. The unsuspected load Turner had taken had removed everything immediately connected with the still, save some empty hop pockets and sugar bags and a suspiciously smelling keg. Jones enjoyed the discomfiture of Lumsden, as indeed did his fellow constables, who were like all the world jealous of a neighbour's good fortune.

"I'm sorry for your disappointment, gentlemen," said Jones with a derisive grin; "but you see, it is not always well to depend on information received from a low scoundrel. Howsomever, I'm sorry to see Mr. Lumsden look so down in the mouth. I don't mind giving him a glass of very good whiskey I happen to have here by me."

"Hang you and your whiskey, too!" was the young man's not over civil reply to this kind offer, and in a few moments the police accompanied by the terribly disappointed

Jerry had all cleared out by the back way. To say that Jerry was disappointed is putting it very weakly—he evinced his feelings in such threats at Jones and, indeed, at the police, who had, he fancied, cheated him in some way or another, that Lumsden was within an ace marching him off to the lockup.

Lumsden was quite as much disappointed as the informer, though he was able to control his feelings a little better. So convinced was he that Jones had been warned and cleared his cellar out, that he determined on doing duty on his own account that night. That is, instead of going to bed or to amuse himself after his patrol was over, after dinner he returned to his beat to watch Jones's Corner.

He did not get to his beat till about eleven o'clock, believing that whatever illegal thing might be done on the old man's premises would not be attempted before that hour. He had acquainted the constable on duty of his intention so that his movements should be taken no notice of and he chose as his place of watch the entrance to a narrow right-of-way opposite old Jones's back yard.

When he took up his post, there was a light in the shop, though it was shut, but all was darkness at the back. Jones was not the man to let his wife and Con sit up burning candles for nothing. After about half an hour's watch, Lumsden saw the light from the shop disappear, and in a few minutes a man crossed the yard stealthily, opened Jones's gate noiselessly, and slipped 'round the corner of the street where the door of the shop was. Lumsden was curious and followed him to the corner. There he saw small, lithe figure dart across the moonlit street and enter Turner's wood-yard. Lumsden went back to his station, wondering what Turner was doing there at that time of night; and just then the town clock was just striking twelve.

It was quite another hour before he saw anything else at Jones's. Then a slinking figure crept along in the shadow of the houses, and deftly climbing Jones high fence, dropped inside. The young constable recognised Jorry Swipes instantly, and guessed at once that the low scoundrel was on the same self-imposed duty as himself, *viz.*, watching old Jones, with the hope of making some discovery of a fresh plant. It was about half an hour before Jerry left the yard, and it was chiming the half-hour after one as he dropped out into the street again and ran down the lane.

Another half hour, and Lumsden saw a light appear for a moment in the kitchen window. The light was very indistinct, for the window was under the back verandah where Mrs. Jones did her poor washing; but it was distinct enough for Mr. Lumsden to see it twice—once when it seemed to come and go away again, and once more when it reappeared and seemed to be suddenly put out. Believing that Jones was rambling about the place making a bestowal of some illegal machinery, Lumsden was about to climb the fence for a nearer watch when he saw something that changed his mind with a strange suddenness. The young man had heard no noise, but he felt, as it were, that there was something moving in his vicinity. Turning involuntarily, he saw, coming down the street full in the moonlight, what seemed to be the shadow of a hearse. A sort of fear crept upon him for a moment, but he recovered himself speedily, remembering his jibes at the dead hearse that very day, and his determination to prove its mortal and tangible nature.

The thing passed him—the shadow of a hearse—and turned Jones's Corner noiselessly. It appeared to Lumsden's eyes just as Jones had described it: a plain box-like hearse with a cover haped like a sarcophagus. The shape of a black horse drew it, and the shape of a man in black, with long black crêpe weepers hanging down from his hat, behind sat in front and held the shadowy reins. There is not one among the very wisest of us without some hidden superstition, however we may to try to deeeive ourselves about the fact; and young Lumsden felt a queer, cold creeping up his back in spite of his declared unbelief in the "Phanton Hearse."

No sooner had it turned the corner and was out of sight, however, but he pulled himself together and hurried after it, determined to see the affair through. He had not far to go. I have said the thing turned the corner. It had barely done so; when Lumsden reached the front of the shop, he saw the hearse standing an front of the window he knew belonged to Jones's bedroom, the vehicle and horse still and soundless, the man sitting on his box as if carved out of black marble.

One moment the young man hesitated, for he was only mortal, but then he strode on toward the hearse, his steps making a loud noise on the moonlit pavement. His heart was beating quickly, but he did not stop until he was so near that by putting out his hand he should have been able to touch the hearse. He *put* it out, and touched nothing! He moved a little nearer, and tried again. Still there was nothing tangible, but he heard a terrible moan that seemed to come from the interior of the ghostly vehicle, and started back.

When he looked again, the whole thing had disappeared. There was nothing in the whole length of the street but the moonlight lying upon pavement and roadway!

Constable Lumsden stared for some minutes, and then being, as I have already said, only mortal he turned quickly, and sought the companionship of his fellow policeman whose step he fortunately heard at that moment echoing down a neighbouring cross street. The constable on the beat that night was an elderly man, and he did not laugh at Lumsden's story.

"I've heard of it often," he said thoughtfully, "but I never saw it, and I don't want

to. They say it is a sure sign of death in the house where it stops. It was at Jones's, you say?"

"Yes, but was it there after all? I wonder if I could fancy it all?"

"You ought to be the best judge of that yourself; but that the hearse *has* been seen there's no manner of doubt. I've been on this beat over eight years, and I've heard of the hearse a dozen times and more."

"Well, whether or not I imagined the hearse, I'm certain the sound was real."

"What sound?"

"Why, the awful groan I heard. It made my blood creep."

"You'd better go and get a sleep," said Cooney, "or you'll not be fit for duty tomorrow."

And the young man took his advice, the sight of the "Phantom Hearse" having cured him of all the interest he had lately felt in "still hunting."

Lumsden lodged with Cooney, who was a married man with a family, and it seemed to the young man that he had not been asleep ten minutes when he was wakened by a rough shake. Cooney was standing by the side of his bed with something in his rugged face that roused Lumsden at once.

"What is it?" he asked.

"It's murder, that's what it is. Get up at once, and be puttin' on your clothes while I tell you. You'll get no chance of pocketing that fifty pounds now. Old Jones was found dead in his bed this morning."

"Good heavens! Who found him?"

"That little chap, Con, who lives there. It seems he had to call Jones every morning before he opened the shop at seven o'clock, and this morning when he went he found the old man so sound asleep that nothing but the last trump will waken him. The boy ran to tell me, and before Smith relieved me, the neighbourhood was in a commotion."

"What time is it now?"

"Near nine. Hurry out and get your breakfast. Didn't you tell me you saw Jerry

Swipes climbing over Jones fence night?"

"Yes."

And then a sudden recollection of the terrible threat Jerry had made against the old man after he was struck down recurred to Lumsden.

"How was he murdered?"

"Stabbed in the breast, or rather stomach, by some sharp instrument. He appears to have been lying on his back asleep from what the doctor says, and was found in a pool of his own blood. By Jove, Jerry seems to have kept his word. He swore he would let every drop out of the old man's heart, and it looks as if he'd done it."

"You think it was Jerry?"

"Can there be a doubt of it after what you saw? At all events, I went straight to his tumble-down shanty and arrested him suspicion."

"How did he take it?"

"Like a man stupid—as indeed he was with the effects of yesterday's drink. There was blood on his clothes, too, but he denies the murder, of course."

"Does he deny he was in Jones's yard this morning?"

"No; he owns to it. He says he went in hopes of finding old man in the cellar. It seems there's some crack in the wall he can see through. Come now; if you've done breakfast, we'll be down and see what we can find out. You can question the boy this time."

We can understand the deep interest of Lumsden in this case. It was his first in the force, and the matter of the suspected illicit work in Jones's place, together with his own intimate connection with it as co-informer, made the whole affair of importance to him. And there was what he had seen last night, too—that solemn hearse that had stood for a few moments at the dead man's house. He could never again disbelieve in apparitions as long as he lived.

Talking the case over, the two men walked quickly to Jones's Corner. The shop was shut except that one shutter had been taken off to light it, and there, in pitiful state, sat Mrs. Jones, with her one decent dress—a black stuff—on, and a white apron she had actually that morning washed and ironed spread under her folded hands. Her withered old face was deathly as ashes, her cap borders scarcely seeming more blanched in colour. Looking at her for a moment, as she stared straight before her into the dim shop, among the confusion of boxes and bags, it seemed to Lumsden as if her little share of sense had been stricken out by the shock, to leave her but one remove from an idiot.

It was not so with poor Con. He had wept until his eyes were like boiled gooseberries, and there was a look of terror in them as they seemed to wander against his will to that awful closed door. He was sitting in the yard, on a box, when Lumsden appeared, and he welcomed the young man though he was a policeman.

"Tell me all about it," Lumsden said, as he leaned against the fence by the boy. "It was you found him this morning wasn't it?"

"Oh! Yes, sir. I haven't got over it yet. I'll *never* get over it."

"Oh, you will; never fear of that. When did you see Jones last—I mean alive?"

"I didn't see him after I went to bed about nine, sir, but I heard him, off and on, for a long time. Someone had taken the key out of his bedroom door; he blamed the police for it, I think. At all events he couldn't find it, and went on awful. I fell asleep after a while, and then when I wakened up, I heard him saying, 'Good night, Turner,' and someone came out the back door."

"Where do you sleep, Con?"

"In that little skillion room at this end of the verandah; Mrs. Jones sleeps in the other one, only hers opens into the kitchen and my room doesn't."

Lumsden considered a moment. If Con had heard Turner so plainly, how was it he had not heard Jerry Swipes so shortly after? And there was that light he had twice seen in the kitchen—who had carried that?

"You heard nothing after that, Con?"

"Nothing, sir; I fell asleep again, and never wakened till mornin' when Mrs. Jones called me."

"Oh, *she* called you, did she?"

"She always calls me; Mrs. Jones is up by daylight, but the master wouldn't let her call him—I had to do it about seven. I always knocked and he was easy wakened, but this morning I knocked and knocked and got no answer. Then I remembered about the key being lost, and I opened the door quietly and called again. I could see the bed then, and guessed something was wrong, and I went a little nearer... Oh!" and Con covered his face with a shudder.

"What did the old woman do when you told her?"

"She only looked stupid, and stared at me, and then when she appeared to understand, she said, 'Yes; that she would put on her apron and mind the shop,' and there she's sat ever since."

"Con, there was someone moving about the place with a light at two o clock this morning—I saw it in the kitchen window myself. Do you think it could have been Jones?"

"More likely Mrs. Jones, sir; she's often awandering about the kitchen at night, and she seemed very unsettled when I went to bed last night."

Having got all the information he could out of the lad, Lumsden went in to see the terrible object in the guarded and darkened room, and then to visit the poor old woman, who sat in state, "minding the shop," while her murdered husband lay within a few yards of her. If the young policeman had any hopes of getting information out of her respecting the light he had seen in the kitchen, he lost them ere he had been speaking to her five minutes.

"This is a sad business for you, Mrs. Jones," said the young man in a low sympathetic tone. "Have you no neighbour that would come and sit with you?"

"He would never let me have no neighbours," she answered woodenly, as if a machine were speaking. "I'm minding the shop. Why doesn't Con come in? I want Con."

"I'll make him come in presently. Mrs. Jones, was it you that had a light in the kitchen at two o clock this morning?"

The sudden way she turned her fishy eyes on him set the young man wondering, and her unexpected reply startled him.

"There was no lights, only dead-lights, and the Dead Hearse was there. I heard 'em say it. It was all quite true. Watch him, and you'll find out."

Lumsden remembered that she had used those very words when he was in the shop yesterday, but he did not know that it was Jerry who had originally said them, and that they had made a terrible impression on the poor ill-treated old creature.

"Do you think that you'll keep on the shop now that the old man is gone?" the young constable asked, out of curiosity as to her reply, and finding nothing better to say.

"Yes. I'll allays mind the shop now—allays—me and Con, with a clean cap and a white apron; and no one'll beat me and knock me about."

The old woman's eyes now glowed with an almost fierce pleasure; she drew up her head, and wagged it at Lumsden in an alarming manner as she spoke. He drew, back scarcely knowing whether to be shocked at her apparent insensibility or not, when Cooney appeared behind him in the doorway.

"I wish we could find that key, Lumsden," he said, not observing the old woman; "it's very awkward not to be able to lock the body in."

"I've got no key," almost shrieked Mrs. Jones, as she stood up and faced the speaker; "why don't you take him away? Tell the Dead Hearse to come and take him away, quick!" and she almost fell into the old chair again, trembling and shaking all over.

"She's not even half-witted," Lumsden said. "What on earth will become of her? Do you think the old man was any way well in?"

"I don't know," replied Cooney, who was closely observing the old creature, who sat shaking in her chair. All at once she got up, and, muttering some indistinct words, tottered away into the kitchen, and from it to her own room, and they heard her locking the door behind her.

"Have you heard anything fresh?" inquired Lumsden of Cooney, who was staring after Mrs. Jones in an odd way.

"I've been talking to the doctor. He says that when he was called here this morning, Jones had been dead five or six hours. Do you remember what you said last night about that groan you heard, Lumsden? You said *it* was real, at any rate, and so it was. It was about that time, or a little before, that he got his death stab. And you know the weapon has not been found, Lumsden. Whoever had that light you saw last night knows something of the murder."

"You have changed your mind about it's being Jerry, then?"

"I don't know; he might have come back again—went for knife, perhaps. But several of his neighbours are ready to that the blood on his clothes was on it yesterday—he sells rabbits sometimes, it appears. And another thing—the doctor says the weapon must have been an unusual one, long and narrow, and sharp at the sides—such a wound as is in his breast could not be made by even an ordinary carving knife. I am going to make a very thorough search of the premises. Con?"

"Yes, sir."

The two constables had been passing through the kitchen while Cooney was speaking, and when Con was called they were standing under the verandah between the two skillion rooms.

"Con?" questioned Cooney, "the old man has been killed with a long, narrow kind of knife, the doctor says; do you know of anything about the house answering that description?"

"A long, narrow knife?" repeated the boy, thoughtfully; "master used to have an old thing like that—I think he used it in the cellar. I saw him sharpening it on the grindstone yesterday morning—it was rusty and had a black handle."

"You haven't seen it since?"

"No sir."

"What are you driving at, Cooney? Is it very likely the murderer would find and leave his weapon here on the premises?"

"I'm going to have a hunt for it, at any rate."

Lumsden went out of the yard and across to Turner's, for he had a mind for a talk with the woodman about his visit to Jones's last night. He found Turner very busy sawing in his yard, but with such a serious face that it was evident the murder of his neighbour had agitated him greatly.

"Yes," he said, as he sat down on a wood heap and wiped his face with the loose sleeve of his shirt, "I'm awfully cut up about it, though Jones was not a man any of his neighbours cared for; but, you see, I must have been the last man that talked to him before he was killed."

"It *was* you I saw last night, then?"

"Oh, yes, it was me; and it's a good job the boy heard the old man bidding me good night, or I might have been suspected myself. I went over to get paid for a little job I'd been doing for him.

"Clearing out the still, maybe?" Lumsden asked suspiciously.

"Nonsense—not that I'll deny the old man *did* once work a private still in his cellar, for he owned as much to me last night. And I want to tell you something else. They say you saw that "Phantom Hearse" last night?"

"Yes, I saw it," was the short answer.

"Well, Jones told me a queer story about that last night. He said that he would never again have anything to do with illicit distilling—he was getting too old, and that the Dead Hearse he had encouraged such talk about all these years was nothing but the conveyance that used to come for the whiskey now and again. Some man was in the secret with him, it seemed, and they had a black cover, and so on, made for the cart so as to frighten people."

"I'll take my oath!" cried Lumsden, angrily, as Turner concluded, "that what I saw last night was no real conveyance. I went as close to it as I am to you, and I put out my hand twice to try and touch it, but I had only air in my grip. And how could a natural thing disappear from under my very eyes when there wasn't a thing from end to end of the street but moonlight like day?"

Turner smiled as he remembered that this defender of the supernatural had only yesterday scouted the very idea of a ghostly appearance, but he only said—

"'Tis impossible to account for these things, but there's an old saying that 'mocking is catching.' It may have been the real thing last night, as a sort of warning for people not to imitate the dead. Have ye found any kind of clue to the murderer?"

"Swipes is arrested, you know."

"Oh, *he* never did it, no more than I did; he's low and drunken, and foul-tongued, is Jerry, but he wouldn't spill blood."

"Who do you think did, then?"

"Ah, constable, if I had any suspicions I'd keep 'em to myself. It's rather a dangerous thing to accuse an innocent person; but I'll go so far as to say that I think both the lost key of the old man's door and the knife that killed him never left his own home."

And Turner turned to his work again.

Turner's opinion that the lost key and murderous weapon were in the corner house renewed the young policeman's interest in it, and he returned to see the result of Cooney's careful search.

"I haven't left a corner hardly," said Cooney, in reply to his question, "and Con has been helping me. We've found nothing

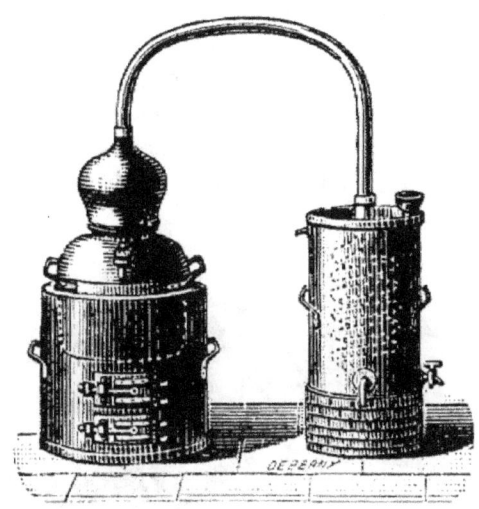

bearing on the murder. Con, go and try if you can get the old lady out of her room. Say she's wanted in the shop; that'll fetch her, I think."

"Cooney, are you going to search her room?"

"Yes."

"You have some suspicions?"

"I can't answer you now—follow me and you will see. I must get into that room by hook or by crook. Won't she come out, Con?"

"She won't answer at all," replied the boy, who was knocking at the door in the kitchen.

Cooney went 'round to the small window of the skillion room—there was a coarse curtain over it, but perceiving that it was simply hung on hinges and opened outwards, the experienced constable soon drew it open, and was master of the situation. Lifting the curtain aside, he saw Mrs. Jones sitting on a box opposite to him, quite immobile. It appeared as if extraordinary emotion of some sort had frozen into helplessness every bit of brain power of which the poor old creature was possessed.

"Mrs. Jones, there's half a dozen customers in the shop; don't you hear Con calling you? Open the door and let him in."

She got up mechanically, still keeping her eyes fixed on Cooney, who was leaning in the open window, but she seemed glued to the spot where she stood, and kept her hands behind her in such a

strange way that the policeman decided on active measures, and he had bounded through the open window and was standing before the now trembling old creature in a moment.

Cooney's first act was to open the door, and then having Lumsden and Con as witnesses, he put a hand on Mrs. Jones arm and drew her forward. The instant she was touched her hands dropped to her sides, and there was a sound of something falling. Lying on the floor behind her were the key of her dead husband's door and the long, rusty weapon the unfortunate man had sharpened for his own murder.

"I thought it was something this way," said Cooney, as he stooped for the articles. "God help her; she's not accountable. How did you come to kill the old man, missis?"

"It was quite true," she said stonily. "Watch him and you'll see. I must go and mind the shop."

Past the horrified Con she staggered, and her shaking hands groped before her as one in the dark. Opposite the door leading into the shop she paused unsteadily, looking

towards that of the death chamber which was on her right hand. Then she turned to the right, opened the door of the darkened room, and glided in. All this time the men and boy were watching and following her. When the poor old creature crossed the threshhold, she put out her hands in an attitude of entreaty, as though to the dead, and falling on her knees by the bedside, her face sank to the reddened coverlid, over which her outstretched hands lay. She spoke no word—not even a moan passed her lips, and when Cooney had waited vainly for a moment or two, thinking to hear some word of prayer or entreaty, he stepped forward quickly and raised her face. She was dead.

"So best," he murmured, "she's gone to keep shop in comfort in the 'big city.' I'll never believe she knew what she was doing."

"It seems to me a matter of impossibility that an arm like that could strike such a blow," muttered Lumsden.

"She struck through no bones, and the way the man was lying made it an easy job. I've been hearing something from Con that made all plain to me. It seems that Jerry Swipes told her to watch the old man yesterday. The fool was only amusing himself trying to excite the poor old creature's jealousy, but a fool's words often makes the devil's opening. It was she that took the key of the door, so that Jones could not lock himself in, and the devil laid that long knife handy to her. May God have mercy on her soul!"

"And maybe that's more than was said for the man she murdered," Lumsden discontentedly remarked.

"Maybe he doesn't want it so bad. At all events, he had no blood on his hands."

No more need be said, save that never from that day to this has the Phantom Hearse been seen near "Jones's Corner."

✗

THE NETHER GARDENS

by Frank Robinson

The nether gardens are filled with riotous blooms
That creep along the ground and hang temptingly
From the boughs of strong-limbed trees that sway
With the rhythm of the wind.

The flowers are of such a hue no mortal has ever
Seen—rainbows of attractive colors that lure the
Ones who linger in the gardens into picking
Them for their—shrouds.

For beware! The flowers in the nether gardens
Were not in Heaven grown nor did they feast on
Holy Water—their drink was something of a coarser
Grade—a thicker drought.

I once knew a mortal who lingered in the gardens
Entranced by the sensuous blooms—and when
I sought for him on the morrow—there was a new
Flower in the gardens—with petals shaped
Strangely like the features of his face.

AT TAKEOFF TIME

by Raymond L. Claney

I'd like to leave for the stars from Iceland
There where they gleam in purple and gold,
In green and orange, and all gorgeous colors,
And the Northern Lights their beauties unfold
Under the eyes of Venus and Mars
From the Northern Isle, I would leave for the stars.

THE GOLDEN KEY

by David H. Keller, M.D.

No one knew what the tower was for. No one knew when the tower was built, or by whom it had been constructed.

Everyone just seemed to realize it was there, all realizing it at once, and all at the same time.

They saw it, rising from the hot burning sands one morning in early March, From further away than fifteen miles, it stood sharply defined, reaching clear and clean against the horizon. It puzzled everyone, yet they did not try to explain its sudden appearance. They just took it for granted as a definite fact, much as they accepted the blizzards, or the Mormon crickets, or the fossil turtles which they often uncovered, half buried in the sand.

It was a good two miles in diameter at the base, of fine structural steel; it rose skyward till its peak was lost in the sky. Even on absolutely clear days no one could be sure where or how it ended, or if it ended at all for that matter; the top was simply out of sight. From a distance, the steel tower looked like a peculiar web, woven by a gigantic spider. Between the heavy bracing girders were smaller iron rods, forming gigantic ladders, constantly decreasing in size as the perspective of the tower rose higher and higher, out of sight.

In the next few months, articles concerning the tower appeared in various magazines and newspapers. It was the general opinion of the Sunday Magazine editors that in some way the tower was connected with radio or television, or the dispersal of atomic energy. Many thousands of words and hundreds of conjectures all ended in the general statement, "No one knows who built the tower or why. The goverrment still refuses to commit itself by stating whether the tower is a military project or not."

During the first year of its existence, many tourists braved the rugged Utah desert to visit it. Some of them even climbed a few of the countless thousands of rungs on the ladders. Many of them took pictures of the tower, mailing them back hone to their friends with the worn phrase, "Having a wonderful time; wish you were here," scrawled over the back of the prints.

Then one day gossip started circulating about the tower. The casual gossip rapidly spread into rumor and the rumor to actuality. The information was passed along, very confidentially, in whispers, and each person told was pledged to absolute secrecy,

Tha information spread through the various states like a hurricane. The story was out. On April first, anyone who wanted to do so could climb the tower. At the very top was a fabulous *golden key*—a key that would unlock all the riches of the world. No object or power was beyond the possession of he who held the golden key.

When the news broke at Salt Lake City, the Bantam Brothers Combined Circus was playing at the Fair Grounds. Jim, John, and Jenny were elated at the prospects of claiming the key for themselves, They knew it was futile for anyone to think that they could beat the incomparable "Three Flying J's" in securing the item. They were not known as "The Aerial Wonders" for nothing. For years they had stunted in one dinky carnival after the other. Finally they arrived at the peak of their ambition, a solitary act, highly spotlighted, in the center ring of the three ring circus. Each night, at a height of one hundred feet, without a net, Jin would throw Jenny through the air to John, who would catch her by the wrists, then send her streaking back across the big top to Jim.

Jim and John were tall, with the slim matchless bodies of trained athletes, Jenny was the vision of Aphrodite with her machine-perfect muscular coordination. But in Jenny's beautiful body dwelt the demon of lust: Jim and John both loved her, with the conviction that she loved each alone. In reality there was room for only Jenny in Jenny's life.

* * * *

The "Flying J's" arrived early on the morning of the second of April, astonished to find so many hopeful adventurers ahead of them, already swarming over the lower rungs of the ladders. Those who had come first were already several hundred feet into the air, climbing rapidly, then more slowly. Many of them had never been on anything higher than a step-ladder, and the hope in their hearts was mingled with nauseating fear in their souls. None of them knew how high above them the golden key might be. Few of them had bothered to prepare themselves adequately for the climb, but all of them held the hope that they would be the first to secure the key.

April in Utah is desert weather—the bitterest of cold at night, coupled with burning blazing heat at noon. Almost all of the seekers for the key had come unprepared for either temperature. Those who had started to climb the tower could not stop even if they wanted to; the pressure of the hopefuls climbing below them made retreat impossibls. The first night they could only cling to the rungs of the ladders or tie themselves securely with their belts. When daylight came, they had to move on upward, forced ahead by the less tired climbers at the bottom. By noon all of them were tired and hungry, and most of them were very frightened. Here and there along the ladders someone would stop for a moment to rest and gaze at the panorama of Utah, stretched out endlessly, all about them, shudder for a moment, and

be pushed on with the climbing tide.

The "J's" had made definite, cold-blooded preparations for their climb, heartless in their Magnitude, to insure their progress upward. Jim prided himself on his ability with the switchblade, John was an expert with his close-range target revolver. Jenny needed no weapons to compliment her hands—hands with the sure grip of steel, hands on which her life literally depended each night in their act. Each of the "J's" carried a canteen of water; each had pockets filled with chocolate bars and concentrated energy tablets.

On the morning of the second day, when they started to climb, they were determined to force their way through the hundreds that stood ahead of them, blocking their way. They shouted. They gritted and snarled their battle cry, "Make way! Let me pass!" Three against hundreds. But the three moving as one.

A coordinated, determined, ruthless force, fearless of height, indifferent to danger. Jenny headed the triple wedge. Deliberately she would squeeze between two men, whispering to each, "Let me get by you; then follow me, I will make a way for you."

Foolishly the men believed her, allowing her to pass, regretting their actions only when it was too late. Behind her came Jim and John. Acrobat shoes had been replaced with heavy leather boots shod with sharp, steel spikes. Anyone refusing to give way had their hands torn by the spikes. A trail of blood was slowly forming behind the climbing wedge.

Not all took the brutal assault without resistance. Among the climbers were experienced structural steel men and ruthless lumber men. In a few hours, the acrobats depended less on persuasion or diplomacy or Jenny's allure. Jim, knife at hand, hamstrung the obstinate, or waved his knife wildly about at those who tried to block him. John threatened others with his pistol. Jenny, if honeyed words gave no result, took the man with the bulldog grip of her fingers, tore him loose and threw him into the air or wrapped her hand around his throat till he dropped lifeless on the masses below.

By noon, they had penetrated half way through the mass of early climbers. Those above them were moving slowly, determined, yet dreading to climb further, but unable to return to the Earth. Many simply clung helpless, or tied themselves to a rung and tried to rest, and at the same time hold their places. For five hundred feet the tower was black, encrusted with crazed, greedy, evil, crawling humanity.

The "J's" paused only for a drink of water, or a few nibbles of chocolate, then were again on their way. The struggle was now more intense. There were fewer climbers, but proportionally fewer and narrower ladders. A thousand feet above the ground the tower was shrinking rapidly in diameter. When darkness came, as though by common consent, all stopped climbing, either to hang tenaciously to the rungs or tie themselves fast with rope or belts. There they waited, shivering, through the dark night, hungry and cold, only to spring into new life again with the approach of false dawn and climb once more upward.

Above the "J's" were determined, desperate, and dangerous men. They refused to obey the command and give way. The well-coordinated trio with their accessories made short work of these stubborn ones. Body after body of the greedy ones, less well-equipped than the "J's", hurtled down, crushing into the swarming, struggling mass below, bouncing occasionally from some of the climbing people, only to fall again, against more of them.

Now the "J's" were laughing, for few were higher than they. The going was much faster now. They were two thousand feet, now three thousand feet high. Below them, what had been the roar of the equally greedy climbers diminished to a whisper. Only about ten climbers were yet to be passed. Another thousand feet lessened the number to less than five. At this point it became noticable that the tower was swaying, gently but presistently, in the wind. Another thousand feet and only one lone man was yet above them, and he only by a few rounds of the ladder. He turned, crazed with the height, dizzy from the swaying of the tower. He laughed down at the "J's", letting go with one hand to wave a cheery greeting to them.

Jim threw his knife and the man stopped laughing. Clasping his side with his other hand, he floated gently away from the ladder, blood trickled from between his clasped hands. He tumbled, over and over, over and over, falling to the earth a mile below. Now nothing remained between the three and ultimate victory. They had arrived so near the top of the tower that they could see the upper three ladders. Two of these, separated at their base by about six feet, faced each other. At the top, a third, single ladder raised upward, its top lost in the clouds that drifted hazily over the tower.

They paused a moment to make their final plans. Far below them came the murmur of discouraged thousands, climbing like swarming bees on the lower rungs. Frequently an exhausted man, loosing his grip, dropped shrieking against other weakened men, knocking them loose, or dragging them with him till they met a merciful death on the hard, parched earth. The nearest climber was three hundred feet below them, his face twisted with hopeless hatred, unable to climb higher, too exhausted to even try to descend.

There were now only two ladders, and three climbers. John offered a suggestion.

"I will stay here, guarding the rear. You go on. When you get to the single ladder, let Jenny go first. She has the best sense of balance of all of us. When you get the key... when you get it, we will share the wealth of the world. Only a few minutes more!"

Jenny looked at Jim. Between the two

of them flashed the truth behind John's suggestion. He would stay behind. After they left him, he would shoot them—and then there would be no need to share. Jenny had to protect her part of the profits. She began to cry.

"First let me kiss you, John," she sobbed. "This may be the last time I can hold you. What if I should fall?"

She worked her way along the rungs of the ladder to John. For a moment their bodies met in a wild, abandoned embrace. She whispered into his ear, "Stay here, my own one, and wait for me. I will take care of Jim. He threw his knife away, and he'll be easy to handle without it. I'll get the key and bring it back to you. We'll get married, John, and together we'll share the wealth of the world."

Jenny kissed him again, running her fingers in gentle caresses through his hair, tenderly down the side of John's face, to his throat. She grasped it in the grip of death. Tortured, gasping sobs wracked him as he tried to break her hold. Fiercely she dug her fingernails into his flesh. When he stopped struggling, she took his revolver, stuck it into her belt, loosened his belt, and let his body fall away from the rung. It bounced off the ladders below.

Jenny climbed around the double ladder to face Jim.

"I had to do it, Jim. It was his life or ours. He was going to double-cross us. Now we're safe. When we get the key, we'll be married, Jim, Just the two of us. No more circus work! No more anything but you and I, Jim—and all the power in the world!"

Holding to rungs of the ladder, she kissed him, and together, one on each ladder, facing each other, they started the journey upwards, toward the final single ladder, and the key.

At last they came to the joining of the two ladders and the beginning of the single one. The clouds were below them now. They were standing in a world of their own, flooded by brilliant sunlight, stronger than any spotlight that had ever been focused on them under the big top. A private world of their own, that whipped them unmercifully with a sharp cold wind; that threw them about wildly with the swaying of the tower that had now grown to furious proportions. A world that ate into their ears with a ringing noise that made them almost want to scream with pain. They looked up. At the top, instead of the key resting on the top rung, as they had expected, they saw a large curved iron rod, fashioned in the shape of a question mark, from the top of which, suspended on a tiny gold chain, the golden key swung gently to and fro, propelled by the swaying of the tower.

Jim surveyed the situation. He bent over the top rung, hands and feet hanging dangerously loose for a minute. Then he locked them together, rocked himself for a moment to gain the best balance. Carefully she crept up over him, teetering precariously for a moment, then slowly she straightened, inching her feet apart until she felt herself firmly placed on his upturned haunches. Grasping the stem of the iron question mark, slowly and delicately she balanced herself in perfect timing with the swaying of the tower. Carefully testing the strength of her frail support, she slowly lengthened her lovely body and reached upward with her right hand for the key.

She missed.

Again she balanced, stretched and reached. This time she grasped the key. Quickly closing her fingers, she tore it from its retaining chain. Methodically she eased herself down to a kneeling position.

"Did you get it?" Jim was excited.

"Yes, my darling, it's in hand."

"Then we have everything that it is possible to possess."

"Yes, Jim, we have everything. But let's not start down right now. After that, I must rest for a moment."

Jim looked away, at the clouds gently

floating by below them, Jenny cautiously took the revolver from her belt. She held the muzzle close to Jim's neck, pulled the trigger.

With a convulsive jerk, Jim threw his body off the rung. He instinctively grabbed for something—*anything*—to save himself.

His fingers closed over Jenny's ankle with the trap-tight grip of the acrobat. Caught off balance, she fell with him, the two plumeting through space to die on the lower rungs, hundreds of feet below the question mark.

Simultaneously with their fall, the tower began to melt, throwing globules of molten steel in wild, pyrotechnic convulsions. Breaking the chain that supported the key was a signal to make the metal turn liquid and rain on the helpless, greedy, evil climbers. They fell like autumn leaves in a gale.

The few able to reach the ground ran in a wild hysterical panic, fear and horror in their soul, nursing their burned flesh.

* * * *

In an hour, it was all over, The surviving evil searchers-for-wealth now sought only life in the hot, burning desert sand.

Two days later, the little area of solid ground that had once held the tower was once again a quiet place, basking in the heat of the desert hell. There was nothing left but the scorched earth, the pieces of molten steel, now hardened again, and the many vultures feeding on the unburned bodies. For miles around, the crazed treasure-seekers still wandered aimlessly over the moonlit desert, leaving the area that had once held the tower much as it had always been.

* * * *

Many months later, as the moon flooded the scorched desert with light, the Responsible One searched slowly among the masses of fused metal and sand. At last he paused, and rising to a terrifying height, held high above his massive head a key and watched its golden surface glisten in the moonlight.

He cried, "Now, who shall I next tempt? What manner of destruction bring to my foolish, greedy little ones who search in vain for a powerless key, hoping it will bring them all they desire?"

THE GOTHIC HORROR

by George Wetzel

Quite often Penhryn had puzzled over the reasons Gothic arts were made so hideous; every cathedral he had visited, every Gothic manuscript read, even medieval tapestry was cursed with this ubiquitous grotesqueness. Once a medieval archaeologist told him it perhaps was the soul—ugly and deformed—of the Age that tolerated it. Perhaps so. Certainly there was a shocking parallel between it and the practices of the witch covens that marked that period; a parallel that suggested many hidden Satanists carved the wood and stone of the cathedrals. For did not the same spirit of mockery and perversion of Mass ritual exist in the gargoyles who leered atop cathedral parapets and from cornices and recesses?

Even now, the tymponum Penhryn studied was such an example of that blasphemy. A sly, cynical hint of bigotry, it seemed to him, was expressed in the too-closely-crowded group of saints and reveling demons. Another infamy like this present symbolism of the Elect and the Damned, he recalled, once carved on the tympanum of Rheims Cathedral, so shocked its 18th century clergy that they had it chiseled out.

His examination of the stone figures on the entrance arch was broken by the verger, commenting pedantically on some ninth century Saxon brickwork in the wall. Penhryn stepped into the cathedral and a palpable sea of silence which even the stone of sound (that was his footsteps) could barely ripple. Mumbling about the church's reliquary, the verger started off; and Penhryn, despite the verger's boresome presence, decided to follow him.

Beneath tons of stone they passed, whose weight elfin Plantagenet-ribbed vaults appeared incapable of supporting. Reaching the Reliquary in the gloom of the west transept arm, the verger unlocked it and brought out of a chest therein the cathedral's mortuary wealth—the the remains of illustrious prelates and canonized saints—that reposed in bejeweled, golden urns and containers. Dryly, the verger spoke of dullsome abbots and obscure saints,

"This particular urn," said the verger, picking one manifestly no different from the rest, "whose osseous contents are those of an early saint, has a quaint history. In 1163 the Popish monks here gathered some henbane found growing in their garden, mistaking it for a kind of parsley."

Unimaginatively, he went on, relating—*despite* his pedantic manner—an interesting account of how those monks who did not eat of it were awakened that same midnight by the Matin's bell. And coming into the cathedral read scrawled across the sacred books what was never originally written there, saw written in chalk on the walls blasphemy, and heard profane things uttered by those who had awakened them.

"The archives," said the verger, "arc not explicit on the outrages; though they did say how the drugged monks, for one thing, made a mockery of Christian ritual by reverencing this urn."

At Penhryn's look of amazement, the verger smiled, reflected a bit, and said: "Oh, we've had other misfortunes here, worse than that. Why, the west tower has come down four times since their time. And fires without number are always breaking out and always had been." The verger went on to recount other calamities suffered by the cathedral.

"Don't you think it odd," interruped Penhryn, "such an uncommon number of disasters has struck here?"

The verger pondered this a moment and then smiled triumphantly "Why, not at all. We missed some serious misfortunes that have plagues lesser churches. Cromwell's troopers let us alone when they desecrated other cathedrals about us."

"But Cromwell was a hidden Satanist," blurted out Ponhryn. "At least Montague Sumners thought he was."

"Which is why," added the verger, "he and his Roundheads desecrated so many British churches."

Penhryn desisted from further argument. The verger did not see he meant his emphasis on the fact that Cromwell had left *this place* inviolate. He pondered a bit. Then, he asked the verger another question:

"I wonder just what do the bones in that urn," he pointed to the one that figured in the curious story of the drugged monks, "look like?"

A look of quizzical tolerance crossed the verger's face. "Just like any other, if not dust already." Then the amused verger added, "They could be fraudulant, you know. It wouldn't be the first time three thigh bones of a saint existed in three separate churches."

What the verger referred to was the traffic in spurious relics during the medieval times, the monstrous incongruities that sometimes existed along with the monkish pilfering of relics from rival monasteries. But that was not what Penhryn had in mind at least not entirely. Better he not voice what he thought of those relics lest he shock the verger. Considering the spirit that motivated the Gothic decorations, it was vary likely just *what* those relics night be.

At that moment a man in faded overalls entered the cathedral, looked about, and spying the verger, came over. A conversation about gardening ensued. Finally, the gardener—quite obviously not comprehending the pedantic instructions of the verger—asked that person to accompany him outside and see the vegetable problem

himself. Penhryn breathed a deep sigh of relief. The verger was a bore, besides openly regarding Penhryn as a ridiculous, superstitious man.

Now at last Penhryn could do what he originally came for—examination of the cathedral's organ. As he ascended to the triforium gallery, a feeling of self reproach arose. He regreted remarking on the oddness of this place; no wonder the verger had smiled. And yet there was no denying of it—the cathedral had an atmosphere of wrongness; it affected him.

Sunlight glorified the mosaic panes up here; and alternately, where no window pierced the stone wall, a chill darkness lurked. Thrusting up its ornate spires and pipes in perpendicular Gothic style was the organ case, beneath the oculus window. Dry dust assailed his nose as he crawled behind the organ to examine its geometric world of square and round pipes. Coming out, after a time, he paused to look over the balustrade into the hollowed-out nave below, and was seized with awe; the Gothic craftsman had been clever, for their arboreal and animal carvings on paw boards, corbel-tables, and moldings showed living things frozen in acts of motion, waiting for some mysterious summons before they convulsed with life again.

Penhryn felt an oppressive sense of heat; and looking up, saw last, lingering sunlight burning through a window. And the sainted figure that down at him seemed to be twisting agonizingly, as though its abode there was some fiery hell. The window frames were wrought in sections resembling flame tongues—a feature similar to the French Flamboyant Gothic style—which furthered the illusion that the window openod into a fiery domain. And he speculated if flame tracery was not also deliberated fashioned, along with the grotesqueness of the Gothic carvings. Another thought, of imitative magic—at least the wish it expressed—came to mind as he looked at the fiery window, and he grew more uneasy Quite suddenly he realized there was *some sort* of blistering warmth emanating from the window—too much for comfort—and he retired into the gloom.

Raising his eyes upwards to the clerestory regions, he noted the irregular alignment of the longitudinal axis, proof that a later repair had been incorrectly engineered. While he studied this mistake, the shifting sunlight retreated roofwards as darkness filled the depths below, and he became aware of the long time he had browsed up here, hoping it was not so long that the verger may have forgotten his presence and locked him in.

The thought terrified him—the spending of a cold night here—but why he could not say, or else did not want to dredge up the reason.

Hastening downwards, he found his worst fears were true. The entrance door had been locked. A kind of reasonless panic threatened to engulf him—his theories about Gothic art were the blame—but by mimicking the verger's pedantic cynicism, he kept a surface calm. Possibly he could find, a broken pane wherefrom he could shout out until someone came.

Penhryn had barely made up his mind when it happened. Hitherto all was a canvas of dead silence but now a sound brushed across it. From the transept of the Reliquary it had come; and as he turner in that direction he sensed, then saw, a stirring in the almost impenetrable dark. Fear had called up that presence.

Memory was fragmentary after that. Some shock drove him to seek the upper regions where a blur of light remained. A priceless stained glass window was smashed. And he plunged to the ground outside.

No questions were asked him when, days later, he came out of a state of delirium. None were needed; he had babbled disjointedly while in that state, enough to cause the cathedral to be closed. An ex-amination was made, discreetly, of certain relics. Later the gardener was observed by some to cast a small paper parcel into the river. And shortly afterwards, several high ranking clergymen held a private church service in the cathedral to which no one was admitted...though the more nosy spoke of hearing a hand bell ring and ponderous Latin phrases uttered.

Penhryn's experience had blanks in it—which was well for him. One thing, not fully erased, was of a "face eaten away by darkness." There was one final thing that, when he learned of it, sent him into a paroxysm of horror.

The investigators, taking much of his delirium babbling into serious consideration, had medical examinations made of the relics. One osseous remain—that which the drugged monks had blasphemously reverenced—had been non-human and unhallowed, a spurious relic passed off as genuine. The substitution was made obviously by a hidden Satanist, mocking the Church, as the Gothic carvers had, and the witch covens.

FEAR

by L. Patrick Greene

Trooper Jennings opened his eyes wearily. Every bone in his body ached, and he groaned with pain as he moved.

Thompson and Andrews, his two comrades on the Border Guard Patrol, came over to his bed as he threw off the covers and gingerly essayed to stand on his feet; he was still weak, and would have fallen had they not supported him.

"Better take it easy for a while, Jennings." "Oh, I'll be all right in a minute." He tenderly fingered his bruised face. "Where's that beast Peters?"

The two men looked at each other significantly.

"Peters said that he would be down this afternoon," replied Thompson. "He's going to demand an apology from you."

"Well, he'll never get it. He cheated last night, and you know it." The boy—Jennings was little more—looked appealing at the two men.

"Yes, he cheated, and you accused him of it. Well, see what you got. The man would have killed you, unconscious as you were, if Andrews here had not pulled a revolver on him."

"And suppose I don't apologize?"

"He said that he was going to bring a sjambok down with him and beat you till you do. And he'll do it."

"And you mean to tell me that you'd stand by and let him do it?"

Andrews flushed.

"See here, youngster! This is not our quarrel. Peters is all you say he is, and then some more. He's a bad man—but he's a strong bad man. Why, he could wipe the floor with the three of us. I know he could. I saw him clear out Joburg's saloon— you

remember that, don't you Thompson?"

"Yes. He caved in three of big Dutch Lockner's ribs—with his fist, Jennings. You know what his native name is, don't you? The Schelm—the Bad One. Natives are pretty apt in their naming, and there's not a negro in this district but would gladly kill him; but they are all afraid of him. He beats them viciously, yet there's not one that will lodge a complaint against him. I don't think he knows what fear is."

"And here's another thing—" Andrews took up the tale. "We are dumped on this Border Patrol and aren't likely to be relieved for another six months. The rainy season is coming on and the place will be a fever trap. We can't afford to quarrel with our only white neighbor, 'specially when he happens to be the storekeeper on whom we are dependent for our provisions. Besides, he could make things mighty unpleasant for us with the natives. It's up to you to apologize."

"Why should I?" he demanded. "I was in the right. I can't back down—you surely wouldn't have me do that."

"Why not? No one would know but we three, and we are not likely to talk about it," said Thompson. "After all, it was only a little thing."

"Well, I'll apologize if he'll do the same. He called me a—"

"Peters apologize! Boy, you must be mad. He'll never do that."

"Then neither will I." There was a note of finality in the boy's tone.

Thompson and Andrew looked at each other in despair. "Well, just remember that we're neutral, though we'll try to stop him from using the sjambok on you."

Jennings buried his face in his hands, striving to overcome the fear that all but sickened him.

"Will he really beat me with a sjambok," he said after a while, "if I don't apologize?" Andrews nodded. "And if you tried to stop him—what then?"

Andrews shrugged his shoulders. "There will be some blood shed. Possibly his, but more probably ours," said Thompson. "He shoots from the hip."

"Well, I won't be beaten."

"That's the way to talk, Jennings. We knew you'd see this thing in the right light."

Jennings held up his hand. "And I won't apologize. See here," he went on hurriedly, "if there's going to be any fighting I'll see that I get a fair chance; and if there's to be any blood shed it'll either be mine or his. I'm going to challenge him to a duel."

"Don't be a fool, Jennings. This is the twentieth century.

"Besides, how'll that help you? You're only a fair shot with a revolver or rifle—you don't propose to fight with carving-knives, do you?"

"I'm not joking. If you'll agree to my plan it'll put me on even terms with him. That's all I ask. Let's go to scoff—I'm hungry—and I'll tell you all about it while we are eating."

* * * *

Peters, rising from his midday siesta, yawned and stretched his arms lazily above his head. A big man, fully six feet in height when he stood erect; his usual posture resembled that of a gorilla. His brutal head, set on a short, thick neck, was bowed forward, and he gazed constantly from side to side through shaggy brows. His eyes, set wide apart, were green at times of repose, but when anger roused him they contracted to pin-points and had in them the baleful, hypnotic glare of a, snake's. His arms were abnormally long and mightily muscled. His body was covered with coarse red hair.

As he stretched himself one of his hands hit the low-thatched roof of the hut and dislodged a small grass snake. It fell on his bare chest, hung there a second, then dropped squirming to the floor. Cursing furiously he jumped up and down like a maniac on the harmless thing, then, satisfied it was dead, sat down heavily in a chair, his mighty chest heaving convulsively, his muscles twitching. His face showed ghastly pale through the red beard of several days growth, and his eyes dilated with terror as they fell upon the dead snake.

Reaching for the whisky bottle, he drank deeply, and then called, in a voice thick with anger: "Thuso! Come here, you black—"

A native came running in reply to his call. "Throw that away," he said, pointing to the snake, "then come back here." After Thuso had left the hut to carry out his master's bidding, Peters rose from the bed and took down a heavy sjambok. "On your knees, dog!" he commanded when Thuso returned.

Abject terror was in the native's eyes as he groveled at Peters's feet.

"Swish." The sjambok came down on Thuso's naked back, leaving a scarlet weal. "Didn't — I — tell — you — to — beat out — the — roof — of — my — hut — every — day?" Each word was punctuated by a blow. Thuso screamed for mercy, but still the sjambok rose and fell. When the screams ceased he ordered two of the natives, who had gathered round the door of the hut, to enter. "Take this carrion and tie him to a tree—but first rub salt on his back. So shall he learn to obey my orders."

"Yah, Inkosi!" They picked up Thuso.

"When that is done, return here and beat out the thatch of this hut lest perchance other snakes are hidden there."

"Yah, Inkosi!"

Singing an obscene song, Peters left his hut and walked toward his store, a rough, galvanized shack. He had not gone very far when he was hailed by Thompson. He turned quickly round and waited for the policeman to come up with him.

"Well, what is it? Does Jennings want to apologize?"

"He says he'll apologize if you'll apologize to him for calling him a—"

Peters's answer was a stream of curses. "Where's this Jennings?"

"He's down by that patch of elephant grass yonder." Thompson pointed toward the river which flowed at the foot of the hill. The veldt all around was devoid of vegetation save for this patch of elephant grass about four hundred yards square.

Then he continued:

"His plan is this. He's waiting now on the other side of that elephant patch with Andrews; I'm to take you to a place, opposite him, on this side. When you're located I'm to fire a shot. That will be the signal for Andrews to get out of harm's way. Five minutes later you'll hear another shot; that'll be the signal for you to enter the patch from this side, and for him to enter on the other side. You are to keep on walking—as much in a bee-line as possible—and shoot on sight. If you don't sight each other on your first passage through you are to keep on until you do."

"And what happens after I kill him? Do you other two fools try to arrest me for murder?"

"No; here's a signed statement from Jennings testifying that the shooting was accidental. You keep that, and he expects one from you."

"You've thought it all out, haven't you?" sneered Peters. "What weapons?"

"Revolver—and as many cartridges as you please."

"All right, I'm ready. Give me the paper."
"I want one from you first."

"You don't think you'll need it," Peters laughed. "What shall I say?" He took a notebook from his pocket and wrote, at Thompson's dictation:

I, Buck Peters, realizing that I must soon meet my Maker, testify that I was shot accidentally, and that Wilfred Jennings is in no way to blame.
(Signed) BUCK PETERS.

"I'll have that back before the day's over," he said. " Now let's go."

* * * *

Andrews looked uneasily at the slender figure of Jennings. The boy was pacing restlessly up and down the bank of the river, puffing furiously at a cigarette.

"For Heaven's sake stand still man, and try to compose your nerves. You'll be easy game if you go on this way."

Jennings checked his pacing. "Do you think he'll agree to my plan, Andrews? Isn't it about time we heard Thompson's shot?"

"We'll hear it soon enough. There's no chance of Peters backing out. Are you sure you want to go through with this thing, Jennings? No one will blame you if you back out, and we can easily find a plan to get you out of Peters's way."

Jennings hesitated a moment before he answered. "No. I've got to go through with it." He shivered as though with a cold.

"Well, don't forget all we've told you. Don't expect to hear any noise. Peters is an expert hunter, and he'll move as quietly as a cat for all his big bulk. Keep your eyes peeled for the slightest movement in the grass, and when you sight him, fire; then drop to the ground and stay there, even if you think you've hit him. He may be bluffing."

"Yes, I know, I know. You and Thompson have been over that with me so many times that I'm not likely to forget it. Phew! It's almighty hot. I'm going to take my tunic off." He started to unbutton the coat of his khaki uniform.

"You keep that on, you silly young fool. Your white shirt 'ud be a nice target!"

Jennings sat down impatiently on a large boulder, and lighted another cigarette.

The air was oppressively still, and the ground seemed to dance in the heat waves; nothing stirred. Even the chattering "Go-away" birds seemed to have been lulled to sleep by the torrid heat. The sun was slowly sinking, casting mysterious, ever-changing shadows on the elephant grass patch. A strong smell of musk filled the air. Jennings sniffed and looked at Andrews inquiringly.

"Cross!" explained Andrews. "Pity you didn't challenge Peters to a swimming race across the river."

A wisp of smoke floated lazily in the still air. Then the sharp report of a revolver came to their ears. Jennings sprang to his feet alert. "He's ready!"

"Yes. I'm going to leave you now, boy. Good luck, old man. We'll be waiting for you up the hill." They shook hands, and a moment later Jennings was alone.

He threw away the half-smoked cigarette and nervously examined his revolver. The impulse to run was strongly upon him. But that was no way out; he couldn't go back—to be pointed out by every one as a coward. That was impossible.

The grass patch before him seemed to loom up larger and larger; it seemed to become suddenly impregnated with a mysterious terror. Fantom shapes had their being there—shapes changed as the grasses swayed slightly in the newly awakened breeze.

A second shot sounded.

Jennings hesitated for a fraction of time, then rushed headlong into the thick elephant grass. His mad rush was abruptly halted as, catching his feet in the entangling vines that entwined themselves round the thick stems of grass, he fell to the ground. His revolver flew from his hand and he lost much precious time before he finally recovered it. When he went forward once again his progress was much slower. As he got deeper into the patch he had to force his way through the grass.

Occasionally he would come to a bare clearing. Then he would cautiously work his way round the fringe. To cross it would have exposed him needlessly. Excepting such places he could scarce see more than three yards ahead of him; the grasses towered high above him, and for all the brightness of the sun he was forced to feel his way forward as one surrounded by a dense fog. At every few yards he would stop and listen; no sound came to his ears save the droning of mosquitoes and the gentle swish of the wind among the grass. Once a giant bustard flew out somewhere ahead of him.

"Peters must have put it up," thought Jennings. A shot rang out and the bustard, turning slowly over and over, fell to the ground.

He attempted to locate the direction from which the shot came, but in vain. The grass was over ten feet high and there was no tree or rock near upon which he could climb in order to take his bearings. Unexperienced in the art of trekking, his progress was a noisy one, though he practised an almost exaggerated caution. The knowledge that he could not disguise his movements filled him with a sudden terror, and dropping to the ground, he tried crawling along on his belly. Finding that this narrowed his field of vision, he soon gave it up.

Strange noises sounded all around him. A dry twig snapped under his foot and he jumped back, expecting to feel the hot searing pain of a bullet. Again, cursing himself for his folly, he went forward. A harsh croaking came to his ears from the sky overhead. He knew it was a vulture, and wondered at its presence. Then the grass became thinner and suddenly ceased. He was out on the open veldt. A strange, elation seized him. He had passed through the lurking peril of the patch. He drew a deep breath as though he would take in courage from the light and cleanness of the open before turning to face the peril once again.

On the hill before him he could see Thompson and Andrews. They waved to him, and he could almost hear what they were shouting. He knew they were words of encouragement. He waved back to them, then turned toward the patch. Again the harsh croaking of the vulture sounded clearly, and looking up he shook his fist savagely at it. Even as he did so the scavenger of the veldt folded its wings and dropped like a stone into the patch.

He scouted for a while along the fringe of the grass until he came to the place where Peters had entered. The trail was plain, and throwing caution to one side, he followed it quickly, hoping to come up on Peters unawares. He gave no thought to the chance that Peters had doubled on his tracks and was lurking in ambush beside his trail. Or if he thought of it, it did not imbue him with caution. He was only conscious of seeing the thing through to a speedy conclusion. After a while he came to a large open space, in the center of which was a stunted tree with low wide-spreading branches.

A vulture perched in the topmost branch of the tree, and in the shade of its branches was Peters. He was lying on his back, stretched at full length.

Cautiously Jennings approached him, his finger trembling on the trigger of his revolver. As he came nearer he saw that Peters's face was distorted with terror—a fearsome sight. His eyes were wide open, but the glaze of death was already creeping over them. Something moved on his chest, and a small black momba—that deadliest of snakes—lifted its wicked head and menaced Jennings. The vulture croaked hoarsely, and Jennings, steadying his shaking hand, fired.

The repellent-looking bird tumbled grotesquely down from the tree, landing with a thud close to the body of Peters; the snake, taking alarm, uncoiled itself and vanished into the tall grass. Jennings then fled from the place.

* * * *

When he came again to the tree, Thompson and Andrews were with him. Marfwe, one of the police boys and a cunning hunter, came with them. They carefully examined the body of Peters, but could see no telltale puncture hole, nor was the body at all swollen as would be the case had he been bitten by the momba.

"What do you make of it, Thompson?" Andrews, asked in wonder. Thompson shook his head. He was watching Marfwe, who was closely examining the tree and the ground around it. "Can'st read us this riddle, Marfwe?"

"Aye, Inkosi. Somewhat is written plainly here, the rest—because I well knew this dead one—I can tell ye.

"To this place came the Schelm—the Bad One. He rested awhile in the shade of the tree—see ye, he smoked a while"— Marfwe pointed to a cigar stub. "Anon he rose to his feet and went back a few paces from the tree. He sprang suddenly for the branch that hangs low, catching it with his hands; ye can see where his feet left the ground, and see ye here where his nailed shoes sought a footing on the trunk.

"And then, Inkosi, this man who feared not the Spirits of Good or Evil, met Fear face to face. A snake—if thy nose is keen ye can sense his scent; if thy eyes are open ye can see his slime— lay along the branch to which the Schelm hung. And the Schelm suddenly loosing his hold, fell heavily to the ground, and the branch, thus freed of his great weight, shook violently, so that the snake also fell. Onto the Schelm's naked chest it fell, and there, feeling the warmth of the man, coiled itself and was well content.

"Then. What then? See ye here."

Marfwe pointed to Peters's tightly clenched hands; showed how the nails had cut into the flesh.

"He did that, Inkosi, to prevent the jumping of his muscles. Had he moved but a little, look ye, the snake would have struck." He pointed to the blood-stained lips almost bitten through in the struggle to keep back the screams that sought utterance.

"Aye, white men," Marfwe concluded, "so this man died; but first he died the death of the spirit many times. It was not the snake that killed him, nor yet the fall from the tree. Nay! But it was the fear that killed him–the fear born of evil that was within him."

✗

INTRODUCING MACK REYNOLDS
by Mack Reynolds

One or two wars ago I found myself hanging around New Orleans waiting to be assigned to a ship. As you know, killing time isn't murder, it's suicide, but we all, at one time or another, find ourselves doing it.

All right. So I spent a lot of time in the New Orleans library and one day reached my hand up and plucked from its shelf a copy of *Writing and Selling* by Jack Woodford.

The first sentence that hit my eye went: "Anybody who can read without moving their lips, can write stories that will sell to the American magazines."

Now, my lips had moved only slightly in the reading, so I said to myself, He must mean me.

I went home and blew the dust off the portable and took a crack at writing a short-short detective yarn.

I know, you think I'm a liar, but that first story sold to *Esquire*. You'll start believing me again when I tell you that I've never sold a slick since. Worse luck.

The war stepped in then and I wasn't able to pursue my newfound ambitions for some years.

Eventually, however, I acquired the three necessities for becoming a writer—a pipe, a tweed coat, and a wife who works. I wrote for six months, full time, before making my first science fiction sale to *Planet*. The story, by the way, has not as yet appeared in print....

About then the New Orleans heat drove us up to the mountains of Taos, New Mexico, where we met Fredric Brown and Walt Sheldon who immediately took me under their literary wings.

Among other things they introduced me to Harry Altshuler their agent and a considerably better one than a tyro like myself could ordinarily hope for. Sales began rolling in. The Ziff-Davis magazines, the Standard magazines, *Other Worlds*, and then, when she started up, *Imagination*. Fifty or sixty stories in the past two or three years to almost every magazine in the field.

Not so many shorts these last months since I've been concentrating on novel lengths for hard covers, but I still turn out an occasional one when I get an idea I particularly like. One of the novels, *The Case of the Little Green Men,* was really meant to be somewhat of a ruse on both the detective and the science fiction fields, but nobody seemed to recognize the fact. Maybe I was wrong.

Also managed to compile *The Science-Fiction Carnival*, an anthology of science-fiction fun, along with Fredric Brown, for Shasta. Should appear this fall. I couldn't resist including one of my own, of course, and picked "The Martians and the Coys" which appeared originally in *Imagination*.

"What am I doing now? Writing a serious science fiction novel, which should take at least two years to complete. No wars of the future, no ray guns, extra-terrestrials, nor even time machines. It's going to be entitled *Tomorrow*—and I wish it could be finished by then! In the meantime I hope you like my story ("The Cosmic Bluff") in this issue of *Madge*.

✗

ODDS ON YOU!
by Mack Reynolds

Mathematically speaking, you are impossibly lucky. So lucky that you can only be said to be the exception that proves the rule. Mathematically the odds are so great against your being here at all that it is unthinkable that you were ever born.

Let's examine the facts.

You have two parents, four grandparents, eight great-grandparents and 16 great-great-grand-parents. Each generation doubles the number of your ancestors. A geometric progression, as it is called.

If we consider a generation to be 25 years, then we see that in each century that goes by we have accumulated four generations of progenitors. One hundred years ago you had a total of 16. But 200 years ago, which takes you back a bit before the Declaration of Independence, there were 26 ancestors of the person who was one day to become you.

It mounts up fast. Three hundred years ago, in 1659, it is most likely that most, if not all, of your forebears were living in Europe, or elsewhere in the Old World, since the Pilgrims had landed less than 40 years before and the settlement of America was hardly under way. But at that time you had 4,096 ancestors. Each of them just as vital as the next if ever you were to be born.

You begin to see what we are leading to. Four hundred years ago these progenitors of yours numbered 65,536. And only five centuries ago—a drop in the bucket in terms of human history—you had more than one million ancestors. To be precise, 1,048,576.

We need carry this no further.

Had any one of these persons not lived, you would never have been born.

There is a gimmick here. The above figures are probably not exactly correct. It is quite possible that they overlap somewhere. If in your family tree you had a case of cousins, or second cousins (or eighth cousins, for that matter) marrying each other, then some of our figures duplicate.

However, we'll eliminate that phase of the question by suggesting that we take any of these million ancestors of yours and trace him back for 500 years. If we do, our mathematics are repeated. And if any one of those million ancestors of his who lived five centuries before his birth, had not existed, you would never had been born.

There are side angles to all this that parlay up the fabulous luck you represent. For instance, today child mortality has largely been conquered, but this medical achievement is one of only the past hundred years or less. Five hundred years ago, the chances of a child growing to maturity to have its own children in turn were less than one in three.

But all your ancestors grew to adulthood. Not one was struck down by childhood diseases, lack of medical care, famine, war, pestilence.

Let us assume that you are of European stock, as most Americans are. In the 14th Century the Black Death, known to us today to have been bubonic plague, swept Europe, killing up to two-thirds of the entire population of the continent.

At that time, you had over a million ancestors living, but not one fell to the Black Death before having raised a family. Lucky you.

Or let us touch on just one of the countless wars that have devastated Europe within comparatively recent history. The Thirty Years War which raged between 1618 and 1648 decimated Europe to a point unheard of in history. Northern Europe in particular was bled white. Whole nations were all but wiped out. Even populous Germany needed centuries to recover.

But your numerous forebears saw it all through. Each raising his children in turn without catastrophe striking.

Lucky? Add all this up and you can do nothing but realize that mathematically speaking it is utterly impossible that you are alive today. A miracle is the only way of explaining your existence.

How are you using this life of yours?

WHAT IS COURAGE?

by Mack Reynolds

The bartender was drawing a beer as I came in. The head foamed over the top of the glass and he cut it off with his spatula. He looked up and said, "Hello, Jeff."

"Hello, George," I said and went down to the end of the bar where I could see who entered the door.

George slid the beer over to his customer, rang up the ten cents and walked down to me.

"What'll you have, Jeff?" he asked.

"Rye."

As he poured the drink, I looked down the bar. Except for one stranger, the usual afternoon crowd was there. The stranger stood alone, reading a tabloid he had spread out on the bar.

"You want water with that, Jeff?" George asked.

"Yeah."

"How's business going?"

"Slow."

He saw I didn't feel like talking and went up to the other end of the bar to listen in on an argument about Louis and Conn.

I was trying to remember how long it had been since we had had a decent case when this kid came in the door. No one else saw him until he said, "This is a stick-up."

You could see he was scared stiff. It must have been his first caper. His face was kind of pale and the .38 he held was shaking a little.

"You guys all put up your hands," he commanded.

George and I got our hands up fast. Kids on their first job are bad. The last thing an old-timer wants to do is hurt anybody, but an amateur is too nervous to do the job right.

"Okay," said George. "Take it easy."

The kid tried to sneer, but he still looked scared and it spoiled the effect.

Everybody had their hands up by this time except the stranger with the newspaper. He hadn't even looked up from his reading when the kid first spoke. He either hadn't heard him or must have bought it was a gag. When he noticed the rest of us, he looked a little surprised and turned around to take a look.

The kid walked over toward him and tried to look tough.

"That goes for you too," he said. "Stick 'em up."

The guy didn't even move. He just looked at he kid without saying a word. For a minute I thought he was going to turn his back and go on reading his paper.

The kid got paler and I considered going for my shoulder holster. Not that I cared if the nut was killed, but I was afraid that if the kid started shooting, he might hit some of the rest of us.

"Stick up your hands, wise guy," he said again, "or I'll let you have it."

He was jittery and his gun hand was trembling, but he was too near to miss.

The stranger let his eyes go down slowly to the kid's gun and then right up to his eyes. He didn't say a word and didn't move a muscle. I never saw such gall in my life. I expected to see the punk start blazing any second.

They stood there like that.

George started to lower his hands. He had probably decided to go for the old service .45 he kept under the bar. A woman gave a short hysterical laugh.

The kid looked more scared than ever and then suddenly turned and made a dash for the door. I could have shot him in the back if I had felt like it.

Nobody said anything for a minute. Then George looked down the bar at me, and I thought there was a question in his eyes.

"If you want him, chase him yourself or call a cop," I said. "It isn't my kind of work."

"I don't want to chase him," George said. "I could've shot when he was running out the door."

He went over to the stranger and said, "What'll it be, buddy? It's on the house."

Everybody started talking at once. Most of them thought we ought to send for a cop. One guy looked out the door to see if the kid was still in sight.

The stranger waited a minute and then asked for whiskey.

George poured him the drink. "I'd think you'd need it," he said and then walked over to the pay phone to report to the police. He left the bottle on the bar.

I looked at this guy. "Buddy," I said, "you either got more gall or less brains than anybody I ever saw." I was mad.

He just looked at me.

"I been in the private dick racket for a long time, and I've seen plenty, but I never saw anybody take such a long chance," I said.

He looked at me for a minute more, then drank his whiskey and poured another one.

"I was so scared I couldn't move," he said.

Your Soul Comes C.O.D.

By Mack Reynolds

In view of the trouble to which he had gone in order to acquire such out-of-the-way items as a piece of unicorn horn and three drops of blood from a virgin, it was rather disconcerting to have the spirit appear even before the prescribed routine. In fact, he hadn't even got his protective pentacle drawn when he looked up to find the entity materialized in his rickety easy chair.

The spirit said, "You don't really need that, you know."

Norman Wallace stared at his visitor, even after all these months of research, unbelievingly. The other was far from what

the young man expected. Somehow, he was reminded of Lincoln, his face almost beautiful in its infinite sadness.

The spirit nodded at the pentacle. "Mere superstition. It couldn't protect you if my purpose was to do you harm. But, more important still, I am quite incapable of such aggression. Man has freedom of choice, free will; we of the other worlds can only help him destroy—or elevate—himself, we cannot initiate."

Norman was shaken, but not quite to the point of speechlessness. He pointed to his assembled drugs, charms, potions, and incenses and said, almost indignantly, "But I haven't performed the rite as yet."

The other nodded and shrugged. "What's the difference? You wished to summon a spirit. Very well, here I am. The desire is of more importance than the act of combining those rather silly items. But, to get to the point, just what is it you desire?"

Norman Wallace took a deep breath and got down to business. He indicated his shabby quarters. "I can bear this no longer," he said. "I want a few years of decency in living, a few years of the good things of life that others enjoy. So—"

"So in your desperation you wish to sell your soul in return for help."

"That's right."

The spirit considered momentarily. "Suppose I give you my support for forty years? Suppose I guarantee you love, wealth, and power to the degree you desire them? At the end of that time your soul is mine?"

Norman Wallace's mouth tightened, but he said, "That's agreeable."

The spirit came to its feet. "Very well, the pact is made."

The other frowned. "Don't we make out a contract or something? Don't I have to sign in blood?"

The faintest of smiles came to the melancholy face of the spirit. "That won't be necessary. The pact has been made; neither of us will nor can break it."

Suddenly he disappeared.

And almost simultaneously came a knock at the door. Dazed, Norman came to his feet and opened it. Harriet was there and immediately in his arms. "Oh, darling, darling, I was so wrong."

He held her back at arm's length in amazement. "You mean that you've changed your mind, you'll marry me?"

"Oh, darling, yes. I thought going away from you, spending a few months in Florida, would let me forget. I was so wrong."

Frowning, he indicated the poverty of his room. "But Harriet, we'd still—"

She smiled now, and laughed up at him. "Remember that little farm I told you my aunt left me? The one in Louisiana?"

He nodded, uncomprehending.

"Oil, darling," she bubbled over. "Enough to give you the start you need."

* * * *

And so it went for forty years.

Wealth to the modest extent he desired it; prestige to the small degree his ambition demanded; but, most important of all, love that ripened and ever grew as the years went by. And a home rich with children, and the respect and affection of his neighbors and his associates.

Not that he ever saw the spirit again, not in all those years. Almost, it was possible for him to look back at his life and think it was all of his own doing. Each success had seemingly been not inordinate good luck, or a result of his own efforts. Sometimes he had even tried to convince himself that the pact he'd made was a figment of his imagination, that the demon he had thought he had summoned was a result of too much worry, too much work, too little food and recreation back in those days of his poverty-stricken youth.

But subconsciously he knew. *He knew!*

And so it was that after his forty years, he sat alone in his study and waited. Harriet had gone on to bed; the children, of course, had long since married and now lived their own peaceful, happy lives.

He wondered now, as he looked back over the years, at the use to which he had put the demon's assistance. He had been promised love, wealth, and power to the extent he desired them. But, somehow, he had wanted no more than sufficient for himself and his family. He had made no attempt to accumulate the fortune of a Midas; nor, for that matter, had he attained his possessions by recourse to the racetrack or stockmarket. He had worked hard during those forty years.

He had been promised power, too. Why had he taken so little? He had been content to assume a position in society that coincided with his natural abilities. He could have been president or, for that matter, dictator of the world. Why hadn't he?

Ah, but he had taken his full measure of the other. His cup had overflowed with love. In all the years, the romance between Harriet and him had never waned. And the children? Well, for instance, the way they had returned to this old home from all over the nation this last Christmas had proven their affection.

And now suddenly he thought he knew his motivation. Somewhere, beneath it all, he had been attempting to forestall the fate awaiting him. Subconsciously, he had told himself that if he were moderate, if he led the good life, if he abstained from demanding the ultimate, his reckoning with the demon would be the easier.

He laughed abruptly, bitterly.

And suddenly fear washed over him. The reckoning was now.

No matter what he had done with the demonic powers awarded him. No matter how he had loved and been loved. No matter how much he repented now.

His soul was the spirit's.

He clasped his hands tightly to the arms of his chair.

Run! *Hide!* ESCAPE!

But he sank back again. There was no place to run. No place to hide. No way of escape.

The spirit materialized on the couch across from him.

Norman Wallace nodded his gray head in submission. "I was expecting you."

"Your forty years are up," the spirit told him.

"Yes, I know." Hopelessness had replaced fear now.

"Is there any reason why our pact should not be fulfilled? You are satisfied that I have suitably kept my part of the bargain?"

The old man hesitated, then nodded again. "I am satisfied."

"Then you are ready to go? You have taken farewell of those you love, made what arrangements you thought necessary?"

"Yes. Yes, I am ready." His voice was firm now. "I suppose it will be hard on Harriet for a time, but then, we must all face the end sooner or later, and only recently my doctor warned me of my heart. Harriet always said she wanted me to go first, that she would hate to think of me alone in life after we have been so close."

The spirit came to its feet. "Very well, let us be on our way."

Norman Wallace arose, too, and the shock was not so great as he might have expected when he was able to look back and see himself sitting there in the easy chair, his face pale and his eyes staring unseeingly.

"Then I am dead already?"

"Yes," the spirit told him, "Your doctor's diagnosis was quite accurate. Come."

And suddenly they were in another place, and Norman Wallace stared about without comprehension.

He said, "It seems that in all my relations with you I have been continually surprised at the inaccuracy of the legends and myths."

"Oh?" the spirit said.

"Yes. When you first appeared, you didn't look like my life-long conception of a demon. Nor in my dealings with you have you acted the way I supposed you would. Now, this place has none of the attributes I had expected of Hell."

The spirit smiled. "My dear Norman, why is it that so many suppose that souls are of less interest to us than to our adversaries? Why should not one side strive for a worthy one as well as the other? I am not a demon, nor is this Hell."

✗

LONG BEER—SHORT HORN

by Mack Reynolds

The Duke said, "Buddy, can you spare two cents?"

The mooch stopped and stared at him. "Two cents? Don't tell me you know a place where you can get coffee for two cents."

"Naw," the Duke said easily, "but beer costs fifteen in this town and I already got thirteen."

The other grinned. "Things are bad everywhere," he laughed, and dug down into his pocket. He came up with a handful of change. "Haven't got two cents," he said. "Here's a dime." He flipped the coin to the Duke and went on his way, still grinning.

The Duke scratched himself thought-fully and looked after his benefactor. It worked two times out of three. If he'd asked the mooch for a dime he'd have got the quick brush-off; asking for two cents, for some reason or other, always startled the other and a couple of minutes blab-bling usually netted him a dime or more. They liked it better, too, if he came right out and said he wanted it for beer, rather than something to eat, or a cup of coffee.

He shrugged. You had to have angles, a new slant, if you wanted to get on in thus world.

Without taking his hand from his pocket, he counted the coins there. He actually had forty-six cents now. Not bad for a half hour's work. Of course, that didn't include his emergency funds, three dollars which he kept pinned to his shirt tail. In some towns they still couldn't pick you up for vagrancy if you had visible means of support, and three bucks was usually the minimum sum considered visible means of support.

He figured he might as well reward himself with a glass or two of beer and made his way down the street to the nearest bar, whose sign announced that it was the Norge Tavern.

He entered and sidled onto a stool. The bartender—a little sign above the cash register proclaimed that his name was Joe—didn't say anything until the Duke slid fifteen cents out before him.

The bartender smiled, as though apologizing for doubting him. "What'll it be?" he asked.

"Beer," the Duke said. What else could you get for fifteen cents?

"What d'ya want it in?" Joe asked.

The Duke said, "Huh?"

The bartender repeated it, motioning with his thumb to a wide selection of glasses, mugs, steins, even metal cups, standing or hanging behind the bar.

"What's the idea?" the Duke asked.

Joe explained in a tone of voice that indicated he had to go through the same routine a score of times each day. "It's the boss," he revealed. "He thinks the place oughta be different so folks'll remember it and come back. He figures instead of just plain glasses he'll have a whole shebang of steins and mugs."

The Duke was impressed. "It's a good idea," he said. "Your boss's got enterprise; he'll get places. That's what you need these days." He scratched himself thoughtfully, then pointed to a large stein. "I'll take that one."

Joe shook his head, still looking as though he had to go through the same routine daily. "That's a thirty-five cent stein. He's gotta put higher prices on the big ones or he'd lose money."

The Duke was disappointed, but his hopes hadn't been too high anyway; he'd thought there must be some angle. "Okay," he said, "give me some fifteen-cent one. You pick it out."

The bartender looked over his collection and said. "Ever drink out of a horn?"

The Duke said. "Huh?"

"You ever drink out of a horn?"

"I thought you blew 'em," the Duke said.

Joe had brought forth an ancient-looking brass-bound horn. It was too big to be from a cow, and that about exhausted the Duke's knowledge of horns.

Joe said, "It's a drinking horn, like in the old days."

The Duke said, "Why didn't they use glasses?"

Joe shrugged. "How would I know? I mean the real old days, like in Norway and Sweden."

The Duke was getting thirstier by the minute. "All right," he said, "anything. Let's have some beer."

Joe took the horn down to his taps and filled it. It didn't seem to hold very much and the Duke wondered if he'd made a mistake, or if it'd been half full of flat beer and Joe had just put a head on it; sometimes they'd do that if they didn't like your looks and wanted you to take your business elsewhere.

The bartender cut the foam off with his spatula and brought the horn back and handed it to him.

"How d'ya set it down?" the Duke asked.

"You don't, I guess. I had it leaning up against a corner." Joe wiped the bar with his rag. "I guess you just hafta hold it until it's empty."

"That won't be long," the Duke told him and proceeded to lift the horn to his thirsty lips. It was good beer, very good; not too cool, but a bit stronger and heavier, he thought, than usual. He wondered if the bartender had given him ale instead of beer.

Two other customers entered, and Joe went down to wait on them. The Duke sat alone and sipped his beer, and his mind faded into dwelling upon the past and the present. He tried to avoid the future.

He looked into the mirror and wondered how many hours he'd sat like this at some bar, drink in hand. A good many. Too many, he thought, but took it back. How better could you spend your time?

The Duke took another gulp of the beer and looked down into the horn. It evidently held more than he'd thought. He'd expected it to be empty by now.

He thought of how he'd started off in school, ambitious, eager, ready to seize the world by the tail and swing it. What had happened? He didn't know exactly; undoubtedly it had been a lot of things, not just one. Graduation during the depression; several years without a job; the marriage with Helen that hadn't worked out; the war, and the years of horror and disillusionment.

And here he was.

He took another deep draught of the beer, figuring on draining the horn and getting another one. A glass this time. The horn was too much bother, you couldn't set it down.

It didn't drain. He looked into the horn with surprise, then took another deep drink—still without emptying it. This horn really held a lot of beer, much more than you'd think. The Duke scratched himself thoughtfully. He figured that maybe he'd better stick to drinking out of it; the bartender evidently didn't realize how much it really contained.

He sighed and relaxed. He had enough money in his pocket to have the horn filled twice again. By the time he drank that much beer, he ought to have a pretty good shine. He could probably panhandle another sixty cents or so later on. Yeah, it looked as though it was going to be a good day. Why, the way he'd been drinking, this horn must hold a quart—more.

He eyed the horn quizzically. The darn thing couldn't possibly contain that much.

Joe came down and asked, "Want a refill?"

The Duke said, "This isn't empty yet."

The other scowled. "The way you been working on it, I'd think it was empty ten minutes ago. You look like you're gulping like crazy, but you must just sip it."

"Yeah," the Duke said, "I just sip it."

Joe wandered off again and the Duke decided he'd better finish the horn off quick and order another. He didn't want this nosey bartender to find out just how much the thing held. He put the horn to his lips decisively.

Now the Duke was a beer drinker from way back. He remembered that time in Albany when a couple of bar sports offered to buy it for him if he could finish off a fifty ounce tankard of beer in five minutes. Well, he'd done it, and if he could do that he wasn't going to have any trouble downing the contents of this comparatively small drinking horn.

He drank deeply, took another breath, and went at it again. There was still beer in the horn. He looked down into it in amazement. As a matter of fact, the thing looked about as full as it'd ever been.

The Duke was beginning to feel it. He told himself he was drinking on an empty stomach, but inwardly he knew that wasn't it. He usually drank on an empty stomach; the alcohol went further that way. Besides, what with liquor being the price it was, he often couldn't afford to eat.

He peered into the horn again, unbelievingly. Why kid himself, he'd drunk at least two quarts out of it already and, by the wildest overestima-tion, the thing couldn't hold more than one.

Joe said, "Something wrong?"

The Duke shot a glance up at him. "Where'd ya get this horn, anyway?"

The other scowled. "As a matter a fact, I let a guy have two bucks on it this morning. He was broke."

"What kinda guy?"

The bartender rubbed the end of his nose with a forefinger. "It was a sailor, I guess. Looked like a squarehead. Said he'd be back later to redeem it; put on an act it was worth plenty. He won't come back, they never do."

Joe wiped the bar reflectively. "He was quite a character. Had an accent you could hang your hat on. Said he wouldn't have left the horn with me if I hadn't been a fellow countryman."

The Duke took another long draught from the horn. "You don't look like a Scandinavian," he said, noting that his tongue was beginning to get thick.

"You mean a Swede?" Joe snorted. "On my mother's side I'm Swiss and Greek; Welsh and Italian, on my old man's. I can't help it if the boss of the joint wants to call it the Norge Tavern, and do it all up with steins and Swede pictures. That don't make me no squarehead."

The Duke took another long drink and stared into the horn. He was tight enough to have to close one eye for accuracy, but the level in the horn was as high as ever. He scratched himself thoughtfully.

"Tell me more about this guy," he said.

"No more to tell," Joe said. "He just gave me a song and dance about this here horn, and when I gave him the two bucks, he beat it. Oh, yeah, he called it the Horn of Thorn, or something like that."

"The Horn of Thorn?" There was a clicking in the Duke's beer soaked brain, a memory from high school days.

"Yeah," Joe said. "Something like that."

The Duke asked, "You mean the Horn of Thor?"

The bartender scowled. "Maybe that was it." He looked at the Duke searchingly. "Hey, are you stewed? You looked sober as an undertaker when you came in here. You ain't one of these guys that gets plastered on one short beer, are ya?"

The Duke ignored him. "Listen," he said, "you wanta sell this here horn? I'll give you three bucksh for it."

The bartender squinted at him. "The guy asked me to keep it for him," he said slyly, "but I'll let you have it for four."

"All I got ish, I mean ish, three bucksh," the Duke told him sadly.

"Okay, it's a deal."

The Duke carefully brought out his shirt tail and unpinned the three one dollar bills. He placed them on the bar, gingerly got down from his stool, still holding the horn, and marched for the door. He wanted to get out of here before the bartender changed his mind.

The Duke headed for a secluded spot in the park, free both from flatfooted representatives of the city and from fellow vagabonds. He found it, relaxed with his back to a tree trunk, sighed deeply, and continued to draw upon the contents of the Horn of Thor.

* * * *

When he awoke in the morning, his head was splitting. He closed his eyes and groaned. How had he managed to achieve such a tremendous hangover? He hadn't been able to afford enough drink to get him that tight for months.

He could feel part of his clothing was wet. Maybe it'd rained in the night and he'd been too drunk to seek shelter. Suddenly, it came back to him. *The horn!* He opened his eyes and glared around, red eyed, looking for it.

There it was, leaning on its side, a continual flow of dark fluid issuing from it. He grabbed it quickly, automatically. All about him was a puddle of flat-smelling beer, gallons of flat beer. He was sitting in the middle, soaked.

It was one thing, last night, when he was tight, but it was another now. This just couldn't happen. He got to his feet and waded out of the puddle, holding the horn upright.

He found a sunny spot and sat down to wait for his clothes to dry and to have a few more eye-openers. He peered into the horn and scratched himself thoughtfully. It still looked just as full as when he first got it at the Norge Tavern. What a deal!

When his clothes had dried, he stashed the horn away, upright this time, beneath some bushes and made his way to the public library.

The librarian gave him the oatmeal look and some information on Norse mythology.

There wasn't much on the horn, but he found enough to bring back what he'd read in his younger days. The Scandinavian god Thor had gone to the land of the giants and had a series of contests with them. The giants went all-out to show up this most powerful of the gods, and Thor had had a rough go of it.

Among other things, they'd given him a horn to drink from. And he, not knowing it was a magic horn, one end connected to the ocean, tried to drain it. Evidently, the giants hadn't had much trouble putting Thor under the table. But, at that, he drank so much that there were droughts all over the world.

What the Duke didn't get was how come there was beer, or ale, or whatever it was, in the horn instead of water. Maybe the whole story had been allegory. Instead of the magic horn being connected with the ocean, it just meant that, through some device or other, it was endless in its contents. As a matter of fact, he couldn't imagine old Thor drinking water.

He made his way back to the park where the horn was hidden, on the way trying to remember some of the science, particularly physics, that he'd studied in school. Of course, he didn't believe in magic; there couldn't be anything supernatural. If it happened, no matter how strange or unbelievable, then it was natural. Maybe men didn't understand the why or wherefore of it; but, if it occurred, there were laws of nature that encompassed the phenomenon.

Sure. Most legends, be they of dragons, or gods, or giants, or what have you, had some basis in fact. It was quite possible that an older race, or races, had once populated the Earth. Who could say to what extent their science had developed? The only traces that remained of them now were obscure ruins in out of the way places of Earth, and the legends that exist of olden gods with their magical devices.

Perhaps his horn drew upon some unlimited source in some other universe, or some other time. How did he know? As a matter of fact, right now he didn't care. What he wanted to know was what he could do with it. He scratched himself thoughtfully. The immediate problem was to get hold of a little capital so he could begin operations.

* * * *

By noon he'd figured it out. Keeping the horn concealed in a paper bag, he made the rounds of the park benches where most of his acquaintances and social equals made their headquarters.

When he saw Duke approaching, Willie the Mark nodded, exerting himself as little as possible in the process.

"What's new, Duke?" he asked, not caring.

"You in on this shindig, tonight?" the Duke asked easily.

"What shindig?"

"The free beer."

Willie the Mark sat up, interest at last gleaming from his eyes. "What free beer?"

The Duke shrugged nonchalantly. "Not exactly free; but all you can drink for two bits. One of these here philanthropists is throwing it in the park tonight. All you have to do is bring two bits and your own glass. Uh...the two bits goes to charity." The Duke scratched himself thoughtfully and added. "He doesn't want to let anybody know who he is, so he's letting me help him on passing out the beer." He made ready to move on. "I'm spreading the word around. If you see any of the boys, let them know. There's plenty for everybody."

"I sure will," Willie the Mark said fervently: "Anybody oughta be able to raise two bits. There oughta be five hundred guys there tonight."

* * * *

Marmaduke Halloway, beer baron extraordinary, looked up from the chair he was occupying in his luxurious study and said easily, "Yes, James?"

The butler said, "Mr. Aiken, your secretary, is here to see you, sir."

Marmaduke Halloway frowned lightly. He disliked having his evenings disturbed with business matters.

"Very well, James," he sighed. "Show him in."

Frederic Aiken hustled, rather than walked, into the room. He was a nervous, quick little man carrying a briefcase under his arm, and, seemingly, the weight of the world on his shoulders.

"Sorry to bother you like this, Mr. Halloway," he apologized.

The brewery tycoon yawned. "I assume the matter is of some importance, since you did."

Aiken said nervously, "Sir, it's just that I am at my wits end. Orders for your Norge Brew are so far behind that even at full capacity our present production would take more than two years to fill them."

Marmaduke Halloway said impatiently, "I realize that, Aiken. After all, I spend a full half hour at the office every day."

"But, sir, we must open another brewery. We must expand. Why, overnight, if we increase production, we could become the leading beer of the nation, of the world! The flavor of Norge Brew is the talk of the industry. Its popularity..."

Marmaduke Halloway shook his head wearily. "Aiken," he said, "I've told you time and again, and the others as well, that I have no intention of increasing the production of Norge Brew. As things are now we are turning out a premium beer. Our prices are half again as high as any other beer in the country. I am satisfied." He felt he had to give some explanation. "Besides, I am afraid the formula might leak out if I let it into too many hands. I want to keep the secret of its production to myself."

Marmaduke Halloway, the fabulous beer baron, scratched himself thoughtfully. "I realize full well that the thousands of barrels a week that flow through that three inch tube that leads from my laboratory don't take care of the demand."

"Not nearly, sir," said his secretary.

WITH THIS RING...
by Mack Reynolds

Newton Brown turned to the passenger sitting in the seat nearest the window and said politely, "I beg your pardon, but could you tell me what year it is?"

The other had been staring out at the scraggy, bedraggled palms and at the endless succession of tiny fruit, vegetable, olive and souvenir stands. He said, "Huh?"

Newton Brown repeated, "Could you tell me the year?"

"You kiddin', Jack? It's 1951." He gave the wistful appearing little man a long searching look, then went back to the scenery.

"Fine," Newton Brown said. "I always like 1951; but, if you don't mind, just one other thing. Where is this bus going?"

The double-seat's other occupant closed his eyes for a second, as though in pain, then opened them and looked around at Newton Brown again. He stared at him for a long time. "You can't be a wise guy," he said finally. "You're too little to go around cracking wise. Maybe you're a crackpot."

Newton Brown repeated, "Please, where is the bus going?"

"It's going to L.A., Jack. The City of Lost Angeles."

"Ummmm. Thank you," Newton Brown said. "That will be nice. It's been a rather long time since I've been in Los Angeles." He added, as though to himself, "It's always a different time and a different locality."

His seat companion said bitterly, "Jack, you better start gathering up your marbles."

They rode in silence the rest of the way to the Union Terminal, and the highway fruit stands and palms gave way to miles of drab streets of the unglamorized sections of the Baghdad of the West.

As the passengers disembarked to lose themselves among the teeming hundreds in the bus center, the driver stood at the door and amiably exchanged good-byes with those of his riders he'd made acquaintance with on the long trip.

Newton Brown was last. As he stepped down from the bus, the driver frowned in puzzlement and said, "I don't remember you. Where'd you get on, sir?"

Nature hadn't cut out the little man from the material of heartiness, but he said now, with a weak attempt at joviality, "That makes two of us, I guess. I'm not quite sure where I got on, either."

The frown had become a scowl. "Do you have your ticket stub, sir?"

"Ummmmm. I'm afraid not."

"Sir, I'm afraid you'll have to pay your fare. I don't know exactly where you sneaked—"

Newton Brown was searching through his pockets. He came up with thirteen cents, a pocket comb with three teeth missing, four keys on a ring and a tiny knife. He looked up at the driver and essayed a wry smile. "It would seem that—"

The driver looked down at the little man's hands and his face went suddenly pallid. He blurted, "I...I didn't know. Please forgive me."

Newton Brown said, "Not at all, not at all. We all are capable of error—all of us."

He turned and ambled easily toward the entrance.

The driver stood staring after him, his face still white and his body shaking uncontrollably.

The dispatcher came over to him, looking worried. "What's the matter with you,

Steve? You look like you just had a brush with a ghost."

"Ghost! Listen, Jake, do you know who I just had ride in with me?"

* * * *

Newton Brown hailed a cab and directed the driver to the Biltmore. He had considered, momentarily, going up into the Hollywood area and stopping at one of the luxury hotels there, but he was feeling slightly fatigued from the bus ride and decided that the Biltmore would be closer and quite as comfortable.

"Here y'are, bud," the cab driver drawled, as they drew up before the entrance opposite Pershing Square. He shot a glance at the meter. "That'll be exactly—"

The little man murmured, "Just tell your company officials that I praised your driving. You seem quite competent in the heavy traffic."

"Huh?"

Newton Brown smiled gently and lifted his hand. Then he turned and made his way toward the entrance.

The doorman, dressed like a Bulgarian Rear Admiral, took in the newcomer's attire, shabby gray suit, nondescript hat, unshined shoes—and noted his lack of luggage. He didn't bother to open the door. Instead, he scowled out at the cab which still blocked the curb, and strode over angrily.

"Get along, bud," he began to the cab driver. "You're blocking the entrance and—"

The other's eyes were bugging out.

"What's the matter, you sick?" the doorman snapped.

"Holy jumping jeeps," the other breathed. "Did you see who that was I just brought up here?"

The doorman snorted, "You must be new to your racket, bud; celebrities are a dime a dozen around here."

"Not *this* celebrity."

* * * *

Newton Brown made his way to the registration desk and faced the impeccably clad diplomat who presided there. "I'll have my regular suite," he said mildly.

The reservation clerk was courteous in the haughty manner achievable only by headwaiters and reservation clerks. He had sized up the bespectacled little man as he'd made his way across the swank lobby.

"Do you have a reservation, sir?" he asked, his tone insinuating that not only did he doubt that the other had such a reservation, but that he ever would have one.

"No," Newton Brown told him. "As a matter of fact, I never make reservations."

"Then I am afraid—"

Newton Brown didn't argue. He held up his right hand and let the clerk see the emerald.

"—but...but, you have a ring on your finger. Surely you know that is most illegal. No one in the whole world is allowed to wear a ring except—" He broke off and his carefully cultivated calm melted away; cold sweat broke out on his forehead. "Oh, no," he moaned.

The little man said, "Of course, I am incognito, although it seems that secrecy concerning my presence is quite difficult to achieve. However, that is no matter. For the present, I shall want tailors, a limousine and chauffeur, and—well, I am sure your manager will be able to anticipate my desires. Inform him of my presence immediately."

"Oh, yes, sire—"

"Ummmmm. Well, I assume my suite is ready?"

"Always, sire. Every major hotel in the city—in the world for that matter—reserves its best—"

"Very well, I'll go up."

* * * *

The suite was acceptable. Newton Brown gave it a perfunctory inspection,

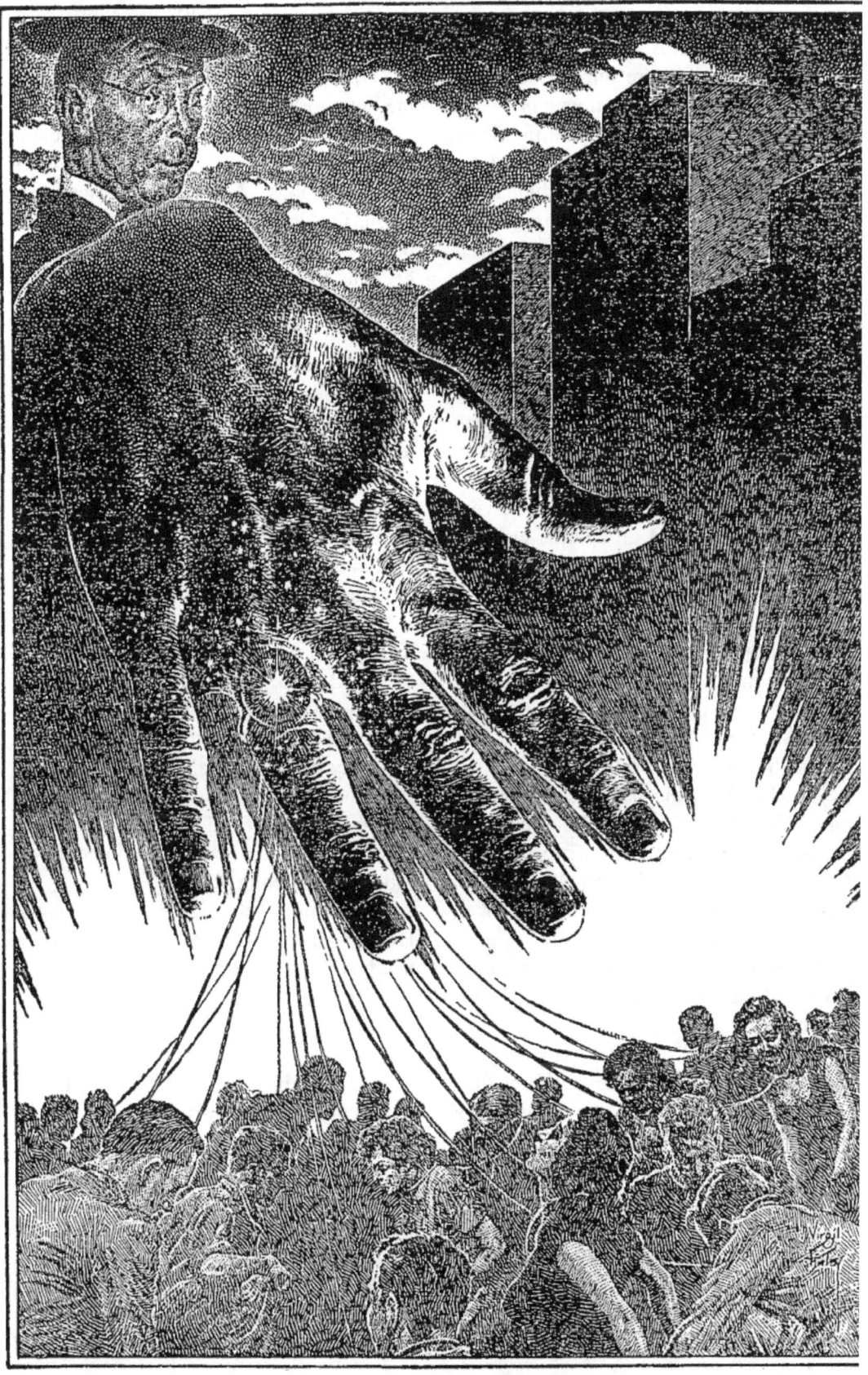

then made his way to the built-in bar and poured himself a stiff shot of Metaxa, noting it was the ultra rare hundred-year-old, and then relaxed for a few moments.

Later it might be somewhat difficult for him to take a stroll, so after a bath and a quick change of clothing to something more suitable to the climate—the manager had immediately rushed tailors and haberdashers to his suite—Newton Brown made his way to the lobby again, waving aside the various flunkies who hastened nervously toward him when he made his appearance.

He strode leisurely out the front entrance and crossed the street to the park to listen momentarily to some of the groups arguing Socialism, Technocracy, Communism, Fascism, Anarchism, and Thirty Dollars Every Thursday. The largest group was also the most vocal. Newton Brown stopped and listened.

In the center, a lone figure was holding out against all the others. "The DeLeonists are right," he insisted loudly. "All the rest of you are trying to reform capitalism. What we need to do is abolish capitalism, not patch it up."

A red-tied fanatic began screaming at him, "You White Guardist! You enemy of the Soviet Union. You—" Off to one side, a newsboy began to call excitedly, "*Extree!* Emperor rumored to be in L.A. Read all about it. Emperor in L.A. *Extree!*"

"Oh, gracious," Newton Brown muttered. "So soon." He turned and began to make his way back to the hotel.

"The Emperor?" one of the park debaters said. He took off his hat respectfully. "Do you really think the Emperor might honor us in this..." The rest of them removed their hats—those who wore them. "The Emperor..." a breath went through the crowd.

Somebody snarled at Newton Brown. "Your hat, shorty. Didn't you hear somebody mention the Emperor?"

The colorless little man tried to hurry past—this sort of thing bothered him a little.

But the way was barred by the bulk of the other.

"What's the matter, chum, don't you like the Emperor? Maybe you think—"

Others were beginning to crowd around, threateningly. An angry hum began to rise.

"Oh gracious," Newton Brown muttered again, peevishly. "I had hoped to at least be able to take a short walk." He held up his hand to let them see the emerald, and a moment later picked his way through their respectfully prostrated bodies. As he began to cross the street to return to the Biltmore, he could hear the sounds behind him of the crowd unmercifully beating the one who had used threatening language against him.

He hesitated in the lobby long enough to ask the trembling and bobbing manager the name of the currently most popular night spot in the Hollywood-Beverly Hills area.

"The Buckingham, I would say, sire."

"Ummmm" Newton Brown said. "Perhaps you'd better inform the management of the Buckingham that I shall probably drop in tonight. And, also, it might be pleasant if you'd ring the studios and, let's see, let us say Betty, Loretta, Hedy, and possibly Judy and Yvonne—have them at my table."

"Oh, yes, sire. And possibly you would enjoy some additional entertainment—additional to the floor show?"

"Ummmm. Thank you for reminding me. Have them send Bing to sing a few songs, and possibly Bob for some comedy."

"Certainly, sire."

* * * *

The Buckingham, of course, had been closed to others than his party. But in spite of the almost super-human efforts made by all concerned, the evening had been just a trifle less than Newton Brown had expected—which was somewhat surprising to him.

The food had been quite acceptable. Of course, it hadn't been left in the hands of the club's only averagely competent chefs. Instead, the city had been combed for the most capable artists of the kitchen and a score had prepared his dishes. Actually, he'd had to send back only the *Raie au beurre noir*. It distressed him when he found out later than the *poisson* expert who had prepared it committed suicide.

Bing had been in good voice; Bob amusing as usual except for a slight nervousness, which was understandable in view of his audience.

It was the actresses who had bothered Newton Brown a trifle. They were a bit too pushing, too desirous of being noticed, each anxious to prove more charming than the next. He finally ran four of them off, after telling them sternly that he had no desire to read of any of them talking an overdose of sleeping pills later.

When he left the club to reenter his limousine, he noticed that thousands had gathered before the Buckingham, awaiting his reappearance and an opportunity to see him in person.

He gave them a gentle wave, to which they responded almost hysterically, and climbed into his car to return to the hotel, which had meantime been cleared of all other guests so that maximum attention of all the staff could be devoted to his care.

On the way back to the hotel, an unfortunate happening marred some of the peace of the balmy Los Angeles night. The chauffeur, of course, had been ignoring red lights as he proceeded down Sunset. He was finally confronted with a red-faced traffic officer who directed him curtly to the curb. A crowd gathered idly to hear the fun.

The cop, conscious of the presence of the crowd, was in high form. He began by snarling to the chauffeur, "Just where is the conflagration, my man?"

The chauffeur said tightly, "My instructions were—"

The officer let loose a long string of profanity, before turning back to the occupant of the rear seat. Sitting there, blinking behind his thick lensed spectacles, Newton Brown listened for a short moment.

"Instructions, eh?" the traffic cop barked. "Who do you think you are to be giving—"

Newton Brown had had enough. He held up his hand so that the crowd could see the ring.

"Dispose of him," he said mildly. Then to the chauffeur, "Proceed."

They could hear the officer's screams for mercy only for a few moments; by then the crowd had torn him to bits and the car had gone on.

At the hotel, Newton Brown noticed that there was a new doorman and a new reservation clerk. He assumed correctly that the previous two had committed *hari kari*.

* * * *

In the morning, Newton Brown had half a dozen of the city's more prominent politicians and educators up to his suite while he lay in bed breakfasting upon *Oeuf a la florentine*. Motioning impatiently for them to get up from their knees, he came immediately to the point.

"Just what is the present international situation?" he asked, idly sipping his coffee.

It was the mayor who answered him. "Sire," he said, "there is a cold war in progress which threatens to become...er...hot, momentarily. The two most powerful nations have been on the verge of—"

"Ummmm," Newton Brown interrupted. "Get Joe on the phone for me."

He took a bite of his toast and marmalade.

He wasted little time on the conversation: "Now, I want this clearly understood. There is to be no war, and this situation that prevails at present is to be ended. In fact, I am somewhat upset about the present tendency of your experiment. As I recall, when you started it, it was supposedly intended to evolve into a super-democracy, a virtual Utopia, and I was inclined to wait and see what developed. It seems to me that you've gotten far away from the road on which you claimed you were going to travel.

"Please. Don't answer me. I hope this word of warning will be sufficient." He hung up, muttering: "It seems that I can't turn my back without this whole space-time continuum going to pot."

He finished his coffee and glanced at his wrist watch. "Oh, gracious," he said, "is it that late?" He made a quick mental calculation, then waved his hand at them. "Out. All of you, out!"

When they had bowed themselves out, he raised his right hand and took the emerald in his fingers and twisted it sharply.

* * * *

Martha was standing above him as he sat at the tiny desk in his cellar laboratory.

"Well, Newton," she flared, scowling down at him. "What have you been up to now? I've been calling you for the past ten minutes to come and do the laundry."

"Now Martha," he began placatingly, "I was just continuing my experiments in alternate space-time continuums."

"I see," she snapped nastily. "You've been off to that alternate universe—or whatever you call it—of yours. Haven't I warned you? How long were you gone, you worm?"

"Only twenty-four minutes, our time; twenty four hours, theirs," he told her fearfully. "Now, dear, there's nothing wrong with my—"

"Oh, I've heard you talking in your sleep," she interrupted him sharply. "Women, liquor, mansions—everything your own way. Off where I can't get at you. I—I—" She couldn't find words strong enough. "Other women marry plumbers or bricklayers, but what do I wind up with? A little shrimp of a crazy inventor!"

"But Martha," he protested pleadingly. "I've devised a method by which I can travel through the neocontinuum to that space-time continuum, or universe, among all the infinite number of universes, which I would enjoy most. As a matter of fact," he added hopefully, "it is remarkably similar to this one in which you and I live.

"This invention can send anyone to that space-time continuum in which he would be most satisfied. Why don't you let me send you to the one you'd like best? Just for as long as you'd be interested in staying, of course."

She glared down at him, her two hundred odd pounds quivering with rage, but since she remained silent, he gathered hope. "All you have to do is wear this ring. Turn the emerald on it to the left to—"

"You worm," she snorted. "I have no desire to go to some other universe. I like this one. And what's more, for the last time I forbid you—absolutely forbid you—to ever go off again. Time after time you've done it. Why, once you were gone three hours! This is the last time, do you realize? Give me that ring, Newton Brown!" She held out her hand. "The next thing I know, you'll be going off to this ridiculous alternate universe of yours and never coming back."

His eyes widened imperceptibly. "Gracious," he said mildly. "I'd never thought of that."

His left hand reached for the emerald on the ring.

⚔

MERCY FLIGHT

by Mack Reynolds

The phone rang and Ed Kerry wasn't doing anything so he picked it up and said, "Yeah?"

He said yeah a few more times, his eyes widening infinitesimally each time, and finally wound up with, "Okay, Bunny." He hung up and said, "That was Bunny, up in Oneonta. She says a guy is coming in from Luna with a kid for emergency hospitalization, radiation burns or something."

Jake was sitting back in his swivel chair, his feet on the desk and his hands clasped behind his head. He growled, "That's the trouble with women in this game; they've got no story sense. She phones all the way from Oneonta on a story that's been run a hundred times. Every time somebody gets good and sick up on Luna, they bring 'em to Earth for treatment." He shrugged. "Okay, so it's a kid this time. Do up about a stick of it, Kerry, and we'll put it on page three if you can work it into a tear-jerker."

Ed Kerry said, "You didn't let me finish, Jake. Something's wrong with this guy's radio."

Somebody on the rewrite desk said, "Something wrong with his radio? He's gotta have his radio or he can't come in."

Jake took his feet from the desk and sat up. "What d'ya mean, something's wrong with his radio?"

"Bunny said he's calling for his landing instructions, but they can't get anything back to him. He's just reached *Brennschluss* and he's in free fall now; it'll be four days before he gets here. That's the way they work it—he's supposed to get in touch with the spaceport he wants to land at, and..."

"I know how they work it," Jake growled. "See if there's anything on the last newswire

from Luna about him."

* * * *

Phil Mooney flicked his set on again and repeated carefully, "Calling Oneonta Spaceport. Phil Mooney, outbound Luna, calling Oneonta Spaceport. Come in Oneonta."

Calling Phil Mooney. Calling Phil Mooney, Oneonta Spaceport Calling Phil Mooney. Come in Mooney.

He cast a quick glance back at the child, strapped carefully in the metal bunk. She was unconscious now, possibly as a result of the acceleration in leaving Luna. He'd had to reach a speed of approximately two miles per second to escape Earth's satellite, and that had called for more gees acceleration than Lillian's sick body could bear. His lips thinned back over his teeth; it would be even worse when they came in for landing and he had to brake against Earth's gravity.

He switched on the set again to give it another try. Instructions were to contact the spaceport at which you planned to land as soon as possible. There was plenty of time, of course, but the sooner the better.

He said, "Calling Oneonta Spaceport. This is Phil Mooney, Luna, Calling Oneonta. Come in Oneonta."

Calling Phil Mooney. Calling Phil Mooney. Oneonta Spaceport Calling Phil Mooney. Come in Mooney.

* * * *

Ed Kerry came back to the city room with a sheet of yellow paper that he'd torn off the radiotype.

He said, "Here it is, Jake. This kid—her name is Lillian Marshall—is the only survivor of an explosion at that nuclear-fission laboratory they had on the dark side. Her old man and her mother were working under this Professor Deems; both of them killed."

His eyes went on scanning the story. "Evidently this Phil Mooney runs an unscheduled spaceline. Anyway, he blasted off to rush the kid to an Earth hospital."

Jake took the dispatch and scowled at it. "Kerry," he growled, "see what we got on this Phil Mooney in the morgue." He rubbed the end of his nose thoughtfully. "They'll probably pick him up all right when he gets nearer."

Somebody on rewrite said, "It doesn't make any difference how far he is; they should be able to reach him even if he was halfway to Mars. Something's wrong with his set."

* * * *

He decided to try one of the other spaceports. As a matter of fact, it made very little difference at which of them he landed. There'd be suitable hospital facilities within reasonable distance of any Spaceport. He was three days out now, and, according to spaceways custom, had to let them know he was coming in. It wasn't like landing an airplane—they want plenty of time to prepare for a spacecraft's arrival.

He said, "Calling New Albuquerque Spaceport. Calling New Albuquerque Spaceport. Phil Mooney, Luna, calling New Albuquerque. Please come in New Albuquerque."

Calling Phil Mooney. Calling Phil Mooney. New Albuquerque Spaceport Calling Phil Mooney. We are receiving you perfectly. Come in Mooney.

He tried once more.

"Calling New Albuquerque Spaceport. Calling New Albuquerque Spaceport. Please come in New Albuquerque. Emergency. Repeat Emergency. Please come in New Albuquerque."

Calling Phil Mooney. Calling Phil Mooney. We are receiving you perfectly, Mooney. Come in Mooney.

* * * *

Kitty Kildare took up her notes and prepared to make her way back to her own tiny office.

"I've got it, Jake," she said breathlessly. Kitty was always breathless over any story carrying more pathos than a basketball score. "My column tomorrow'll have them melting. Actually, I mean."

Jake shuddered inwardly after she left. Ed Kerry came up and drooped on the edge of the desk.

"Here's the dope on this Phil Mooney, Jake," he said. "He's about thirty. Was in the last war and saw action when we had our space-forces storming New Petrograd. Did some fighting around the satellites, too. Piloted a one seater, got a couple of medals, but never really made big news."

"Got any pix of him?"

Ed Kelly shook his head. "Like I said, he never really made the big news. Just one more of these young fellas that saw plenty of action and when the war was over was too keyed up to settle down to everyday life."

Jake picked up the thin folder and riffled through the few clippings there. "What's he doing now?" he growled.

"Evidently when the war ended he got one of these surplus freighters and converted it. Name of his company is Mooney Space Service; sounds impressive, but he's the only one in it. Probably going broke; most of those guys are—can't make the grade against the competition of Terra-Luna Spaceways and the other big boys with the scheduled flights."

The city editor scratched the end of his nose speculatively. "Maybe we ought to have Jim do up an editorial on these unscheduled spacelines. Something along the line of how heroic some of these guys are; that sort of stuff. Do up the idea that they're always ready, fair weather or foul, to make an emergency trip...."

Kerry said, "There isn't any weather, *fair* or *foul*, in space."

Jake scowled at him. "You know what I mean, wise guy. Meanwhile, get some statements from some authorities."

Ed Kerry said painfully, "What statements from what authorities?"

The city editor glared at him. "So help me, Ed. I'm going to stick you on obituaries. *Any* statements from *any* authorities. You know damn well what I mean. Get some doctor to beef about the fact there aren't suitable hospitalization facilities on Luna. Get some president of one of these unscheduled spacelines to sound off about what a hero Mooney is and how much good these unscheduled spacelines are—and that reminds me of something—"

He yelled to a tall lanky reporter at the far end of the city room: "Hey, Ted. Get Bunny on the line up in Oneonta and tell her I said to look up some of these unscheduled spacelines guys and see if she can get a photograph of Phil Mooney from them. Maybe he's got some buddies in Oneonta."

* * * *

There was one thing about being in free fall. You had lots of time to sit and think. Too much time, perhaps.

You had the time to think it *all* over. And over and over again.

There was the war which had torn you from the routine into which life had settled, from friends and relations and sweethearts, and thrown you into a one man space-fighter in which you sometimes stayed for weeks on end without communication with anyone, friend or foe.

There had probably been no equivalent situation in the history of past warfare to the one man space-scouts. The nearest thing to them might have been the flyers of 1914, in the first World War—but, of course, they were up there alone only for hours at a time, not weeks.

"You develop self-reliance, men," was the way the colonel had put it. "You develop self-reliance, or you're sunk. You're in space by yourself, alone. You can't use your radio or they can locate you. If something happens, some emergency or some contact with the enemy, you're on your own. You have to figure it out; there's no superior officer to do your thinking. You're the whole works."

And the colonel had been right, of course. It was a matter of using your own wits, your own ability. Fighting in a space-scout was the work of an individual, not of a team. Perhaps it would be different someday in the future when machines and instruments had been developed further; but now it was an individualistic game, each man for himself.

And probably it was because of this training that he, Phil Mooney, was unable to get back into the crowd after the war had ended. He was an individualist who rebelled against working not only *for* but even *with* someone else.

He should have known better. Industry had reached beyond the point where one man goes out by himself and makes a fortune—or even a living, he thought wryly. It's the day of the big concerns, of tremendous trusts and cartels, who didn't even have to bother with the task of squeezing out tiny competitors like himself. He was out before he started.

The *Mooney Space Service*. He snorted in self deprecation.

Oh, well.

He pulled himself erect and made his way to the bunk. The kid was awake. He grinned down at her and said. "How's it going, Lillian ?"

Her eyes seemed glazed, even worse than they'd been yesterday, but she tried to smile back at him.

"All right," she whispered, her child's voice so low he could hardly make it out. "Where's mother..."

Phil Mooney held a finger to his lips. "Maybe you'd better not talk too much, Lillian. Your mother and father are...they're all right. The thing now is to get you to the hospital and make you well again. Understand?"

* * * *

Kitty Kildare was saying indignantly, "What's this about no insurance on Luna?"

"Use your head, Kitty," Jake grunted. "What company'd be crazy enough to insure anybody working on Luna? By the way, that was a good piece on Mooney and the Marshall kid."

"Did you read it?" Kitty Kildare was pleased.

He shuddered. "No, but the letters have been pouring in. Maybe you ought to do another. Take it from some other angle this time."

"That's why I wanted to know about the insurance. Do you realize that this child, this *poor*, sick, defenseless child, is penniless? Actually, I mean. Bad enough that her parents have left her an orphan, but, Jake, that child is penniless."

"All right, all right," he told her, "work on that for tomorrow's column."

Ed came up with another radiotype report, just as Kitty was leaving. "This guy Mooney's calling all the other spaceports now, Jake. Evidently he's getting desperate; he's only two days out. And by the way, here's a new angle. This guy Harry Marshall, the kid's father, was a war-time buddy of Phil Mooney; they went to cadet school or something together."

Jake growled thoughtfully, "He hasn't got a chance, but it makes a tremendous story. Get somebody to rig up a set in the radio type room, Ed, and we'll see if we can listen in."

* * * *

There was a desperate, tense, taut inflection in his voice now.

"Calling New Albuquerque Spaceport or Oneonta Spaceport. Phil Mooney calling *any* Earth spaceport. Phil Mooney calling Oneonta, New Albuquerque, Casablanca, Mukden, *any* Earth spaceport. Emergency. Emergency. Request landing, instructions. Have Lillian Marshall, eight years old, needing immediate medical care, aboard. Please come in any Earth Spaceport."

Calling Phil Mooney. New Albuquerque calling Phil Mooney. Ambulance waiting on grounds. Receiving you perfectly. Come in...

Calling Phil Mooney. Casablanca Spaceport calling Phil...

Calling Phil Mooney. Mukden Spaceport calling...

Calling Phil Mooney. Oneonta Spaceport calling Phil Mooney...

* * * *

Ed Kerry looked up over the set in the radiotype room at the city editor. He wet his lips carefully and said, "He's only got one day now. They've got to pick him up in hours or he's sunk."

Jake said, "I never did understand how that works. Why can't he land himself? I know he can't, but *why?*"

The reporter shrugged. "I don't quite get it either, but evidently the whole operation is pretty delicate stuff. They bring him down with radar, somehow or other. It's not like landing an airplane. Landing a spacecraft is done from the ground up—not from the spacecraft down. The pilot has comparatively little to do about it. At least, that's the way it is with nine ships out of ten."

The set began to blare again, and they both listened tensely. It was Phil Mooney.

"Listen, you guys down there. If you're sitting around playing craps or something, I'm going to have a few necks to break when I get down."

The two newspapermen stared at each other over the set. Ed Kerry ran his tongue over his lips again.

The strained tone had gone from the voice of the spacepilot now and had been replaced by one of hopelessness. He said, "I don't know who I think I'm kidding. I know darn well that something's wrong with my receiver and I can't find out what it is. Maybe my sender is off too, for all I know. All I can pick up is some girl singing something about white roses. White roses, yet! I want landing instructions and I get white roses."

Ed Kerry jerked his head up and snapped, "Holy jumping hell, he's able to pick up some commercial station!"

Jake came to his feet, stuck his neck out of the door and yelled at the top of his voice, "Phil Mooney is receiving some commercial station! Some dame singing something about white roses! Check every station in the city! Find out if any of them are broadcasting some dame singing about white roses."

* * * *

Ladies and gentlemen, we interrupt this program for an emergency situation. Undoubtedly, you have heard on your newscasts and have read in your papers of the tragic case of Lillian Marshall, child victim of an atomic explosion on Luna which orphaned her and necessitated her immediate flight to an Earth hospital.

For the past three days the spacecraft carrying her, piloted by war hero Philip Mooney, has been having trouble with its radio. Due to circumstances surrounding landing of spacecraft, the two have been given up as lost in spite of the fact that almost hourly it has been possible to receive messages from Mooney.

It is now revealed that he is able to pick up this program on the Interplanetary Broadcasting System network. We are not sure which of the nearly two thousand stations of our system he is receiving, but we will now attempt to reach Phillip Mooney with relayed messages from the Oneonta Spaceport where expert medical care is

awaiting little Lillian Marshall.
   Come in Oneonta.

* * * *

Calling Phil Mooney. Calling Phil Mooney. Come in, Phil. This is Oneonta Spaceport, relaying through the Interplanetary Broadcasting System. Come in, Phil.

"Phil Mooney, calling Oneonta. I'm getting you, Oneonta. Come in, Oneonta. Over."

Okay, Phil. Now this is it. We should have had you two hours ago, but we'll hake out all right. Your velocity is a little too high. Give it six more units on your Kingston valves. Get that? Over.

"Got it. Six more units on the Kingstons. Over."

All right now. Switch on your remote control, Phil. We'll take it from here. Stand by the coordinators...

* * * *

It was night, but a blaze of lights illuminated the Oneonta Spaceport. Hundreds of landcars stood on the parking lots, thousands of persons crowded the wire fence which kept all but port personnel from the field itself.

The old space-freighter sank easily to the apron and in seconds the rocket flames died. A surge of humanity ebbed over the field toward the craft.

Phil Mooney opened the pilot-compartment's hatch and stuck his head out, blinking in surprise at the mob beneath him.

"I don't know what this is all about," he began, "but I've got a sick kid aboard. There's supposed to be an ambulance..."

Police wedged through the crowd, convoying a white-haired, white-jacketed man. He called up to the spacepilot, "We won't need an ambulance, Mr. Mooney. I've already made arrangements for facilities here at the airport for immediate treatment."

Phil Mooney made his way to the ground and scowled, still obviously startled by the swelling crowd.

"Who in *kert* are you?" he asked.

The other motioned for two assistants to enter the ship and bring out the child. "I'm Doctor Kern," he said. "I'll see..."

"Doctor Adrian Kern, the radiation expert?" The pilot frowned worriedly. "See here, doctor, the Marshalls were friends of mine, and I've taken over the care of little Lillian, but I'm—well, I'm afraid I couldn't afford to pay you...I mean..."

The famous doctor smiled at him. "I've been retained by the Interplanetary Golden Heart, Phil. You needn't worry about my fee. Besides," and he smiled easily, "I'm not going to accept any fee for this case. You see, I was listening to Marsha Malloy singing 'Love of White Roses' when your call came through. I believe it was the most poignant experience I have ever been through."

A girl next to the doctor gushed, "I'm Bunny Davis, Mr. Mooney. The managing editor of our newspaper chain has authorized me to buy your story for five thousand. If you'll just—"

Phil Mooney blinked. "I—I—"

A heavy-set man in a business suit grasped his hand and shook it with fervor, while flashbulbs went off blindingly. "Phil," he said huskily, as though moved by deep emotion, "as president of the board of directors of Terra-Luna Spaceways, I wish to take this opportunity to offer you a full—"

"Hey! Give us a smile, Phil," a man on top of a television truck yelled.

* * * *

He was headed back for Luna the next day.

They'd been indignant, of course. There was Hollywood, and the television networks, and that Terra-Luna Spaceways guy who wanted to get in on all the publicity by offering him a vice-presidency. And the newspaper editors, and the magazine editors, and all the rest of them.

Approximately a billion persons had

been tuned in to the Interplanetary network when the emergency landing instructions had been broadcast to him through that system. A billion persons had sat on the edge of their chairs, tensely, as his ship had been brought in.

He and little Lillian had received more publicity in the past twenty-four hours than anyone since Lindberg.

And the child would be all right now. Before he'd left, checks totaling over a quarter of a million had come in for her. Donations from all over the Earth and from Mars and Venus and even some from the Jupiter satellites.

And offers of adoption. Thousands of them, from rich and poor—even including Marsha Malloy, the video star who'd been singing that song, "Love of White Roses."

Yes, Lillian would be all right. He wouldn't have been able to pay for the medical care she'd needed; but now she had the most capable experts on Earth at her disposal.

They had been indignant when he blasted off again for Luna. They'd wanted to make a hero of him. This leaving on his part they interpreted as modesty—which, come to think of it, would make him all the more of a hero.

Phil Mooney slipped a hand down to his set and flicked it on. He dialed over a dozen different stations. The news programs were all full of him and of Lillian. You'd think, to hear them, that he was the noblest, the most daring, the greatest man since Alexander the Great.

He grinned wryly. One of the reasons he'd been so anxious to leave was to get away before somebody thought to check his set to see what was wrong with it. Why, if anybody had found that it was actually in perfect shape, they'd probably have lynched him.

Yeah. The colonel had been right. In the space-forces you learned to be self-reliant. When you got in a bad spot, you figured it out yourself. You're on your own; it's you against everything and everybody. Anything goes.

His grin broadened. Maybe he wasn't a hero—the way they were all painting him; but at least Lillian was all right now, and no longer penniless the way her parents' death had left her.

—And he wasn't doing so badly himself.

ALEXANDRINES
by Clark Ashton Smith

Knowing the weariness of dreams, and days, and nights,
The great and grievous vanity of joy and pain;
Frail loves that pass, where languors infinite remain,
Fervors and long despairs and desperate, brief delights;

Knowing how in the witless brains of them that were,
The drowsy, wiving worm hath prospered and hath died;
Knowing that, evermore, by moon and sun abide
The standing glooms made stagnant in the sepulcher;

Knowing the vacillant leaves that tremble, flame, and fall,
The sweetly-wasting rose, the dawns and stars that wane--
Knowing these things, the desolate heart and soul are fain
Of the one perfect sleep which filleth, foldeth all.

GIVE THE DEVIL HIS DUE
by Mack Reynolds

"Why, you look exactly as I imagined you would," exclaimed Nostradamus Perkins, student of the occult.

"You've got a vivid imagination, is all I can say," the demon told him bitterly, looking down at his cloven hoof, back at his barbed tail, and gingerly feeling the horns on his head. "What in hell did you think I'd look like if not the way you imagined me?"

"Why, I…I don't believe I get your point," Nostradamus Perkins said.

"Skip it, then," the demon told him, still fingering the horns as though fascinated with them.

"Not at all," the student of forbidden mysteries snapped, careful not to step out of the pentacle he'd drawn with colored chalk on his living room rug. "I have you in my power and expect to extract from you whatever knowledge I desire."

The demon looked at him questioningly. "You've got me where? Say, what space-time continuum is this, anyway? I've had some strange specimens call me up in my day, but this really tears it!"

Nostradamus Perkins said hesitatingly, "You mean you don't know where you are?"

The demon was trying out the tail, wagging it sharply from left to right, back again. "Of course not," he said reasonably. "Why should I know where I am? You're the one who did the materializing."

"Well," the student snapped, "you're the devil; at least I suppose you know where you came from."

The other eyed him in puzzlement. "'You're quite devilish yourself," he said. "Now what's all this about, anyway, and what was the purpose in going to all the rigmarole involved in dragging me up here? Not that I don't appreciate the business, of course."

Nostradamus shook his head firmly. "That won't do. I know better, Satan."

"The name is Ozidaminos," the other said mildly.

"As I said," Perkins insisted, in what he hoped was a commanding voice—actually this whole matter wasn't going the way he'd planned at all; for one thing, the demon was so damnably amiable— "as I said, you are now in my power and must do as I command."

The demon stopped playing with his tail and scratched the end of his nose with a claw-tipped finger. "I continually get the impression that I came into this conversation late," he murmured. "Now, let's start at the beginning. Just what have you got in mind that I can't refuse doing?"

"I want to sell my soul," Perkins told him.

"Your what?"

"My soul," the other repeated, his voice was beginning to reflect some of the puzzlement that had been in the demon's for the past five minutes.

Ozidaminos, for the first time, took in his surroundings. He noted the pentacle in which the other was standing; the bizarre looking brazier smoking to his right; the skull sitting on the table beside the old and tattered manuscripts; the charts of the Zodiac on the walls; he sniffed the incense.

"I'm beginning to recall this set-up," he said thoughtfully. "It's been a long time, but it seems to me that the last one to give me this song and dance was wearing a funny looking cloak embroidered with stars and moons." He paused a moment in thought. "As I remember, he wanted to sell me his soul too, in exchange for the knowledge of

how to change lead to gold."

"Did you tell him?" Perkins asked, breathlessly.

"Sure," the demon said, "but I doubt if it did him any good; he didn't have either the equipment, the materials, nor the manpower to build the plant. I gave him the specifications; for all I know, he's poring over them still. Frankly, I've often thought since that he was a bit around the corner. What would be accomplished by changing lead to gold? The amount of work involved is considerably more than if you dug the gold in the first place."

Nostradamus Perkins was impatient of the trend of the conversation. "I don't believe you," he said, "and, besides, we're getting away from the point. The point is that I have you in my power and have a contract I wish to make with you."

The demon complained, "You keep bringing up this I have you in my power stuff. Would you mind explaining?"

Nostradamus glared at him. "Do not think to throw me off, vile demon," he said sonorously, "I knowest full well thou must needs..."

"Listen," Ozidaminos protested, "stick to one dialect, will you? Do you think it's fun having to pick a mind for a whole language and then have the guy switch on you? What's this knowest and thou stuff?"

"Don't interrupt," Nostradamus Perkins barked. "I have summoned you and have certain powers..."

"You sound more like that customer with the stars and moons robe every minute," the demon told him, returning to fascinated experimentation with the tail. He was trying to wag it in circles now.

"Will you stop playing with that confounded thing!" the student of the occult screamed.

The demon eyed him reproachfully. "It wasn't my idea, you know," he said mildly. "I never had one before. Suppose somebody suddenly tied one of these things on you.

Wouldn't you have the curiosity to investigate a bit?"

Perkins looked as though he was about to prance around the room in his agitation, but restrained himself before crossing the chalk line of the pentacle. He shrilled his protest:

"Here I spend years—*years!*—in learning how to summon a devil, and what do I get?"

"You got me," the demon said. "What did you have in mind?"

"I had *you* in mind," Perkins shrilled desperately. "I wanted to sell my soul, but I'm beginning to wonder whether or not you could make the agreement I wanted."

"This soul stuff escapes me," Ozidaminos said soothingly, "but I'll be glad to give you what you want." He added with caution, "If possible."

The other took a deep breath and a sly look entered his eyes. "Very well," he said. "Do you have a contract?"

"A what?" the demon asked, stamping his cloven hoof on the floor, interested in the clattering sound it made.

"Good heavens, don't do that," Perkins told him hurriedly. "Do you want to break my lease?"

The demon said mildly. "You certainly are difficult to get along with. I was just experimenting with this fantastic foot you gave me. What's a contract?"

"What do you mean, I gave *you*? And you know full well what a contract is; I sign it with blood."

The demon stared at him, wide-eyed. "You must be jesting," he said. Then, "No, now that I recall, the guy with the moons and stars on his cloak had the same idea."

"Will you please stop talking about this man with the moons and stars?" Perkins shrilled.

"Sorry," the demon said. "Where were we?"

"The contract!"

"Oh yes, the contract. Tell me more about it, and don't get so excited. You'll get ulcers."

Perkins began to prance again. "I am willing to sell my soul in return for one wish!" he yelled in agitation.

"All right," the demon said, in a tone that suggested he was humoring the other. "What do you want?"

"'The contract,'" the other suggested slyly. "I want to sign the contract first."

"Listen," the demon told him, "I haven't the vaguest idea of what you mean. You summoned me, showing you believed in me; very well, I'm grateful, now tell me what you want and it's yours."

"In return for my immortal soul," the other said dramatically.

"If that's the way you want it," the demon said, shrugging.

"Done!" said Nostradamus Perkins quickly, as though in fear the demon might change his mind. "And here is my wish. I demand immortality!" He began to laugh, almost hysterically.

"Okay," Ozidaminos said, "immortality it is. What's so funny?"

The other took a long moment to get over his fit of laughter. "Don't you see?" he cried. "I've beaten you."

The demon rubbed the end of his nose with the claw-tipped finger. He said ruefully, "This is a hell of a way to make a living. What's happened now?"

Perkins shrilled in glee. "Don't you see! *Don't you see!* I've beaten you. You've given me immortality; now you can never collect my soul."

"Your code of ethics is lousy," said the demon. "Luckily, it doesn't affect me. But, frankly, and from the friendliest of motives, I'd suggest you change your mind about that immortality stuff. I can give it to you all right, and since I've given my word, will, if you want. But—are you sure?"

The other laughed long and loud. Until, as a matter of fact, somebody started pounding on the apartment wall with a shoe.

"Do not think to confound me, Satan. Thou knowest full well that thou canst not forswear thy pledge…"

"There you go with that screwy dialect again," Ozidaminos complained. "You sound as if you've been reading corny books or something."

"Your agreement must be lived up to," Perkins finished.

The demon shrugged again. "It's all right with me. You're asking for it; but you might pick out something a bit less hard on yourself. After all, I'm here to give you a hand."

The other stopped laughing and bent a prejudiced eye on him. "You're here to rob me of my soul," Perkins rasped. "But you'll never have it; I've beaten you."

Ozidaminos shook his head at him, in bewilderment. "This soul you keep talking about. Just what is it?"

Nostradamus Perkins gaped and started to say, "But, that is why you came…" Then he broke off, a hint of suspicion in his voice. "But, why did you come," he asked, "if it wasn't for my soul?"

The Demon shrugged smugly. "I came because you summoned me. And, to be frank, I needed it pretty badly. There has been so much doubt in this world of our existence that we of the other world are badly beset. Old Ishtar and Aeshma Daeva, for instance, have practically faded away, and Zeus and his gang—you'd hate to see them, knowing the weight they used to throw."

"I…I don't understand."

The demon yawned. "Oh, surely you must, otherwise you wouldn't have known how to summon me for a favor. Surely it is elemental that everything is in the mind. Matter exists, life exists, everything exists, but in the human mind. We of the other world are dependent entirely upon your beliefs in us. You summoned me. Good. I am grateful. I am willing to exercise certain powers I possess, and which you lack, to give you your desire. In return, I know I am secure, for as long as you live, you will believe.

"As a matter of fact," he added with satisfaction, "now that you have immortality, I am guaranteed at least one believer for the rest of eternity." He took to contemplating his tail again, a shade of repulsion on his face. "You should have seen how the Greeks used to dream me up," he said wistfully. "I was really something worth seeing; you know, golden armor and everything."

Nostradamus Perkins said in bewilderment, "Ishtar? Greeks? Believers?" He scowled, certain doubts beginning to run through him. "Are… are the inhabitants of your 'world,' as you call it, Gods or Devils?"

"What's the difference?" Ozidaminos asked disinterestedly. "One man's God is another's Devil—it's in the viewpoint. Actually, we're all about the same. Of course, you humans make up a whole new set of rules and regulations every few hundred years, and there's a lot of…er…propaganda thrown around, but, substantially, we're all about the same."

"But…my soul?" Perkins protested.

"Never heard of it," said the other. His head jerked suddenly. "You'll have to pardon me," he said, "I just got a call." He hesitated, seemingly distressed. "Sorry about that immortality business," he added. "However, you asked for it and it's yours. Frankly, I don't think you'll enjoy it, especially after the first million years or so. I doubt if there'll be any members of the human race left by then—except you, of course. But, anyway, thanks again for calling me up."

He disappeared suddenly.

For a long time Nostradamus Perkins sat and pondered the desirability of immortality. His eyes slowly widened as some of the ramifications came home to him. He didn't go mad, although that might have been preferable—in the long run…

MACK REYNOLDS:
A SELECTED BIBLIOGRAPHY

NOVELS

1950s

The Case of the Little Green Men (1951)

1960s

Episode on the Riviera (1961)

A Kiss before Loving: A Contemporary Novel (1961)

Mercenary from Tomorrow (1962)

The Earth War (1963)

The Kept Woman (1963)

The Jet Set (1964)

Space Pioneer (1965)

Planetary Agent X (1965)

Of Godlike Power (1966)

Space Pioneer (1966)

Time Gladiator (1966)

Computer War (1967)

Death Is a Dream (1967)

The Rival Rigelians (1967)

Dawnman Planet (1967)

After Some Tomorrow (1967)

Code Duello (1968)

Earth Unaware (1968)

Mercenary from Tomorrow (1968)

Mission to Horatius (1968)

The Cosmic Eye (1969)

The Space Barbarians (1969)

The Five Way Secret Agent (1969)

1970s

Computer World (1970)

Once Departed (1970)

Blackman's Burden (1972)

Border, Breed nor Birth (1972)

The Home of the Inquisitor (as Maxine Reynolds) (1972)

The House in the Kasbah (as Maxine Reynolds) (1972)

Looking Backward from the Year 2000 (1973)

Computer War (1973)

Code Duello (1973)

Depression or Bust (1974)

Commune 2000 A.D. (1974)

The Towers of Utopia (1975)

Satellite City (1975)

Amazon Planet (1975)

The Cosmic Eye (1975)

Ability Quotient (1975)

Tomorrow Might Be Different (1975)

The Five Way Secret Agent (1975)

Mercenary from Tomorrow (1975)

Day After Tomorrow (1976)

Section G: United Planets (1976)

Rolltown (1976)

Galactic Medal of Honor (1976)

After Utopia (1977)

Perchance to Dream (1977)

Space Visitor (1977)

Police Patrol: 2000 A.D. (1977)

Equality in the Year 2000 (1977)

Trample an Empire Down (1978)

The Best Ye Breed (1978)

Brain World (1978)

The Fracas Factor (1978)

Earth Unaware (1979)

Lagrange Five (1979)

1980s

The Lagrangists (1983)

Chaos in Lagrangia (1984)

Eternity (with Dean Ing) (1984)

Home, Sweet Home 2010 A. D.
(with Dean Ing) (1984)

The Other Time (with Dean Ing) (1984)

Space Search (1984)

Trojan Orbit (with Dean Ing) (1985)

Deathwish World (with Dean Ing) (1986)

*Joe Mauser: Mercenary from
Tomorrow* (with Michael Banks)

Sweet Dreams, Sweet Princes
(with Michael Banks)

Fiction Collections

The Best of Mack Reynolds (1976)

Compounded Interests (1983)

*Nine Tomorrows: Science Fiction
Stories from the Golden Age* (2009)

www.ingramcontent.com/pod-product-compliance
Lightning Source LLC
Chambersburg PA
CBHW080816250626
47159CB00010B/3405